Wolves of Cold Creek

# Sky's

# Tail

Brittany Putzer

Cover designed by: Charles Putzer Jr.

Cover model photo by Nobert Buduczk on Unsplash

Formatted by: Frankie Page

Editing by: Kat Pagan, Pagan Proofreading

ISBN: **979-8-218-12820-3**

Published in the United States of America.

This is for those suffering within the confines of familiarity. Don't be frightened to fight for whatever (and whomever) it is you desire. Let no one hold you back, friend. Your happily ever after is but a page flip away...

# Trigger Warning

*Sky's Tail* is a wolf-shifter romance and contains scenes that may be upsetting for some readers. The content includes triggers such as (but not limited to): same-gender sex and foreplay, murder, death, miscarriage, profanity, violence, graphic sexual activities, demanding alpha men, needy headstrong women, witchcraft, guardian angels, and sexual assault. If any of these items are upsetting to you, please do not read.

# CONTENTS

# Sky

# Dark Stranger

"**W**atch out!" my soon-to-be fired employee screeches in my direction.

I balance the plate, but my heels lose traction and I slide across the floor. The once perfectly executed venison with juniper berries now scalds my arm and stomach. But the pain doesn't match the sting of my embarrassment.

"Sky! Are you okay?" The waiter gawks, attempting to hold back a giggle.

"Don't just stand there! Help her up!" a male voice roars, using his napkin to fling off the green beans and mashed potatoes. Before I can right myself, my wannabe rescuer scoops me up bridal-style and dashes us to the bathroom. "Fucking idiots." He runs cold water over my burns.

"Shay is fired."

The man pauses. "Who the hell is Shay?"

"My ex-employee—he just doesn't know it yet." I pause and hold my breath. "This bathroom is disgusting and smells like piss."

BRITTANY PUTZER

The stranger's chuckle rings out. "That's just men for you, sweets. We're fucking animals."

I take a moment to assess him. My knight in leather armor. I nibble my lip as I take in his decorated, corded arms. I clench my thighs, while his calloused palms warm my belly, and freeze when my gaze lands on his neck tattoo. "What are you doing?"

"Well, I was minding my own business, enjoying my dinner, when you crashed beside me. Spraying me with..." He flicks off a glob still resting on his leather vest. "What the fuck is *that*?"

I sniff his chest. "Honey cinnamon butter. We rub it on our dinner rolls."

"You should probably lick it and test that theory."

Then everything hits me. Did I just *smell* a customer? I clear my throat and leap out from between his legs. "Thank you for your assistance. I'm sorry for the poor dining experience. I will refund your meal and make sure this never happens again."

"No."

What the fuck? I'm the one who was burned, not him! Oh shit. Is he going to sue me? I square my shoulders. I'm the owner of the Wolves' Den steakhouse, and it's my job to handle this delicately. Preferably without losing my new establishment. "I apologize. How can I make this right, sir?"

He doesn't hide his hungry assessment of my hot mess. "You."

I sidestep him as I again take in the tattoo screaming at me from across the small space. "That's impossible. You're one of *them*."

Frost Tala, an alpha residing in Cold Creek, warned us about the *Fangs*—a pack of rebel wolves. They live in the decaying streets of Carson City and are trouble with a capital T. I lick my lips. But maybe he's different? He did just *save* me from third-degree burns.

He tucks a loose strand behind my ear. His fingertips tickle my collarbone. "Anything is possible. All you have to do is be brave

2

enough to *take* what you want." A cocky grin brightens his face. "And what is it that you want, beautiful?"

"For you not to sue me," I mutter more to myself. "I just opened this restaurant, and I can't afford to have a mishap like that."

"Do you really think a little spilled butter would cause me to bitch to a fucking lawyer?"

"Maybe?"

"The food is the best I've had in a long time." He leans against the wall, blocking my exit.

"Thank you?"

"I'll be returning here at least once a week. And bringing my friends."

I panic. The leader of my fur-family wouldn't approve of the rival gang encroaching on our territory. "Please don't."

He lets out a hearty laugh. "I'll leave the fur-buddies at home then, but you can't stop me from coming." Who is he kidding? I'm a nobody in my pack. I couldn't stop him even if I tried. I swallow and take in the quiet room. What's keeping him from hurting me now? "Quit wrinkling your forehead. Nobody is going to ruin your business. You have my word."

"As a rebel?"

"As a fellow shifter."

"So, if I allow you to come once a week to eat, we are even, and you'll forget this little incident?"

"Is the meal on the house?"

My mind whirls. Can I afford that? How much can this muscled hunk eat? Probably less than a dragged-out court case. "If that's what you want, then, yes, I'll provide one free entrée a week."

He closes the gap and pins me to the counter. "What I really want

3

is *you* writhing underneath me." He squeezes my rear, pushing me to his chest. "I savor the thrill of the hunt, so I'll work my charm for *that* and accept the meat for now."

"What charm?" His erection twitches at the challenge. "You're that confident in yourself. How do you know I haven't found my mate yet? Or that I won't squeal on you to my alpha?"

His grip tightens, and I squeak. "Because I feel your hot core dripping at my touch, sweets." He bites my lobe. "And if you mention me to your leader, I'll have to punish you."

A shiver runs down my spine. Decisions, decisions. What is a wolf to do? Being the only female in your family has its perks: I always get what I want, when I want it. And right now, I want this bad boy pounding into me until I howl.

# Sky

# Expectations

"This can't happen again, Fredrick."

"What the fuck have I said about calling me *that*?" The slap on my ass burns but I can't help my grin when he pins my arms above my head.

"Oh, I'm sorry, Freddy," I purr as I run my leg up his back. "What would you like me to call you this time?"

I'm rewarded with a husky chuckle before his palm glides over my heel and fondles the anklet he gifted me a few weeks after we met. It's decorated with jade crystals and in the center rests a glass orb of sand. Plus, I can shift with it safely around my leg, and it doesn't get in the way of me working at the restaurant. His kisses have me arching my neck to grant him unbridled access.

"I wish I could remain buried between your legs, but I need to return before my alpha realizes I've crossed the boundary again. He nearly broke my neck when he smelled you on me last time."

"Our own little *Romeo and Juliet* tale." I clench my jaw. Why did

I think *this time* would be different? That he would finally leave his abusive pack and join mine. Just because our ancestors are at odds with each other, it doesn't mean we have to be too. His pants smack him in his face before I push him towards his exit. "Just go. You got what you came for."

I pad over to my discarded clothing. This is what my life has become. I work my ass off at the restaurant and every month, when I'm ovulating and my wolf yearns for a thick cock, Freddy appeases my primal desires. He does what he needs, then hightails it to Carson City where his own fur-family lives.

"Sweets, stop pouting. I'll see you for lunch tomorrow." When I don't meet his hypnotic gaze, he slams me against the wall and kisses me deeply, his tongue demanding access at the seam of my mouth. Once I am melting into him, he whispers against my lips, "This is all temporary. You know that, right? Once our packs pull their heads out of their asses, we can have it *all*." I moan as he rubs his hand over my hips. "Are you still willing to cater our annual gathering?"

"Yes, I've got the menu all planned out."

His member pokes my stomach. "You see what you do to me? How can I ever desire another when *you* are the whole package?" He nips my chin, then pushes off the wall. "But I favor my neck over my dick, so I really need to go. Rain check?"

I flip him off as he sneaks out my window with an arrogant grin on his face. "No, lover boy. This is the last time *this* is happening."

Before he swings his legs out, he cocks a brow. "You say that *every* time." Then he leaps to the ground.

Why do I do this to myself? I am an intelligent *smoking*-hot businesswoman. I can have any shifter I want. Yet, here I am, having the *one* I shouldn't. The only good news is: Freddy is around so much his scent doesn't alarm my family.

My girl bits throb. Being in heat is the worst. Why can't my fur-double be satisfied?

My ruby heels click on the polished tile of the empire I've built. The Wolves' Den. Where shifters and humans can sink their fangs into utter perfection. I hire the best chefs in the state to cook the most delectable entrees with local meat and produce. I flick the lint off my impeccable suit. I even added the *prey of the day* to my menu. Which allows the packs to exchange their extra kills for cash. This setup keeps my customers happy with fresh proteins and my pockets fuller because I'm outsourcing less items.

"I'm reporting you to the boss. You're late, Sky Bear."

I roll my eyes at the hostess. Okay, so it's technically *our* empire. Carly is my rock. My partner in this messy business. "I'm not in the mood for your antics," I say so only she can hear, then smile in greeting at the regulars piling in while lifting my hand in a wave. "Thank you for joining us."

"I can help you with *that*," she coos.

I scowl but stop as she licks her mouth. I look over the gorgeous blonde and bite my lip. Yes, she could help with *that*. As a shifter, I am expected to marry, have the next generation of fur-brats, and bow to those who outrank me. Yet, here I am, fucking the enemy and tasting pussy on the side.

*But what's a girl to do?*

"No, thank you. I've had my fill. I'll be in the office if anybody needs me." No more rule-breaking today. I order my stilettoes to walk away from temptation.

"If you change your mind, you know where I'll be, boss," Carly sings before turning to a group of newcomers.

I steer my eyes forward, not trusting my mouth right now. I fall into my leather chair and rub my temples. I should have taken the day off like Mom suggested. This sex drive is ruining me. But I have deadlines and I'm not one to back down, especially when it comes to the domain I've built. After I graduated early from the local university, my family helped me purchase, fix, and open this place. Especially my brothers. With their supernatural brute strength and stamina, they did most of the heavy lifting.

Even though my older brother Sable is an engineer and owns his own mechanic shop, he took the time to locate the best appliances and software, while my younger brother Aspen—who's still working his way through school—designed the menus and website. Plus, he schedules any promotions I need with his incredible writing and social media skills.

Afterwards, my dad bused all of his starving college students here for a free meal during our soft opening. The kids were so impressed their word of mouth had the restaurant at max capacity on opening day. And my sweet mother is my rock and best friend. She is always by my side, doing whatever she can, between appointments and her crazy doctor schedule at the reservation hospital. She is constantly sending patients, staff, and pack members my way. As well as making sure we are following all the FDA regulations. Opening day was the most exciting moment of my life. I was either going to sink or swim! But thank Luna I was able to paddle above water.

I tap my pen against my lips. That was the night I met Freddy. The moment he walked in, I knew I was in trouble with his leather jacket, tight jeans, and no-fucks-given attitude. And don't get me started on his motorcycle. That engine vibrating between my thighs is a delicious sensation. Although our strong-willed personalities clash a lot, the under-the-covers moments make up for it. Now, don't get me wrong, he isn't my mate. The one shifter Luna set aside *just* for me. He is simply a yummy chew-toy. A distraction until my *one and only* graces me with his presence.

If only our fur-friends could get along like we do… But decades ago, the current leader of the Fangs' brother attacked the Talas' alpha for his position. The rogue wolf lost, but instead of accepting his defeat, he planned an ambush. Frost Tala defended himself but injured the other shifter. When the wounded pup's brother heard the commotion, he rushed over, only to watch his sibling bleed out at his feet and demand he avenge his death. After that, in his brother's honor, Spike Fangs gathered a few sympathizers and initiated his own pack in Carson City. Frost felt horrible that the incident resulted in the wolf's death, so he continues to allow the rival pack to inhabit that territory peacefully.

I glance at the family picture on my desk and run a fingertip over my own brother's face. Sable knew who his mate was the moment she was born. I envy him. I have been searching for mine since I can remember. And *nothing*. The closest I have gotten to satisfying that urge is my Kindle and a battery-operated boyfriend combo. I groan. Speaking of, it looks like I'll be using both when I curl up in bed later. I redirect my panty-driven tension and swivel to my computer screen. I tap in my password and busy myself with order forms, payroll, and inventory.

"Hey, boss."

I rub my dry eyes. When did Carly enter my office? I tap my smart watch. I have been sitting here all day and now it's time to count the registers. I push back my chair. Crap, my limbs are *asleep*. I bend and shake them to get the blood flowing.

"So, your fuck toy stopped in earlier looking for you. He also said that you are ignoring his texts and phone calls." Carly passes me a Styrofoam container, then sits on the edge of my desk. She swings her silky legs as she pops a bubble with those plump lips of hers. "Do you want to talk about it?"

I lift open the steaming carton and drool as the smell of red meat hits me like a ton of bricks. Carly slides her hot-pink fingertips over the lid, closing it and drawing my attention back to her. Then she glides her claws along my arm, making goose bumps rise in her path.

"You look tense." She massages my shoulders. "I guess the dog couldn't scratch the itch, huh?"

I moan as she tweaks a knot. My bestie and I went to college together and we spent many experimental nights sweating under the covers. We have no secrets between us. Even though she is a normal human, she knows who I am, or rather *what* I am. And yet, for some reason, she accepts me. Fangs and all. Not that other two-leggers don't accept us. Heck, we're scattered all over in their midst. The police force, hospital, fire department... you name it. We coexist as equals in this crazy community.

"You know how it goes. He accomplished what his mangy mutt desired and left."

Freddy doesn't like to savor the act. When he reaches his climax, that's it. Zipper goes up and he's out. Most of the time, I touch myself to elicit my own happy ending long after he's gone. Even with all of that, there's always something tugging me to him.

"Sky, he isn't worth it. You *know* that. Why don't you sink those teeth into Jackson? I bet he'd be into that threesome we've always talked about." She slips off her heels to run a foot over my thigh.

"No way! Jackson is like a brother to my dad, which makes him my adoptive uncle—*gross*."

"Yes, but from what the other fur-girls have mentioned, he knows how to keep you wet and satisfied." She wiggles her toes against my zipper.

"But life's supposed to be about *more* than just amazing sex." I pinch my nose. "I need to get my shit together. I'm not getting any younger... and you know what is expected of me."

Carly drops to her knees and snatches my chin. "Don't you dare sacrifice your happiness just to give *them* theirs! You don't owe them shit! Stand up for yourself! Tell them to fuck off! There is *nothing* wrong with wanting to be with a man. So there sure as hell shouldn't be anything wrong with wanting to be with a woman either."

I envy her passion. But she has no idea what it's like to have the shifter 'gift' or the obligations that accompany it. It's difficult when you're sexually attracted to men and women. I want the best of both worlds. I don't want to settle for one or the other.

"I just want you happy." Her fingers trace circles on my neck. "You are beautiful, intelligent, and you do not need to answer to anyone."

"I appreciate your advice, but I really should eat something and close up. I have an early day tomorrow."

"I'm hungry too."

"Oh, well, we can share. You always give me way too much food anyway." I stand and offer her the meal. Carly pinches and tugs my zipper. As my pants fall to my ankles, my mouth drops into an O shape. "I thought you said..."

The goddess between my legs pushes me into the chair. "I said I was hungry. I didn't say for *what*."

My heart races as she runs her fingertips across my silky thong. She slips a finger under the elastic and caresses my opening. I throw my head back at the delicious sensation and arch my hips, giving her more access. She palms my clit while her pillow-soft lips brush mine. Soon her chewing gum dances between our tongues and the taste of sweet watermelon glides over my parched throat. I grind against her wrist before squeezing her breast.

"Oh, no. I'm taking care of *you*. Just sit back and enjoy the ride."

My lips part in protest, but she shreds my underwear and licks my lower lips before flicking my core. I get lost in the forest of dark pleasure. I lose track of my orgasms and the annoying checklist of what I'm doing *wrong* in my life—having sex with the enemy and indulging in same-sex shenanigans among the items that make the top. Carly lifts her head from my glistening thighs. "Your food is probably cold. But we can get you some more."

A wolfish smirk spreads over my face before I tackle my prey to the carpet. "I have my meal right here." I shove my hand down her pencil skirt and grasp her drenched center. "Hot and ready to go."

"Only for you, baby." She tilts her head. "I love you, Sky."

My heart soars. This woman is my world. "I love you too, Carly." I shove her clothing aside and stare at her juicy pussy. "Be prepared to scream." I dive into her aching core, lapping up every drop of her sweet nectar. My fingertips tweak her nipple. Her gasp echoes around the office as we continue our tumblings until we are both satisfied.

# Freddy

# Beta Duties

My fist jabs into the man's smug face again and again. Bones crush. Tissue pulverizes. Damn, this feels good. Releasing all this pent-up energy while blood warms my knuckles. The grunt of his pain causes my lip to twitch and reenergizes my movements.

"Stop," Spike commands. I take a step back with a bow to my alpha. "Tell me again… where were you?" He flicks a tooth off the guy's crimson-stained shirt.

"I swear I was just checking the perimeter, boss. Like you asked." The guy pisses his pants, and the ammonia scent sends Spike into a frenzy.

He pummels into the man's chest. Once his knuckles are swollen and decorated with flesh, he spits on his victim. "Bullshit! Freddy saw you cross over into *their* territory! And I smell them on both of you!" His words bounce off the cement walls of the basement. "Then Scarlett informed me that you made a pass at her." He flicks his blade and the metallic edge dances in the glimmer of the fleabag's pupils. "And nobody touches what I've claimed." Spike slams the tip through the man's pants.

He screeches as blood pools at our feet. "I was just joking with her. I wasn't going to touch her. I know she is out of bounds." Blood spurts as his hand slides off his arm, having been severed from his body, and red paints the dreary walls. His college ring slides from his now-detached finger and clinks onto the floor.

Spike strides towards it, placing the amputated digit in his pocket with a satisfied nod, as its owner sucks in his last breath and twitches. Then the satisfied alpha glides his blade over the corpse's shirt. "Dispose of him where he was attempting to sneak off my territory. That way, it'll remind those who believe they can cross me to *think* again."

I lift my chin at the shadows in the corner of the room, and two men step forward to clean up our mess.

"Scarlett is of age and will need a mate assigned to her," Spike addresses me as the men drag the body from our sight. That damn *nickname*. It's grating on my last nerve. It's bad enough that *he* stole Maya as a pup from the Tala pack and demanded that my family conceal her identity for eighteen years, while she resided in the orphanage. But now that she's living with us, she's all he yaps about.

"Yes, of course. Who did you have in mind for a mate for Maya?"

"You."

My gaze follows the blood trail as the dead man is pulled out the door. Spike pretends to hate the little runt he took in, but I know he favors her. "I assumed you would claim her as your mate, sir."

"You assumed wrong. She's just a piece of ass. You know what her father did to me. My brother's death will be avenged. I'm only doing this to remind Frost of his place."

"But you and Maya would make a powerful union. You were both *born* to be alphas." I stroke his ego.

Spike rubs his chin. "I'll see how Tanner feels about *Scarlett*. He is moldable and easily manipulated." The flick of the match illuminates his scarred face as I light up a cigarette. "We have a ceremony to prepare for. Don't stay out too late."

I let a breath out as he blends into the darkness. I almost had to reveal the secret I've been keeping from him for years. *Almost.*

I tug my fallen comrade through the woods. The little shit was in the wrong place at the wrong time. He found me near Sky's territory, and I had to make a cover story to save my own ass. What really rescued me was the fact that the idiot tried to get into Maya's pants, and she ratted him out. Otherwise, he and I would both be eating dirt right now.

I need to get my shit together. I enjoy fucking Sky and the intel I gather from her is priceless, but I'm beginning to question if it's worth having my merciless alpha breathing down my neck. He was once a member of the Tala pack of Cold Creek. But after the alpha, Frost, killed his brother in a battle, he went berserk and ran off to the closest city with some of his loyal followers at his heels. Carson City was already a decaying pile of shit, even before he got his claws into it.

I take a drag of my cigarette and watch the red embers flicker as my mind continues to wander. My parents brought me here and I somehow climbed the ranks. I flick the butt into the air, and it sizzles in a puddle. Who am I kidding? I know exactly why Spike handpicked me to be his beta. I'll do whatever dirty deed needs doing. Including going behind his back...

"Are you gonna help!" The red-faced shifter barks in my direction as he digs the shallow grave.

"Why would I do that when I have a sniveling bitch like you to do it for me?" I kick gravel into his eyes. "Now hurry up before I lose my shit and decide to shove you in after him."

By the time I return to the pack's warehouse-style hideout, it's well past midnight. I shiver and fight the urge to shift into my fur coat. A light flickers in the distance and I glance at the illuminated off-limits penthouse. I wonder who Spike has up there. I scoff as I pad to my room on the ground floor. I know exactly who he is sinking into, and he can keep that bitch. It's only a matter of time before Frost gets word of the newbie pup and visits. Whenever we recruit a new female, he comes lurking in the shadows to make sure it isn't anyone from his family. Which is why I've been bedding the little fur-princess. She keeps me informed on the happenings of the other packs. If shit is about to hit the fan, I'll have time to hightail it to safer grounds.

I light another cancer stick. Thank Luna Spike planned our ancestral ceremony for tomorrow, and we can link Maya to us before Frost realizes who she *really* is: his stolen daughter. At the big event, we'll all drink from the chalice and pledge our loyalty to the Fangs. It's the same thing every year, except we're welcoming the pups and acknowledging them as official members. The only thing I'm looking forward to is the buffet beforehand that I talked Sky into catering. It'll be the hit of the party.

"You really know how to keep a girl waiting, Freddy." The soft purr comes from the nude female sprawled out on my bed. My internal tail wags. There she is. The golden goddess herself and my big secret. My mate. Angelica. We saved her when her drug-obsessed father sold her into prostitution. My fur pokes through the surface at the thought of the child I carried in my arms that night. She was bleeding and shivering from the trauma. I shake my head of the images. She's blossomed into a furious creature, who uses her former suffering to fuel her fire. She will do whatever it takes to see to our prosperous future.

"I had to dump a body to keep my cover." I start undressing, eager to get under the blankets.

She snatches the button on my pants. "Were you seen leaving her house?"

"Who the fuck do you think you're talking to?" I give her a lopsided grin. "I'm the king, baby! Nobody is going to bring me down."

We maintain discretion, to keep our strategy hidden. The truth is, we are going to dominate every pack in Cold Creek. Starting with the Fangs. My girl climbs the hierarchy, consuming every crumb of information she can get her paws on. We're ravenous for power. A force to be reckoned with. She's great at soaking up confidences while playing the ditsy blonde, and I'm the master manipulator with the muscles to instill terror in our adversaries' eyes. It's a match made in heaven. Or hell, depending on how you look at it.

Her jet-black nails inch over her hips. "I've been waiting too long. I almost thought you were going to stand me up." She slinks out of the bed, her fingers gliding into her dripping pussy. Her eyes flutter as she leans into my chest. She slaps her palm under my nose. My wolf stirs at her arousal, and I pin her against the wall. "So, you like that? How about you lick it, dog?"

I make quick work of kneeling for my queen. I run my nose over her lower lips. She melts into the wall as she opens wide for me and whimpers. My tongue suckles her sweet syrup. A shiver runs through my body as my wolf begs to claim her. I swirl and slurp at her opening until she is on the edge. She tugs my hair to her clit. I bite down and she arches her hip as she explodes.

I tease her entrance with my tip and she mews. "You want *this*? Get on your knees and beg, bitch," I counter. Her eyes never leave mine as she takes me balls-deep. "That's right. Take it all." I wrap her hair around my fists and thrust into her. "Be my good girl and don't make a mess." She nips my sensitive tip and I tug her back. Her laugh draws goose bumps over my arms. "You need to be punished," I seethe as my dick throbs. I drag her over my thighs.

"We don't bite." My open palm smacks her ass, and the sound vibrates around the room. The red handprint marks her as mine. I repeat this process until her arousal coats her thighs. I flip her over, so her pussy is on display.

"Please," she pants.

"You're going to mouth-fuck me, and no more biting. Understood?"

"Fuck you, beta."

A grin spreads across my face. I love it when she *challenges* me. It makes the sex so much sweeter. I jam a thumb into her core and thrust until she's clenching, teetering on the edge of combustion. "Are you ready to comply?"

She leaps off my lap and shoves me against the bed covers. "I do what I want. When I want." She pierces her pussy with my cock and rides me like there's no tomorrow. I reach for her bouncing tits. She slaps me away and snarls. Then she tweaks her own nipples and throws her head back. She keeps her eyes closed as she chases her release. I allow her wetness to seep over my aching balls. Her lids flutter open and she disengages. "See? I don't need you."

She's playing with fire, with her continued challenge to my wolf. I howl into the darkness as fur shreds through my pores, and I release a guttural command for her to follow suit. She immediately obeys and our wolves dance circles around each other. With claws drawn and teeth bared, I pounce and thrust into her hard and fast. My fangs sink into her scruff and my paws grip her sides. She strangles my cock as she reaches another climax, and I fuck her until my seed releases. Exhaustion overcomes us and we curl up together.

The roughness of my tongue brushes through her fur. Her chest vibrates and I bend to cleanse her holes of our fluids, making sure to keep those pristine and taking care of. No one can satisfy me like my fur-goddess. We come from a hard life, but our souls are fused together by the shared desire to be on top. To never again eat the scraps off others' plates.

"Did you like the present I sent you last night?" Spike asks as we gather the pack for the ceremony.

"You really shouldn't have."

"A simple *thank you* will do just fine."

"Thank you. But I'm not interested in Angelica."

Spike's chest heaves as he growls, "She is a perfect match: strong, obedient, clean bloodline…"

Before I can respond, Tanner enters, interrupting our conversation. He lowers his head to our alpha. "I've collected Scarlett."

"Good job. Now make sure everyone loads into the vans. We will be leaving within the hour."

The pup exits without a backward glance. He's young but Spike is right: he is very moldable. Too bad he has no fucking clue what's really going on.

"Are you sure you want to bind Maya to our pack? This will start an all-out war with Frost and possibly the others in Cold Creek."

"It's exactly what I want. That little shit deserves what's coming to him. And your idea was on point last night. I'll impregnate Maya and the children she bears will be of *my* bloodline."

*Of course, I was right.* "You are allowing your pain to cloud your judgement," I mutter under my breath. And gasp for air as Spike's hand clenches around my airway.

"Did I *ask* you for your advice? No. And you will do well to remember that!" He squeezes until black spots dance in front of my vision. "Are you ready to apologize and make it up to me?"

All I can do is nod. I crumble to my knees as he releases his hold.

I wheeze, trying to return oxygen to my vital organs. I'm strong enough to fight *him*, but not the whole pack. I'll remain his bitch until the time comes. Then we'll rain blood down on this city. I screw my eyelids closed, as the lightheadedness swirls around my skull, and hear his zipper lower.

"Now show me how sorry you are. And make it quick."

Is he fucking serious? "Spike…" I croak out.

He snatches a fist full of my hair and jolts my head back. "Do you think I'm a fool? I know you've been crossing the border. What I don't know is *why*."

Shit. "I can explain."

"Oh, you will. But first you will submit to me. I've never allowed another man to suck me off before, but I'm always willing to try new things. Now open your mouth."

I'm waiting for the punch line. Isn't it forbidden to have sexual relationships with those of the same gender in a pack? But, then again, this isn't a relationship. It's foreplay. I wonder what the laws say about that.

"I'm losing my patience," he warns.

I stare at Spike's hard-on. Damn. There's no way out of this. Before I can lift my mouth more than an inch, he shoves his cock past my lips while he tugs my hair back. I gag and attempt to free myself, but he keeps his grip on my scalp, grunting as he thrusts.

"You'll remember this the next time you decide to cross me. I am your *alpha,* and you will obey me or suffer the consequences."

My eyes water and my throat burns. How long can he last? My hands go towards his legs to push him off, but his growl signals that it's a bad idea.

"Try that shit again and I'll widen your asshole," he grunts. "Now be a good bitch and swirl your tongue around my tip. Yeah, like that. You know, I may have to do this more often—hey! Watch those fangs!" His preseed tastes like salty gym socks. And his balls keep hitting my chin. "Squeeze your cheeks tighter. Now massage my testicles and I should come. But if you squeeze too hard, I'll force you to swallow my load."

I definitely don't want any more of his fluids dripping down my throat. This shit tastes nothing like pussy juice. Spike pulls out just in time for his cum to splatter all over my face. Once he catches his breath, he releases my hair. Then he passes me a rag and pats my shoulder.

"You are a good man and I consider you my brother, Freddy. I hated every second of that. So please don't make me punish you again."

I bite back my heated response. He *crossed* a line with this shit. Fuck being his beta. He has made me his *enemy*.

"And you *will* be married to Angelica tonight." Spike offers me a hand up. "Who knows? Maybe we can share her. I'd love to see how Maya and Angelica get along under the covers." He slaps my back and strides away. "Clean up and meet us at the van."

I spit on the ground. If I were wiser than I was enraged, I'd run to Frost and tell him all the bullshit our self-imposed alpha has planned. Or stab Spike while his back is turned. But I'm on fire and ready to set his world *ablaze*. I'll take over his pitiful pack, slit his toy's throat, and force him to watch her bleed. Then I'll turn that same sharpened edge on him.

# Azure

# The Guardian

The wind caresses my hair as I stare into the valley. *A storm is brewing on the horizon.* My nose twitches at the thought. *And trouble is trailing close behind.* My fellow shifters are up to something. But what?

"Azure? Hello?" A hand materializes in front of my face. "Are you even listening to me?"

I meet my twin sister's gaze. "I'm sorry."

"Were you having another vision?"

I rub my forehead, afraid to tell her the truth. Something is *amiss* with my Luna-given powers. Normally I receive flashes of future events so I can prevent them, but my mind is foggy, and my dreams are nonexistent. "I may need to cut this visit short." My arm hair rises. "There's something developing in the northern quadrant."

"Oh, isn't that where that poor pup came from?"

"You're thinking of Cold Creek, Lily." I clench my jaw at the memory. A young wolf named Sable hunted me down to assist him in locating his mate, Maya. At the time, I didn't realize something was blocking my abilities and I couldn't sense the missing pup, so I informed him that it was a lost cause and to move on. But ever since that day, I've regretted it. Because maybe she is alive, and I'm so broken I can't sense it.

Lily warms my hand. "You'll get through this, big brother." A smile tugs at my lips. I never have to say much to her. She knows me too well. "Now, hold your nephew and tell me when you're settling down."

I cradle the infant, embracing his warmth. My sibling is an amazing mother, even though the conception of her bundle of fur wasn't ideal. She was raped by a nomadic shifter when she was vacationing in the snowcapped mountains. And every day I regret not being able to protect her from that brutal attack…

*"We're sorry, but we haven't been able to locate your sister."*

*Dread crawls up my spine. "What do you mean?" I snatch the receptionist's shirt. "Where is she?"*

*The woman pales, but it's an officer who answers. "You need to come with us."*

*I turn my glare on the man in uniform. "Not until someone tells me where the fuck my sister is!" I release the mute girl and shove my phone into the officer's face. "She left this voicemail a few hours ago." I wait for him to listen to it. Her plea for help still shakes me to my core. She begs me to come, to find her, but she's cut off before she can explain what's happening.*

*"Come with me, son. You need to see this." He leads me to a cabin and waves me inside.*

*I stumble as my eyes scan the blood-covered walls. "What the fuck?" I whisper, then sniff the room. "No." I pivot to the man. "Is this…"*

*"The blood belongs to one of the resort's delivery boys."*

*I let out a breath, then rip through the area. Her scent is faint. She was here. But why would she leave her belongings? Unless...*

*Fur breaks through my skin as my legs pound the snow-covered landscape. I'll find you, Lily! I bite the inside of my cheek. Why didn't I have a vision of this? I could have saved her! I shake my head of the negativity. It's not too late! She'll be fine.*

*A scream rips through the wind-blown forest and I bullet to its location. I skid to a stop at a cave's entrance, and my heart stutters. Bone and flesh decorate the stone surfaces, while new horrors flash in front of my eyes everywhere I look. A massive wolf is huddled in a corner with Lily's bloodied frame draped over its carcass. I clutch her limp form to my chest as crimson drenches my skin, then cradle her as I cry into her hair. And with all the energy I can muster, I beg my sister to breathe.*

I tickle the child's cheek with my nose to remind myself of the blessing that emerged from that horrible day. "In Luna's time, I'll settle down. That's when I'll find my mate and not a moment sooner. Have faith."

My nephew giggles before tugging a fistful of my hair.

"I do have faith." My twin crosses her arms over her chest. "I'm just impatient. I don't want to be an old lady when I'm chasing my nephew or niece."

"I'll keep my eyes open."

"Are you going to bring her back here? Or stay with her pack? Oh! Or travel together? That would be so romantic."

"Can I locate her first?" I arch a brow. "You could always bring your pup to my mate's territory."

Lily glances around the small clearing and distant woods belonging to the local pack. Our parents already crossed the rainbow bridge and not much is holding her here. "Maybe." She rubs her arms and I know she's too afraid to leave the safety of our family home. "I just want *you* happy."

A familiar tingle runs up my spine. My head shoots to the sky. I calm my mind and a flash of an image appears. It's distorted but I can recognize the location. "I'm needed in Carson City." I kiss the small bundle in my arms. "I'll call you soon." I pass over my nephew and hug my sister. "I love you, Lily, and I'm proud of you." I don't clarify the sentiment. She knows what I'm referring to: birthing a bastard's pup and making the best of it with a smile on her face.

"I love you too, Azure. Keep your nose up, brother. I know your mate is out there."

I hate that our visit has to be cut short. But my job is never done. I'm a protector. I maintain peace between the packs and humans so we can continue to coexist. And now, I'm also in search of my true love.

## Sky

# New Dreams

It's been a while since I talked to Freddy, and that troubles me. Not only do I miss our tumblings in the sack, but the fleabag is also one of my loyal customers. I rub the charm on my anklet and I swear a spark tingles my finger.

"You know wrinkles aren't very attractive. You'll never get a mate looking like that," my younger brother Aspen teases.

I shoot him a glare.

"Don't worry, her *stellar* attitude will win them over for sure." My eldest sibling Sable ruffles my hair as he passes. And I thrust my burger into my mouth to keep my rude comment contained, at least until our parents leave the room.

"Speaking of mates, Sky, sweetheart, when are you going to visit the other packs to help narrow down your search?"

I swallow the meat lodged in my throat, then sip my crisp wine, before replying to my mother, "I'm with *my* pack."

"Sky, you know what your mother means," my father adds. "You have been keeping yourself so busy with work lately. When are you going to visit the Tala shifters?"

I leap to my feet and snatch up my plate. Why is everyone jumping on my back? When I agreed to this family dinner, I was not expecting to be interrogated. I toss my meal into the trash can before slamming my plate in the sink. The meat was dry and not even seasoned well anyway. The resounding clang bounces off the walls while I stride to my room.

Our family is close. Maybe *too* close at times. We love each other no matter what. Yeah, we could live on our own, but we've never felt the need to. Our home, carved into the side of a cave, is more than large enough to accommodate us. With its rustic appearance, it has all the comforts we need with a touch a magic strewn in. Especially with the natural rock walls and stone flooring.

I lift my blouse over my head and grab my work shirt out of my closet. If my family wants to be a bunch of jackasses, fine. I'll go start on inventory at the restaurant. Once I'm dressed, I grab my keys off my nightstand. As I pass a picture of me and Carly at our college graduation, my lip trembles. What's really bugging me has nothing to do with my fur-kin. The truth is, I'm terrified that when I do find my furever husband, he'll demand I never see my best friend again.

A knock on my door pulls me out of my self-loathing. "Hey. What's up with you?" Sable leans on the doorframe. "You are moodier than normal."

"I was being verbally assaulted out there. Am I not allowed to defend myself?"

Sable snatches my wrist as I try to pass him and smashes me into his chest. "Come on, tell me what's up. If not, I'll just squeeze it out of you." He crushes me in his embrace, forcing the air from my lungs. "Or how about I tickle you until you pee yourself?"

"You better not. I need to check in at the restaurant. Don't make me tell everyone about that time I caught you jerking off to…"

"Hey!" Sable glances down the hallway as he releases his hold on me. "They have wolf ears! Shit. Why are you so moody? Oh, I know what this is… You are going into heat soon, right?"

"Gross. Stop tracking my cycles!" I stomp on his foot with a huff.

His chuckle rings out. "I'll be at the shop until late, but call me if you need me to pick you up some chocolate on the way home!"

Once I'm safely in my car, I blink at my reflection in the rearview mirror as my brother's words wash over me. "No. No. No." I rummage through my purse and slam my finger over my phone's screen to unlock it. I swipe to my cycle tracker and my breath catches. My android slides from my grasp and hits the floor before my fingertips graze my flat stomach. I nearly shit my pants when I hear rapping on my window.

"Hey, honey. You forgot your wallet on the counter. I had to stop Aspen from stealing your cash. Skylar? Please let me in. You are scaring me." I tug the car door handle open, and the air is forced from my lips as my mother awkwardly embraces me in the vehicle. Her fingertips glide over my hair. "Whatever is going on, we can resolve it."

I take in a steadying breath. She's my biggest supporter and we have no secrets between us. She's more of a bestie than a mom. "I'm possibly pregnant with a pup from the Fangs' beta… Freddy."

I'm not met by the look of hatred I was expecting. Instead, my mother's eyes twinkle and she lets out a girlish squeal. She stops abruptly and narrows her eyes. "Is this an April Fool's joke? Because it's not funny. Although, it's not as bad as the year that you and your brothers moved all the furniture to the top of the cave."

"What?" I sputter out.

"It took your dad a week to put everything back and he broke my mother's urn." She rushes through a reflexive sign of the cross. "Luna rest her soul."

I bite my tongue. As I recall, Dad broke it on purpose just so it wouldn't be a shrine on the fireplace anymore. "Mom, it's not even April. Why would I make this shit up?"

"Watch your mouth and get out here and give me a hug." I exit the car, and she lifts me in the air and twirls. Once she finally sets me down, I put a few inches between us, so her baby craziness doesn't rub off on me. "Now, I know this isn't an *ideal* situation, dear. We had hoped you'd find your mate and settle down, or at the very least pick a shifter from our pack before getting pregnant. But don't worry. It'll be okay. This pup is going to be so loved, and if anyone gives you crap about it, I'll always have your back."

"I don't know for sure yet *if* I'm actually pregnant."

She guides me to the passenger seat. "I'll take you to Dr. Fuego to find out. She's the best and very discreet. We'll know if you are, in no time at all. Then we can formulate a plan."

Although my mother is a doctor, she doesn't practice on us if she can help it. And Dr. Fuego is a fellow shifter who specializes in family medicine. Mom prattles on and on about baby equipment, pregnancy, and safety. All the information she is feeding me elicits a migraine. I feel like I'm five years old again and going in for my school physical. But I'm so numb I don't even give a shit.

"I appreciate you being here for me and all. But with the constant conflict between our packs, I don't know *if* I'm keeping it." She slams on the brakes and stares at me. I glance around at the empty street to make sure we don't get rear-ended. "Have you lost your Luna-loving mind? At least pull over if you are going to brake check me. Remember this is *my* car not yours."

"Skylar, tell me you did not just suggest killing this fur-child."

I rest my head against the window. The fog of my breath covers my reflection. I know I won't terminate the pregnancy. Because deep, *DEEP* down, I'm looking *forward* to this new addition. Something to watch grow, to take care of, and maybe even an excuse to move out of my parents' home and closer to the steakhouse. "I'm just not sure how our alpha will react to the pup."

"A pack should encompass family, love, and support. If the alpha's values don't match that, maybe it's time for new leadership."

"…plus, Freddy isn't necessarily a family kind of man," I add after the fact.

"Fine. Then *we* will take care of this little blessing ourselves. And if you are serious about not wanting it, then at least *consider* putting it up for adoption. Dad and I would be more than willing to raise the little peanut. And there are tons of other shifters who would do the same. Some would even be willing to financially compensate you." She pats my hand as I digest her advice before she puts the car in drive again. The silence blankets us for several more minutes, until my mother clears her throat and asks, "If we didn't tell Freddy about the child, would he be able to guess it's his?"

I sneak a peek at my mother to see if she is being serious. She is. "Wouldn't that be completely dishonest? What would Mrs. *Manners* say?" We laugh at my attempt to make a joke and then we are silent again. Lost in our own thoughts. Of course, I would tell Freddy. Right? My phone rings, catching me off guard. "Carly? Is everything okay? Did Sam not show up for work again?"

"Actually, Sam made it in on time. You, however, are late. Again."

"Tell me about it," I mumble into the mouthpiece.

"So, you are on your way?"

"No, I have a doctor's appointment I forgot about. I'm sorry. Are we busy?"

"Nothing I can't handle. Are you sick? Do you need me to get you anything?"

"Mom is taking care of me, but thanks for the offer. I'll call you later and we can catch up."

"Get well soon, Sky Bear."

*Yeah, it's going to be a long nine months.*

"Well, Skylar, I have the results from your urine analysis," Dr. Fuego reports as she enters the examination room.

I clench my mom's hand. Whatever the doctor says is going to change my life. If it's positive, I'll be a soon-to-be mother. If it's negative, well, then this whole ordeal has made me realize I *do* want to start a family. With or without waiting for my nonexistent mate.

*Just not right now*, I pray to Luna.

"Have you been under a lot of stress?" Dr. Fuego asks, pulling me out of my internal anguish.

"Well, we have been dealing with some complicated situations," my mom responds for me as she pats my leg.

The doctor types some notes into the computer. "Well, your pap was done a few months ago and it was normal. I also see you had your annual blood work drawn the same day, and that too was regular... interesting." She trails off as she chews her pen.

I wait for her to continue. When she doesn't, I nearly jump out of my skin. "So, is the test positive?"

"Oh, I'm sorry, dear." She laughs and shakes her head. "Your test came back *negative*. I'm just making sure there aren't any underlying issues in your medical history that could be delaying your menstrual cycle."

I can't help the pang in my stomach. *No* baby? My fingertips twist the hem of my shirt. I'm not going to be a mother after all. I slip off the exam table and grab my purse, before I make a fool of myself in front of my mom's college buddy. "Thank you again, Dr. Fuego."

"If your period doesn't come in a few weeks, follow up with me, please," she calls out at my departing back. Her voice bounces off the cold, sterile walls of the clinic as I make my way to the front door. I was worried about nothing. And now Mom knows my dirty little secret. Boy, did I screw up. What she must think of her baby girl…

I slam the car door shut on my barrage of negative thoughts. I'm a grown-ass woman. What's she going to do? Spank me? When the woman in question positions herself behind the wheel, she passes me my copay receipt, buckles her seat belt, and starts driving towards the house without a word. We sit like this until she shifts into park again. "You are my daughter and I love you more than you know. Nothing can *ever* change that. I'm not going to tell you what you should do, because that is up to you. You are an adult, after all."

"I never realized how much I wanted a child before this happened," I blurt out.

"Are you talking about *with* Freddy, or just in general?" I shrug, and she continues. "Let me put it this way: is Freddy the mate Luna assigned you?"

I can't answer her, so I just shake my head. I know Freddy isn't the *one*. But some shifters never meet their mate. What if I'm a hundred years old when I finally do? We aren't immortal! Our eggs have an expiration date.

"I can't pretend to know how you feel. But I hope you do know that I am here for you. I'll help you search to the ends of the earth for your partner if that's what you need." She kisses my cheek before she slips out of the car.

The charm on my anklet sparkles, catching my attention. Images of the moments Freddy and I've spent together flash through my mind. The one thing that seems to get in the way of us dating is his involvement with *Spike*.

I clench my jaw as I make a choice. I'm not waiting for this mystical being to make an appearance! I'm going to ask Freddy to step up. Maybe if we give our relationship a real shot, it'll blossom into a happily ever after, and he'll realize what an idiot his alpha is and leave the Fangs. *Then* I'll approach him about Carly. I mean, they aren't exactly friends right now. They banter here and there. But I'm sure he'll be willing to let my best friend play with us too. She's a great person and everyone likes her.

I shoot a message to Freddy, asking him out, and chew my lip as I wait for a response. The thumbs up he sends me in return makes my eyes roll. Leave it to him to take a serious conversation and turn it into something meaningless.

I look to the heavens and beg Luna to not let this decision ruin my life.

# Freddy

# The General

A chair whizzes past my head and splinters into a thousand pieces.

"This can't be happening! Where is *she*?" Spike roars. The pack members clamp their mouths shut, no one brave enough to explain that we lost Maya's scent in enemy territory. "I want her brought back here immediately!"

"Sir, I'll take a group and retrieve her," Tanner (the kiss-ass that he is) speaks out first.

Spike grumbles as he slams his feet into his boots. "If you want something done right, you have to do it yourself. You and you, come with me. The rest of you, stay here and be on standby. The enemy has captured one of our own and I have every intention of rescuing her from their claws." He brushes past me as he throws over his shoulder, "I've alerted our pack members within the police station about our situation. If we get picked up by the authorities, be ready to bail us out."

"Yes, sir," I reply. Once the door slams closed, I release a breath and tug out my phone. Sky texted me and I didn't want Captain Douche to see.

"Where's Spike?" Angelica asks as she enters and frowns down at the broken chair. "The General is here to see him."

I curse. The General and Spike have been meeting for a while now, and of course, I'm only told what I need to know. And that equates to zilch. But I've noticed that Spike has been receiving hefty sums of cash from these new friends. Something *big* is going on. I send a reply to Sky, agreeing to meet her after work. She said Sable met a new friend, and she wants to tell me all about it. This whole *dating* thing was her idea and it's already been rewarding. I rub my chin. That charm I gave her is working better than my aunt said it would. Having her in my back pocket *when* things go south with Spike was a brilliant idea. Especially if her family finds Maya before we do.

"Who are you texting?" Angelica asks, peeking over my shoulder at the screen.

I walk towards the meeting room to talk to the General in Spike's place. "Don't worry about it."

Angelica snatches my wrist. "Maybe we should stop messing with her. You almost lost your neck because of that twit. She's not worth it. No matter how much you think she'll save our ass when things get rough."

I pull free as I eye-fuck my mate in her tight tactical pants and clingy red tank top. She's hot when she's jealous. Another member of the pack strolls by and arches a brow at us, so I keep our cover by taunting her. "Angelica, just because Spike *forced* us to be together doesn't mean I'm going to stop doing *whomever* the fuck I want. Deal with it," I snip. The onlooker rolls his eyes and I wink at my mate. I shove my hands into my pockets as I put distance between us. I need to get away from her before I shove my cock in her pussy and make her scream. I adjust my pants and shake my head of the thoughts. If things were different, we could have our villainous fairy-tale ending. But we are stuck here, playing mind games so we

44

can survive.

"General, it's good to see you again," I announce to the group huddled in the conference room.

The older man knots his brows as he rises from his chair. "Where is Spike?"

"He had some business to attend to, so he asked me to apologize on his behalf and act as your liaison." I settle into Spike's place at the head of the table. "Or you can talk to him next month. It's up to you."

He scowls as I rest my boots on top of the table. "Tell your alpha I'm getting anxious waiting around for what he promised."

My ears perk up. What did Spike promise? I need to play my cards right if I want to elicit more information. "There were complications—things that were out of our control."

"I don't give a damn! We paid up, and now it's his turn to deliver. Or so help me, I'll bring my fist down on this shithole you call a home!"

"Easy, General. If you have any suggestions on how we can expedite the mission, by all means, share it with the rest of the class." I watch as his wheels turn, and I know I've made some progress. This fucker is about to give me something. *Everything.*

The General unbuttons his uniform jacket and sits beside me. He slowly folds his hands together while his eyes slide to mine. "I suggest you set more traps and check them often."

I rub my chin, pretending to take his advice to heart. "Where should we place them? In order to be most effective?"

"Set them up in closer proximity to the dens. You may have luck placing some between the pack boundaries. And instead of checking them every few days, do it daily."

I swallow back my surprise. We are trapping... what exactly? "And where do you propose we keep them until drop off?"

"In a cage preferably," he sneers. "I don't give a shit how or where you store them. We will retrieve the mutts and transport them to the facility so we can get the trials started. The sooner we have more DNA samples, the quicker we can start cloning their abilities for field testing."

He's talking about experimenting on shifters? For his military unit? Why would Spike allow this? Those are the questions filtering through my head; however, I respond with, "We will do our best to get it done."

"You will do better than that, Fredrick. Because if you don't, we will begin collecting from *your* pack, starting with that sweet wife of yours."

My wolf loses his shit, and suddenly I have the General in a choke hold against the wall. With five guns pointed at me from his surrounding security. I squeeze his throat and feel him squirm beneath my fingertips as his eyes bulge out. Fur pokes through my skin as my fangs elongate.

The guns cock in near unison.

"Funny how you think you are more powerful than we are," I snarl. "You better watch how you fucking talk to me. Because, unlike you, I have very *little* self-control." I release him and he drops to his knees. Exactly where he belongs.

"We'll see how long *that* lasts, mutt. Tell your leader I won't ask nicely *again*." He slams his shoulder into mine as he walks past. "You have bigger balls than he gives you credit for." He pauses by the exit and flicks a card at the floor. "Fetch this, dog, and call when you're ready to rank up. Unless you prefer being the bitch of the pack."

My threatening growl vibrates the tension-filled air. I leap forward, but my arm is grasped and I'm pulled back. When the red fades from my vision, I scowl at Angelica. She returns my glare before she hisses her defense, "What were you planning on doing? *Killing* him? Well, brainiac, if you do that, you damn the entire pack. Snap out of it!"

I gulp down a few breaths until my head clears. My phone vibrates in my pocket. "James, what's up?"

"Spike and Jake were just picked up by the police and they need you to bail them out."

"Did they get Maya back?"

"The Canis family is offering her sanctuary in Tala territory, and it's only a matter of time before they realize who she really is. Spike demands that you attempt to collect her one more time, then come to the police station. Shit, gotta go, bro. The captain is coming."

The click signals the end of our conversation. I roar my frustration into the empty air and stomp towards Spike's loft. I kneel in front of his safe and spin the dial to the magic numbers.

"That's supposed to be for the pack's benefit. We all worked the streets for that." She doesn't need to remind me of what we've had to do to make this money. We offer the dealers our services for a hefty cost. They give us cash and we shift and take care of their loose ends. They don't call us the Fangs for nothing. We do their muscle work, without *bullets*. Normally it's just throwing around dead-beat junkies who can't pay up. I swivel to see Angelica leaning against the doorway, tapping her fingers on her arm.

"You aren't allowed in here. Get out before you are caught."

She runs her talons across Spike's bed. "I'm the beta's wife. I get some privileges too." She glides her fingertips to the buttons on her blouse, and one at a time, she frees them. My eyes dart to her cleavage and my pants grow tight. I slam the safe shut while I shove the cash into my pocket. This woman is going to get us killed. Angelica's devilish grin spreads across her face. "Come on, baby. You can't tell me you don't want to stick it to him? And what better way than to stick it to me... *on his sheets*?" Her hands glide down to my erection while she licks her lips. She pumps my cock as she leans into my neck. "Let's prove to him that he can't fuck with you."

47

I groan as she pinches my tip while she bites my earlobe. This is witchcraft and I'm falling under her spell. My dark siren. "I need to bail out the boss," I grunt, trying to convince myself.

This stops her actions, and she purses her lips. "Why would you do *that*?"

"Because, currently, Spike is our alpha and holds all the cards."

"For now." She rubs her chest against mine. "Can't we just leave him behind bars to rot. Then we can rise to power." She slams her lips to mine and we get tangled up in a mixture of saliva and teeth. The taste of copper fuels our passion. We fall to the bed, and I pin her to the covers. Her silky legs run over my thighs. "I can't wait until you break that bitch and you are back where you belong, buried in my pussy only."

A shiver trails up my spine at her dirty talk. "Trust me, it'll happen. Be patient. You are the only queen I want beside me. And *Spike* commands too many shifters to leave the bastard locked up. Plus, he now has the government under his thumb. I need to bail him out. And you better hope I don't report your little stunt." I squeeze her ass.

Angelica runs her tongue over my stubble. "Fuck me and let our juices taint his safe haven. Let's remind him who really deserves to rule."

Our lips meet again in a frenzy, and I can't stop my hands as they fumble to remove my pants, then hers. My dick glides in easily. The pack is still downstairs with their big wolf ears, so I slap a palm over her mouth to contain her enthusiasm. Her moans are muffled as I thrust faster.

"Harder, Freddy!" She attempts to push past my hold.

I throw my head back and empty my load inside her with a grunt. Angelica shoves at my chest and I fall to my back on the bed. She takes my rod into her mouth and sucks me dry but doesn't swallow. She crawls on her hands and knees, giving me a perfect view of her glistening, satisfied pussy. She stops at Spike's pillow and spits our

48

shared liquid onto it, then flips it over.

*Fuck, that was hot.*

The night air brushes my fur as my claws dig into the earth. Can I make it to the Tala pack before they discover who Scarlett really is?

"Halt right there, trespasser."

I shift and stand chest to chest with Jackson—the Talas' annoying, ass-kissing beta. "I need to speak to your alpha, dog."

He wrinkles his nose but calls over his shoulder. "Alpha, we have an intruder in the east quadrant."

His highness strides towards us, but it's Maya who notices me first. "Freddy?"

"You *know* this man?" Frost Tala prompts, throwing a thumb towards me.

I bristle at his upturned nose. "Not only does she know me, old man, but she is also coming back with me. She's Spike's mate and doesn't belong here any more than I do."

Maya pales and steps forward. *Yes. That's right. Come with me.* The pompous Canis prick shields her from my view. "Don't worry. We won't let him take you," Sable insists.

Frost draws his dagger and points it at my chest. "I should cut your tongue out for such lies."

"It's the truth. That's why she was lost in the woods. It was the day we had our ancestral gathering. She drank of the ceremonial wine, and Spike asked for her hand."

"I never agreed to marry that son of a bitch. *He* asked, and *I* said no." Maya feigns confidence but I see her knees shake. I need to push harder to break her. Otherwise, war is inevitable.

"She's a filthy liar! I heard her agree. And then, when Spike walked away to tend to an emergency, she ran off into the woods— *drunk*."

Frost glares. "Don't you dare speak about my daughter like that, you ingrate. If she says she didn't agree to his proposal, that's exactly what happened. Now leave."

Fuck. How did he uncover her true identity? We are screwed. Unless… "Even if she didn't agree, she has slept with him numerous times."

"We are not speaking of lost virtues here, boy. We are talking about marriage proposals and pack members. My daughter never agreed to be his mate. Now turn around and walk out. Jackson." The incompetent beta steps forward. "Follow him. Ensure he makes it home."

"This isn't over," I grumble, then curse to myself. I'm sure as fuck not looking forward to explaining to Spike that I failed to reclaim his prize.

I speed through the traffic lights and pull into the police station in record time. Once I collect Spike, we make our way back to the Warehouse. I explain how Maya refused to return, and that Frost knows who she really is. The steam pulsating from the alpha's ears has the short car ride feeling like an eternity.

"Where is Tanner?" I ask.

"Dead," Spike retorts.

"What the fuck?" I push out, trying to hide my shock.

"When I attempted to collect what was mine, the Canis family refused to hand her over." He grinds his teeth. "They were calling her *Scarlett* still, so at the time, they didn't know who she really was."

All these years of concealing the little brat, and now the lies are coming unraveled.

"You are going to fetch me the Canis girl—Skylar. She's at the Wolves' Den steakhouse, a couple of blocks from their residence. I'll have Angelica snatch a few more *weaklings* from Frost's pack. This will get his attention and *lure* Maya back to us. Then I will cut that bitch up and feed her mangled body, piece by piece, to her father. She will regret the day she chose them over me!"

That's it. Spike has lost his damn mind. This is *suicide*.

"Don't look at me like that. The General is sending reinforcements. Just do *your* job," he snarls. "This is our time to rise above them all!"

Should I cut my losses and hightail it out of here? Or wait to see if the two packs weaken each other enough in time for a *new* leader to take over?

"What are we doing with the captives?"

"That depends on the aftermath of this fight." Spike scratches his stubble.

This will not end well. Surely he knows that. I study his face. The rage burning behind his eyes is beyond anything I've ever seen. His fury is going to be his undoing. I can't wait to witness him crumble under the weight of his mistakes. But I'll be damned if he's taking us with him.

## Sky

# Taken

"I'm telling you… I found her outside by the stream." My little brother tugs me towards our guest room.

"I only came home to grab my charger, not to see the wounded animal you picked up on your hike." I skid to a stop. Lying in the bed is a sleeping woman. Where the hell did she come from? I rub the bridge of my nose. This boy is going to be the death of me. "You aren't supposed to bring in stray humans, Aspen. You don't know where they've been."

"What was I supposed to do, Sky? Leave her there to die! She was freezing, and nobody was around to help her. Oh, she's waking up. Wait, where are you going? Shouldn't she see another female when she comes to? She might be frightened."

I curse as my phone rings. I pat his head and make a mental note to tell Mom about his new pet. "Shelley is calling because I'm late for our meeting. Don't touch the human. It might have lice," I shout over my shoulder as I head towards the car. I answer my screaming cell. "Shelley, I'm so sorry. No! Please don't leave! I'll be there in five minutes!"

She hangs up on me. I double-check my GPS. Traffic. Great. I strip out of my business attire and shift to fur. One advantage to having special abilities is I can skip the commute by cutting through the forest. I snatch my purse between my teeth and bullet past the trees. I can't miss this appointment again or I'll lose my organic vegetable supplier. The woods are a blur as I gallop at full speed. Forgetting about everything and releasing the beast.

Later that night, I drag my ass into the cave. I dump my belongings on the dresser and run my hands through my hair. I made it just in time to stop Shelley from walking out. I really need to hunt down *more-forgiving* distributors.

"Did you know your brother brought home a *human*?"

"Dad, please. It's been a rough day."

"Why didn't you tell us what he was up to?"

"Because I'm not my brother's keeper." I groan at his scowl. "I meant to call Mom, but I had to shift and haul ass to a meeting that lasted forever."

"That woman needed our help and now she could be lost in the woods."

"But how? She was safe in the cave when I left."

"Well, she escaped."

"Then she wasn't a stray after all, and she's returned home. Come on, don't give me that look. We are not a homeless shelter." I stomp to the shower.

"Skylar, when are you going to delegate tasks so you can focus on *more* important things—things other than just the restaurant? Like your pack." Dad's never spoken negatively about my dedication to my business. He must really be freaking out over this stranger.

"I'm sorry I forgot to call about the girl. If you are really that concerned, I'll search the woods." But we both know I'm not the best hunter—I barely passed the exam as a pup.

"Sable is already on her trail." Dad pivots, then stops. "I just want you to slow down and *enjoy* life. There's more to it than working, you know? Good night, Sky. Sleep well." He closes my door behind him.

A howl breaks through my dreams, and I lurch out of bed and dash to the front porch, frantically searching for my brother.

"You heard it too, right?" Aspen brushes the slumber from his eyes.

"We all did," Dad announces with Mom by his side.

"I checked his room, and he isn't there." Mom rubs her arms. "He never came home last night after searching for that girl."

"We need to look for him. Mom and I will take the woods. Aspen, you follow the stream. And, Sky, you stay here in case he returns," Dad instructs.

We all split up. I pace the kitchen. "Where are you, Sable?" His agony-etched wail reverberates in my head. "Please be okay."

After an hour of pacing, I watch as Aspen returns with my parents, carrying our wounded fur-member. My heart sinks as I trail behind them before they lay his wolf form in his bed.

"Thank you, Scarlett, for rescuing him," Mom addresses the stray human. I take in the girl's blood-soaked shirt and wonder what happened. "Sky, can you please grab our guest some clothes and a fresh towel." Mom elbows me in the ribs. "And please, Scarlett, feel free to shower and rest. We will have food available soon."

Mom pushes us out the door before closing Sable and Scarlett inside. She meets Dad's concerned gaze, and something passes between them. Dad nods and strides to the kitchen. "I'll heat up dinner."

"Sky, do as I asked and grab a fresh towel and some of your clothes," Mom demands. "I'll talk with your brother while our guest's in the shower."

I collect the requested items, then walk in to see the woman slowly backing away from my brother's wolf form. She meets my eyes and clears her throat. "Thank you for the clothes. I'm guessing they are yours?"

"Yes, they're mine, but it's the least I can do, considering you saved Sable."

"His name is Sable? Does he come around here often?"

Wait… she doesn't know? I can't help the laugh that erupts from my mouth at the sheer lunacy. But then my wolf brother barks. What's he up to? "Yes, he practically *lives* here."

I pivot and meet Dad and Aspen in the kitchen while Mom morphs into fur and sneaks into Sable's room. "She must not be that bright. She has no clue who he really is," I scoff as I pick at a dinner roll.

"*She* has a name. It's Scarlett," Aspen announces as he grabs

56

some bowls from the cupboard.

"Don't get attached to your pet. She's going back to where she came from." I stab a spoon at him.

"Sky, please be nice," Dad warns. "She is our guest and will be respected."

"I don't know why you're being so mean to her, considering Carly's human too," Aspen grumbles.

"Carly never brought one of my siblings home bleeding. Or stole any of my clothes."

Mom's snow-white wolf pads into the kitchen before she morphs back to two legs. "That poor woman." She throws a dress on. "Let's feed her and get to know her a bit more. Aspen, can you help our guest to the table?"

"How is Sable?" I question.

"His wound is already starting to heal."

"Why can't he shift back to his human skin?"

"I'm not sure." Mom's lips thin. "But I intend to figure it out. Either way, I'm confident he'll be on his feet soon."

We sit around the table while Mom serves beef stew. The awkwardness of having a stranger in our midst weighs heavily on us. I'm glad Sable will make a full recovery. But what does he see in this woman?

"So you just walked out, without hearing the drama?"

"Yup. Sable shifted in the middle of the night, and the girl woke up screaming when she saw him naked beside her."

Carly cackles. "I'm so jealous! I miss all the good stuff!"

"I snuck out of the house before she had a chance to screech again." I shake my head. "Now my family is trying to convince her that she isn't losing her mind. Before I forget: Carly, I need you to cover for Sam." I scribble on the disciplinary form addressed to the chronic slacker. "This is his last chance. After this, he's fired. I don't care if his father works with my dad."

"Sorry, honey, you need to find someone else to cover for King Douche." She slaps my butt as she sings, "Because your girl has a date tonight!"

"What?" My head shoots up as she collects her purse. "With whom?"

She fluffs her hair with her fingertips. "Don't act so surprised."

"I just want to know who you are going out with. Please don't tell me it's that married military guy?"

My bestie narrows her eyes at me, then points a digit my way. "I told you I only went out with him to prove to his wife that he was a lying, cheating piece of shit."

"I saw the pictures you sent to his spouse, and you seemed to be enjoying him a little too much to be actually punishing him."

Carly grins and lifts her shoulders. "I am a sucker for a man in uniform. Plus, he had amazing stamina." She purrs as she reminisces. "He just wasn't using it to service the woman he swore to love until death, and was too big of a pussy to be honest with her about needing more."

"You are just a regular, everyday hero. Aren't you?"

"That I am! And tonight, I'll be putting my services to good use with a cheating professor." She glosses her lips. "Hopefully he'll match GI Joe's endurance." She walks to the exit before throwing over her shoulder, "I'll call you when I light the cigarette, right after I text my naughties to the fiancée." I grumble as the door clangs behind her. Ever since she got her heart broken by her high school sweetheart, she has been hell-bent on taking down all the cheaters. I just hope it doesn't get her in trouble one day.

I scan the employee roster. Why does everybody call out when I need help the most?

My cell phone pings. I read the text from my mom and curse. Apparently, my brothers got into a scuffle, and they are at the hospital getting stitches. She doesn't give many details, only disclosing that she'll be home late. I bet it has to do with their new buddy *Scarlett*. I swear that girl is trouble. But I'm the only one who can see it. Well, I guess I can't enlist my brothers' help today.

I raise my chin. It's up to me to feed the Wolves' Den's starving, dinner-rush customers. I think I'd look damn good in a cape right about now.

After hours of nonstop waitressing, the crowds finally slow. I rub my swollen ankles in the break room. I forgot how physically exhausting it is to constantly serve customers. I check my cell and see I have missed calls from my brother. I grumble and skim his message. Oh shit! He said the woman who rescued him is really his mate *Maya*! Somehow, she was under the influence of a powerful spell. And now that it's broken, she no longer exhibits red hair and emerald eyes; instead, her features have returned to the lighter signature hues of the Tala pack. But of course, he didn't give me much more information beyond that, claiming he can't wait to explain the whole tale to me in *person*. My cell vibrates and I glance at it eagerly, hoping it's my sibling. Disappointment floods me when I notice it's Freddy.

He sent a text asking me to meet up. I rub the back of my aching neck. We agreed we would try this whole relationship thing, but it's mostly been us texting. No dates. No flowers or sweet gestures. *I want to be pampered, damn it.* I shove the device in my pocket and stomp through the dining room, where I spot him at his normal table in the far corner.

I slide into the booth across from him. "Hey, boyfriend."

"I've been looking everywhere for you. Where were you?"

I arch a brow at his tone. "I didn't know I needed to wear a collar for you."

He rubs his hands over his face. "Sky, I don't want to fight."

"Well, you come in here. Demand to speak to me. Then growl to know my whereabouts. Those all fall into the whole *fighting* territory."

"I'm in trouble with Spike."

"What do you mean *in trouble*?"

"He knows about us. Without your help, I'm a dead man."

"How did he find out?"

"He smelled you on me. I thought I threw him off, but I was wrong. Please, don't make me beg."

"First, tell me what you need me to do."

"Not in here. Meet me at your car." He leaves the booth without a backward glance. He's never this antsy. Curiosity gets the better of me and I follow him. Even though my feet beg me to turn around and soak them, I demand they march outside. When I turn the corner, he's leaning on my car with his arms crossed.

"You have five minutes. Go."

"I need to take you as a temporary hostage."

I laugh, but my expression quickly sours when I realize he's serious. "Fuck that."

"Sky, baby. You know I won't let him hurt you."

"Hell no." I pivot towards the employee entrance. "Find another way to get Spike off your ass."

The force of his body takes my breath away as he shoves me against the wall. His eyes shine with desperation. "I came here to ask *nicely*. But don't take that as weakness. If you do not come willingly, I will have no choice but to force you."

"So your true colors are finally showing through. You're exactly like your piece-of-shit alpha."

"You know me better than that. Or I thought you did." He runs his nose over my neck before nibbling my earlobe. I squeal at the vibration running to my toes. "*Who* do you think he'll attack after he kills me? *Think* about it. Really think about it."

"Spike wouldn't dare touch me or my family."

"I've spent my entire life under his reign, and I can say, without a shadow of a doubt, that he can destroy everything you care for. His lust for bloodshed knows no bounds. I swear no harm will come to you, sweets. I'll bring you there, prove to him I'm loyal, and then when he drifts off, I'll call your pack to rescue you. Then *they* can put an end to his tyranny once and for all." I hum softly at his honey-laced promises. "With *your* help, we can bring him down and save countless lives."

My heart clenches as his words ring out into the night air. My dad said I've been too focused on my job and ignoring those around me. Could this be my chance to demonstrate that I do care? That I'm not selfish?

"Don't make me regret this."

He guides me into the woods. "Don't worry. You'll be home before breakfast." Suddenly a rough cloth is thrown over my head. I kick out before my arms are zip tied behind my back. "Easy. It's just for show." Freddy's muffled voice answers.

"You better get this sack off my head, or I'll scream bloody murder and alert my pack!"

"Why don't I knock the bitch unconscious?" a female hisses in response to my protests.

"Angelica, let me handle her." Freddy guides me with his palm on the small of my back. "Sky, I promise I'll protect you."

Once we are farther away, I grumble at Freddy, "Who was that?"

"Someone Spike sent to babysit me."

As we near the city limits, I question if I'm making the right choice. However, as I twist my bound wrists, I also realize it's too late. I'm at his mercy.

Freddy

# Hostages

*T*hat was close. I thought Angelica was going to reveal who she was and blow my cover. I guide Sky to the loft to stash her away before Spike can get his claws on her. I open the secret compartment and take the bag off my lover's head. "Just sit in here until I return."

Her jaw drops, likely to argue with me, but she stops as she peers over my shoulder.

"Look at the present you brought me."

I freeze. Spike is right behind me. I turn to face him. "And the others are on their way."

He shoves me aside and grins at his prey. "Your *father* took something that belongs to me. And now I'm taking something from him." He runs his fingertips down her jawline. "Too bad you don't even compare to her beauty." He slams his body against hers. "I'm going to enjoy breaking Daddy's little girl. By the time I'm done with you, he'll rue the day he stole from me."

"Spike, your package is here," Jake mutters from the door.

Spike grins at Sky before striding out. As he brushes past us, he informs me, "The General sent some helpers. When the other hostages arrive, place them with her until I say otherwise."

I can only nod as I watch him leave the room. "Did he hurt you?" I question a pale-faced Sky.

"You didn't even *flinch*," she whispers, unable to meet my eyes. "He could have killed me."

"Hey, that's bullshit. I knew he wouldn't hurt you."

A female clears her voice from a few feet away, and I turn to see Angelica with the other hostages. She pushes the girls into me before barking her orders. "The boss wants us downstairs. Now."

I give Sky a reassuring squeeze and lock her and the other captives inside the dark room.

"So, that's *her*?" my mate seethes.

"What are you talking about?" I grumble as I take the stairs to the main floor.

"The one you play doctor with."

"Angelica, you know *why* I keep Sky in my back pocket," I whisper. "We have a job to do, so how about you pull your head out of your ass and focus. The General's involvement in this shifter war is suspicious. Remain vigilant."

We spot Spike near the entrance of the compound talking with a group of men, and he nods us over. "These are some of the gifts the General sent to assist us. They are trained special ops soldiers, under his direct command. When the alphas visit to collect their girls by force, *they* will keep them busy." He nods towards the humans. "I'm stationing them down here, because that's where the animals will attack first." The uniformed freaks scatter to their assigned areas. Spike clutches my mate's arm. "Angelica." He points to one of the soldiers in the corner. "Work your magic on the leader and find out what his boss is up to. I have a feeling that man has a few tricks up his sleeve."

My fur-wife arches a brow. "What is it you want me to do?"

"The norm, baby girl." He runs a finger over her lips. "That mouth of yours can elicit so many dirty little secrets."

Angelica meets my gaze. For once, she is speechless. I turn to our alpha. "Are you seriously sending *my* wife to suck off some random guy?"

"Do you both think I'm an idiot?" Spike snarls. "I have eyes everywhere. I know what you did on *my* bed, and you're lucky you're still *breathing*. If you want to keep it that way, you'll do exactly as I say."

Angelica clenches her jaw before shaking her hips towards the soldier, who is all but drooling over the fresh meat. I stomp behind Spike as he climbs the stairs, my wolf itching for a fight. "You force me to take her as my wife, and then you send her to another man."

Spike's growl vibrates off the loft's walls before he glares at me. "Your actions have consequences, beta. The sooner you realize that, the better." Before he can continue, movement from the back of the room catches our attention. I gawk at a very *naked* Maya. It looks like my aunt's magic has finally ebbed and the world can now see her for who she really is: the future alpha and stolen pup of the Tala pack. The doors slam open downstairs.

"Boss, we have some company!" I blare before running towards the shifters from the Tala pack as they flood into the Warehouse. The smell of blood and the rush of adrenaline weigh down the atmosphere. My fur rips through my skin. I zero in on Sable as the brute shoves his way towards the stairs.

*Yes, go rescue your sister and your long-lost mate.*

A tingle tickles my spine as my ears prick. Fuck! I gallop towards Angelica and slide to a stop. A soldier pounds into her from behind while she attempts to scream, but his palm is clasped over her mouth and tears stream down her cheeks. My hackles rise, my fangs slice through his jugular, and my tongue smears crimson over my fur.

"Don't expect a thank you," Angelica grumbles as she readjusts her clothes. "The General is not going to be happy that you killed one of his soldiers." The wetness on her face breaks me. I love this fur-demon. I morph into two legs and meet her gaze. I devour her mouth, and together, we swallow the life fluid of our enemy. Revenge never tasted so delectable.

"The General should have sent soldiers who can think with more than their *dicks*," I snarl against her neck.

Angelica grins. "Spoken like a true alpha. Baby, let's show them who they're messing with, and make them regret stepping into our territory and touching what doesn't belong to them."

Her faith in me fuels my desire to kick ass. We howl, shifting into our fur-forms, and return to the battle. The scent of rotting flesh dances in the air. I bite any enemy daring to get too close. As the skirmish rages on, I notice it's not just Frost's shifters amongst us but other warriors who've snuck into the mix. I collect their scent but recognition eludes me. What are these *creatures*? Flashing lights alert us that emergency services have arrived. They break up the brawl and cover up the dead bodies. I stick to the shadows, so I'm not caught in the mess, and scan the massacre, wondering if any of the Fangs survived.

"Freddy…" I hear my garbled name and quickly realize my mistake. My mate isn't by my side. I tear through the crowd, not giving a fuck who sees me now. That's when I spot her. On the ground. In a pool of crimson.

"Angelica." I collect her in my arms and grab a passing EMT. "What the fuck happened? *Who* did this to you?"

She takes in a labored breath. "They aren't happy."

My fingers graze her cheek. "Who?"

"They won't stop until we're all extinct."

The medic works quickly to stabilize Angelica, shoving me out of the way. I never release her cold wrist. The organ that's been locked deep within my chest splinters. I didn't think this could happen. I thought I had a big enough barrier around my heart. But as her life force oozes from her body, my sanity slips away with it. How could I have wasted so much time scheming that I neglected the most significant creature in my life? Rage takes over as they guide us to a waiting ambulance. The medic tries to separate us, but I squeeze Angelica's hand. "I'm her fucking husband," I snarl.

A smug grin illuminates her pale face before her head falls back against the gurney. I know she is never going to let me forget I admitted it out loud. For finally taking *ownership* of her crazy ass. But I'll proclaim it to the world if it means she'll remain by my side.

They transport her to the reservation hospital and the shifter doctors work diligently. I pace the waiting area while Angelica is in emergency surgery. After an hour, a nurse approaches me. I resist my urge to slam him against the wall and demand answers. "I'm sorry, sir. We lost her."

My mouth falls open. She's too strong, too ruthless, too much of a pain in the ass to die.

"I'm so sorry." He hands me paperwork to fill out with a bag of Angelica's belongings. Then leaves me to my grief.

I sift through her wallet and my fingers still on a piece of glossy paper. I examine it further. And sway. An ultrasound of a little peanut shape slips from my hand and onto the sterile ground. Was Angelica *pregnant*? I can't ignore the pain over the sudden loss of the unknown. The icy barrier returns to my heart, and I stomp the image into the floor. I glance one more time at the door—the same door they rushed my wife through not all that long ago. I wait for her to burst out and punk me. But only silence remains. Nothing is left for me in Carson City. Her body will be added to the countless others who followed Spike's ruinous leadership.

My phone pings, and I stare down at a text from an unknown number:

**The old mutt has been put down and your leash has finally been removed. It's time to meet up again, alpha. I'll be in touch.**

The fucking *General*. I clench the device in my palm. He let these events play out exactly how *he* wanted. But why? My cell vibrates again and I see it's from Sky. Shit. I was so distracted with Angelica I forgot about the princess. At the same time, I notice the police stomping around the corner. I sneak out the back exit as I text my new target, letting her know that I'm on my way to check on her. Once my feet touch the sidewalk, I shift and bullet into the darkness. I disregard my sanity as it splinters further.

My pack is *gone*. My mate is dead. And the General has sunk his fangs into my throat.

I have two viable options. I can either spend the rest of my life in a cell, or I can work for the General and attempt to pay off my alpha's debt. Maybe he'll trade my silence for his protection and help keep me outside that set of prison bars.

Once I'm close enough to her den, I breathe in Sky's familiar scent. And my wheels start turning.

Maybe there's a *third* option. If I continue to play my cards right, I can get Sky to vouch for me to *her* pack. I can rationalize my actions without anyone knowing the wiser. Then I can have their support. But I need to say and do *all* the right things. My acting needs to be Oscar winning.

I change to two feet as Sky runs to meet me in the front of her family's cave. I open my arms wide.

*Here goes nothing.*

# Sky

# Fallen Reign

*Earlier that night…*

**W**e've been submerged in darkness for I don't know how long. Scuffling and shouting come from the other side of the locked barrier. Suddenly, light blinds us as the door is yanked open.

"It's safe. You can trust us. Please, we need to hurry."

I stare into the eyes of my brother's mate as she tugs at our restraints. "Sky!" Sable crushes me. "Are you okay?"

"Yes, I'm fine." I rub at my sore wrists.

Maya guides us along the fire escape to the ground floor. "We have to shift if we want to make it back before they come after us." She reaches for Sable's hand.

"I can't go with you. I need to help the pack buy you more time. I'll meet you at home." He turns to leave, but I watch as she tugs him to her and kisses him deeply.

"You better come back to me." Her lip trembles and her devotion soaks her cheeks.

"Go, please. Or all of this was for nothing." He soothes her.

She turns to us. "Is everybody ready?" Her voice cracks and I know she's attempting to hold her emotions in check.

"I can't believe you sacrificed yourself for us, for people you don't even know."

"Isn't that what an alpha does?" She plasters on a fake smile. "It's in my blood."

I clear my throat. I tried to be the hero and failed. We morph into our fur-personas and bullet through the forest until we return to our homes. I embrace my younger brother, glad he's safe.

One of the first items on my to-do list the moment I enter our cave is to shower and rinse off the memories of the day. So much has happened. Did Freddy call my family? Like he said he was going to, so they'd rescue us... Or did they come on their own? As I dry off, I text him. Then I stand outside and wait for him to arrive with the answers I desperately need.

When the little prick is close enough, I pull back my fist and ram my knuckles into his jaw. "What the fuck is wrong with you?" I claw at his chest. "Don't you ever pull some dumb shit like that again." When the rage dulls, I take in his appearance. He is drenched in crimson. My heart skips a beat before my hands glide over his arms. "Were you *shot*?"

He slams me into his torso. "You slug me, then ask if I've been shot?"

I shove him aside. "You're lucky that is all I do to you, Fredrick."

"I *agree*." Freddy has never submitted this easily. He is a stubborn son of a bitch. "Can we go inside so I can change and explain myself? Or would you rather banish me from your life now?"

How am I supposed to trust him after everything that's happened? But did any harm come to me while I was under his care? No, he kept his word. Then again, it was Maya and *my* brother who rescued us. Not my delinquent boyfriend. I stomp towards my house and feel him following at my heels. We make our way inside and towards the sanctuary of my bedroom, stopping by Sable's door to gather some of my brother's old clothes before shoving them against Freddy's chest.

"Before we talk. You need to clean up. You stink."

He peels off his blood-drenched shirt. Muscles rippling. Tattoos gleaming on their perfectly sculpted canvas. I bite my lip at the strip tease he performs. "It's not polite to stare. Especially after you just decked somebody in the face."

I roll my eyes and turn away, allowing him to jump into the steaming water. "You kidnapped me, let Spike put his hands on my person, and left us locked in a dark closet! You deserved the smack I gave you!"

"I had everything under control. I told you that."

I snort as I sit on the bathroom counter, swinging my legs as I watch him glide the bar of soap over his chest. Even though I'm upset, I'm also jealous of those white suds slithering into every nook and cranny. All too soon, the water is shut off and he steps out. The steam rolls off his abs in waves, giving the rogue wolfman a godlike appearance.

"Do you have something to say?" he taunts. His cocky grin sours my peep show.

"I thought you loved me." I can't help the quiver in my lip. It's been a *long* night. So much has happened. I hate feeling the need to be loved by this monster, when he's clearly engaged in some fucked-up shit. But I know there's more to him than meets the eye.

75

Heat spins from his body and onto mine. My breath hitches and he shoves me against the mirror. Our tongues dance in a quick, clumsy tango while his hands tug at my shirt, but I slap his wrist in an attempt to keep my head clear. "I need answers."

A knock on my bedroom door interrupts us, and I'm reminded that I'm not the *only* one who is seeking explanations. After the events of tonight, lives will be changed. Freddy grabs my waist and lifts me off the counter. The action brings me back to the day we met. An eternity has passed since that brief moment in time. "Sky, I shouldn't have to tell you every single day how much you mean to me. You shouldn't be so insecure about what we have."

"I know you don't *need* to remind me, but you *should*." I push him. "Because, trust me, if you don't, I'll easily find someone who will treat me the way I'm supposed to be treated. Like a queen!" I turn on my heels and leave him to chew on those words while he gets dressed. I'm done playing games. He either wants to be with me, or I'm moving on. I answer my door and blink at my parents as they glare past me.

"Where is he?" Dad booms.

I take in the lacerations covering his frame and the fresh bandage on his forehead. For a second, I forgot he was at the Warehouse with Frost and the others, all fighting to rescue me.

"You have every right to be mad, Dad." I clutch his elbow as he brushes past me. "Freddy came here to explain what happened. Please. Hear him out. Before you give him a death sentence. For *me*."

My dad narrows his eyes as the man in question saunters over. "I just want to tell my side of the story—that's it. If you want to kick me out or call the police after that, I won't stop you." Freddy raises his hands in surrender.

"Couch. Now," is all my father can say past his fury. As we follow them to the living room, I see the fur poking through Dad's arms. His wolf is ready to tear Freddy to pieces. Maybe this isn't a good idea.

We settle on the couch and stare at the rogue shifter expectantly. The tale he weaves is sad, to say the least. Freddy explains how Spike has been abusing the pack members and making them break Luna's laws in the process. How his alpha forced multiple wolves to give up on finding their true mate and settle with a replacement of *his* choosing. They had no choice but to follow his demands, because they feared for their lives. "Spike's tyranny is over. I just want to be *free* to make my own decisions," he concludes.

Dad scratches his chin. "Are you asking to *join* our pack?"

Freddy grabs my hand and squeezes. "Wherever Sky is, I want to be. We've had to hide our relationship, but now we're free to date openly."

My heart warms and I can't help the smile that spreads across my face. Maybe I misjudged him? Perhaps without Spike's interference, we can finally be together. "I would love that too." I kiss his knuckles. He might be a pain in the ass, but he's mine. The growl that erupts in the air bounces off the cave walls and shakes me to my core. Freddy's torn away from my hold, landing on the ground with Maya on top of his chest, her hands wrapped tightly around his throat.

"Get off him!" I tug on the crazy woman.

"Yes, get off him, so I can tear him from limb to limb!" My brother snarls.

"Listen, it wasn't what it looked like, okay? Sky came with me to the Warehouse *willingly*," Freddy croaks between his desperate gasps for air.

"Bullshit! My sister would never trust a dirtbag like you! Especially after what you pulled tonight!" Sable's words sting. I can own a restaurant, vote, and drink, but I'm not competent enough to make my own choices? And even if I do make some bad judgement calls, it's my life! Doesn't my brother have faith in *me*?

"He's telling the truth." I stand over Freddy. "Back off and stop being a hypocrite, brother! You're trying to marry *Spike's* bed buddy, and no one's batting a lash. Why can't you hear Freddy out, like you did for her?" *Let them chew on that.* I overheard pack members discussing Maya's history with the fallen alpha, and it wasn't all that different from the wolf they are now looking to persecute. Who are they to judge?

My soon-to-be sister-in-law sidesteps us. And clutches her chest. Sable's eyes bulge like I've grown another set of ears before he shoves a finger in Freddy's face. "Explain yourself! Before I decide my sister has lost her damn mind and kill you without even shifting."

"Everybody, please sit and take a deep breath. Freddy was just finishing up telling us what happened." Dad's eyes land on each of ours, and his alpha tone laces his every word.

We slowly lower ourselves onto the sofa, ready to pounce at a moment's notice. When the tension becomes too thick, I blurt out, "Freddy and I have been dating."

"What the hell! He is just tricking you, using you to get information," my brother is quick to counter in that overprotective tone he likes to use on me.

"Freddy warned me what was going on before it even happened."

"Then why didn't you tell *us*? We could have protected you."

"Because everything happened so fast, Sable. We had to make it look real, or Spike would have suspected us, and we both would have been killed." My brother has stopped hearing me, and I'm exhausted. "Listen, you don't have to believe us. But it's true." My own fur and blood won't even give me a chance to explain, and I don't know how to deal with those emotions right now. "I love him and nothing you say will change my mind," I hiss with finality. I tug Freddy to my room without a backward glance at Mr. Judgmental-

Fur-Prick.

"Sky! We aren't done talking about this!" I slam my door on Sable's negativity.

"I should leave," Freddy announces as he sinks into the covers on my bed.

"Are you giving up on us already? I thought you weren't a little pussy?"

His eyebrow quirks. "Pussy, huh?"

"You know what I mean." I wish I could ask Carly to come over, but with all the fur-brutes on edge, I'd rather not. I climb into his lap and run my nose over his jawline. I hum softly at the familiar woodsy scent as it calms my nerves.

He wraps his arms around me. "I've made enemies."

"We all have."

"Yes, but I don't want them to hurt you or your family."

I snatch his chin, forcing him to meet my gaze. "You are a part of *my* family, you idiot."

"Sky…"

"After everything Spike put you through, I'm glad that fleabag's dead. Now that you are finally free of his control, you can have your happily ever after."

So many emotions pass through his eyes. Is he questioning my motives? My loyalty? He crushes his lips to mine and dominates my mouth with his tongue. A shiver runs down my back. I arch my chest against his as my nipples pebble, begging to be fondled. His calloused palms run circles over my thin shirt and a moan escapes my lips. The waves of pleasure lull me into bliss. He pins my hands on the pillows before he nips and sucks my neck. I rub against him, trying to get more friction on my throbbing parts, and am rewarded with a growl. Two fingers dip into my center and pump. I squeeze them with my core to increase the fullness. My toes tickle his tip. Even with his sweatpants on, I can feel the wetness of his precum.

Freddy tightens his hold on my wrists. "Shit. You're going to make me explode."

I giggle. "Just like a teenage boy, huh?"

He releases my palms and rips my shirt in half. I suck in my breath. That was... surprising. I know he likes it rough. But damn... that was my favorite pajama top. His fingertips tickle my belly, and I bite my lip, forgetting the damaged clothing. Until he clutches the hem of my pants.

"Freddy," I warn. I quickly shimmy out of the thin material before he can destroy it too. His chuckle rings out and I glare at him. Does he not realize how much silk costs?

"They are just clothes and you have plenty." He bites my lobe. "You need to be punished for ruining my fun." He wraps a hand around my neck and squeezes. I meet his burning gaze and attempt to swallow. *What has gotten into him?* He's never tried to strangle me. Before I can vocalize my protest, he slams his shaft into my hole and mercilessly gyrates as he grunts.

I can't move. I can't breathe. With one swift thrust, he comes, then collapses on top of me as he releases his hold. Once I catch my breath, I pound on his chest. "What the fuck!"

He lies on his back. "What? I thought you'd like that. You never complained when I spanked you or pinched your nipples."

I toss a pillow, aiming for his face. "That was nothing like what we normally do."

"*Exactly*. I spiced it up." He catches the projectile midair. "Weren't you getting bored of the same old sex?"

"If I wanted to try something new, I would have *discussed* it with you first."

He yawns and covers himself with the blankets, before turning away from me. "I'll try to remember that next time. Now stop screeching. You'll wake everyone up."

"Why aren't you taking me seriously? If this is how it's going to be, then there *won't* be a next time!"

"What exactly do you want from me?"

I rub my sore neck. "To start, I want an apology."

"I'm sorry."

"Like you mean it, you jackass!"

"I'm not going to be sincerely apologetic for fucking you like that. It was great."

"Great for *whom*?" I wave at my throbbing pussy. This man is hopeless.

"Well, if you calmed down, you would have enjoyed yourself too."

"But I wasn't enjoying myself! And your head was too far up your own ass to notice. You are so selfish!"

"*Really*? You're upset because, for once, you didn't climax? Wow. Look who's selfish."

His accusation hits me like a ton of bricks. I guess I don't have to come every time we have sex. It'd be nice, but it's not logical. Still… he should have noticed how uncomfortable I was. Then again, I never *verbalized* my pain to him. My head throbs as I overanalyze the situation.

Freddy snatches my wrist and pulls me to him. Then he clutches my hips. "Fine, I'll take care of you too, if it's bothering you that much." His tongue flicks across my clit and my anger melts into a moan.

"You know that's not what…" I ride his hand, and soon my body is ready to reach its sweet release. I bite my lip and clench my thighs together in anticipation. Then he stops.

He swipes his wrist over his lips. "I've changed my mind. I'm not going to reward that self-centered attitude."

I watch in disbelief as he casually strolls into the bathroom, leaving me a withering mess. I stare at my pulsing pussy and consider my options.

# Old Dog, New Tricks

The splash of faucet water cools my hot face. I snarl at my reflection. *Get a fucking grip. You are blowing this opportunity.* Sky's juices still linger on my taste buds. But, for a second, I forgot *who* she was and imagined I was buried in Angelica. I wanted to pretend my mate was still with me. I contain my grief and lock it away. If I dwell on it too long, I'll drown in my self-imposed misery. I pat a towel over my cheeks.

"Your mate is *gone*," I remind myself. "Step up and do what you must to survive. That's what Angelica would expect of you." I demand the tears to stay at bay, then I walk out of the bathroom to get some much-needed sleep. But what I see stops me in my tracks. Sky's lids are closed, her breathing is heavy, and her hair is fanned out around her head, giving her a near angelic appearance. Her wet fingertips rest on her now enlarged clit as her fluid drips onto the bedsheet. Is she… *masturbating*? Her scream of ecstasy confirms it. Damn. Well. The joke is on me now. My hard-on becomes unbearable as I watch her like a perv.

Sky's eyes flutter towards my shadow. "I don't need you." Her words toss ice over my spine. This is not my plan of action. If this is going to work, I need to keep in mind that Skylar is *not* Angelica. I swallow my pride.

"Sky, it's been a long night," I push out. "I rushed and was a little rough earlier. If you don't like it like that, I will do my best to keep that in mind."

She sits upright and her hair cascades over her breasts. "I can't imagine what you went through with Spike and the others. *But* that's no excuse to hurt someone. Especially if they mean anything to you." Her voice cracks at the end and I feel her insecurities rise. But she walks to me, swaying her hips as she glides her hand through my chest hair and towards my belly button. "And I do mean *something* to you, right?" She pauses her caress an inch from my growing erection.

"I'm fucked up in the head. You don't want someone like me." I toss a little reverse psychology at her.

She kisses me gently. "Everybody deserves a second chance at a happily ever after."

I knead her ass. "Not everyone."

She strokes my member. I thrust as I groan against her teeth. She teases and pulls, and just as I approach the edge of release, she stops. "I've changed my mind." She flips off the bedside lamp and slides under the covers. I grin into the darkness. She gives it as good as she takes it. Maybe I *can* mold her into what I want? I mean, I'm already teaching her so much. I throw the blankets off the bed, leaping on top of her, and growl like a hungry predator. She stares at me, like a deer caught beneath the wolf's paws.

"Spread your legs." She opens wide. "Good girl." In one quick movement, I flip her, so her belly rests against the mattress. Then I bite her neck. "You know you like it rough. Don't try to deny it

86

again." I kiss away her protests and her cries turn into whimpers. "Do you want my cock?" I slide the tip over her wet entrance. She nods, but I pull her hair. "*Answer* me. I don't want to upset you again with my harshness."

"Yes."

I inch forward, then spear into her. She needs to remember *who* I am. I run my thumb over her other hole and tease it. Her cheeks tense, but I soothe her by murmuring into her ear.

"Freddy..." she begs as she attempts to wiggle away from the pressure.

I shiver. Yes, I like manipulating her. "I'm going to shove my thumb into that tight ass," I groan as my climax nears. Before the words leave my mouth, I do as I promised. As she squeaks in discomfort, I release my load. Her pain is my undoing. After my spasms cease, I rub her clit as I devour her mouth. Soon she melts against the bed, moaning my name into my lips. Once she explodes under my heavy petting, we fall asleep in a mess of limbs and fluids.

My wife haunts my dreams as she bleeds out in my arms. A thousand times over. My soul splinters and begs Luna to take me too, but the goddess ignores my pleas. I wake drenched in sweat before the sun rises. I rub my lids of the gore imprisoned behind them and glance at Sky's sleeping frame. I envy the peaceful life she's been born into. I slip out of bed and put clothes on. When I make it to the kitchen, I stare out the wide window. Tall pine trees decorate the lush surroundings. It is definitely not the city slums.

A projectile thumps me in the back of the head and I pivot to meet my wannabe assassin. "Son of a bitch." I rub the welt. "What the hell is your problem?"

"You don't have anybody here to protect you now, you little shit." The she-demon extends a knife. "Come on, for old times' sake."

Fur pokes through my pores as she attempts to manipulate me into battling her. But I'm not Spike nor her pussy-whipped mate. "Do you really think I'm dumb enough to fall for your bullshit, *Scarlett*?" I know how much she hates her old nickname. Especially now that her new one holds more status.

"Call me Scarlett one more time and find out. I won't allow you to ruin this family. They don't see the real you yet, and I don't intend to wait around until they do. Leave, now."

"You should know better than to threaten *me*. Especially now that Spike isn't around to protect his Little Wolf."

I watch the torment flash across her face and she charges forward. What the fuck? Is she attacking me? Before my brain can fully comprehend her absurd behavior, my back slams into the kitchen table. There's a crash as the wood splinters beneath our combined weight, and we flop onto the floor. We tumble for the upper hand, while I keep my attention on her blade. Who does she think she is? Some ninja wolf warrior? This situation is becoming more complicated by the minute. I need to convince her of my innocence or this whole plan will slip through my paws.

I pin her swinging wrists and snarl. "Enough of this! What makes you think I must prove myself to *you*? You bounce from bed to bed to get men wrapped around your finger. You have no right to judge me." I pause as I sense the presence of other wolves. Now, to lay it on thick for my audience... "I *love* Sky, and we have been dating for months. How long were you dating Spike before you slept with him? Or how about Sable?" She blinks, and I know I have her full attention. "We were both compelled to do things we never would've done otherwise, Scar—*Maya*," I correct. "Don't think you are the only one who deserves a chance to be happy. Or a chance to prove who you really want to be. That you're not the person somebody *forced* you to become. I deserve it too. So, pull your head out of your ass and let me have a damn chance."

The wheels are turning, and I know I have her as the fight simmers behind her eyes. "Get your lard ass off me before I kill you." We disengage. I brush shoulders with Sable. Then wrap an arm around Sky. "You two were just going to sit there and watch him crush me?" Maya questions our crowd of onlookers.

"Trust me, if Sky wasn't here to stop me, I would have ripped his throat out for touching you." Sable throws a glare my way before tugging on his mate's wrist. "Come with me. I want to show you something." Sable guides Maya out the cave door. Then I turn to see Sky's mouth ajar.

"Did you just say you love me?" she stutters.

I grab her waist. "Oh, so you heard that?"

Sky leans into me. "Yes, I did." Then she abruptly jerks my hand, tugging me outside. "Hurry or we'll miss it."

"What exactly are we going to miss?"

Sky's brother Aspen runs past us, shouting, "Sable is going to ask Maya to marry him."

They both shift and take off into the tall grass. Is Sable really going to ask her? Didn't they just meet? My fur pushes through my skin as I follow the group into the early morning sun. This could benefit me too. Once Maya is engaged, she will convince Sky that she should be next and that will solidify my plans to gain the pack's protection. Then, when the time is right, I'll gather an army and take revenge on the General for destroying my family.

As the shifters pick up their pace, I follow suit and the wind tickles my ears. It's amazing how far their territory goes. There's so much room to gallop in the privacy of the trees. The Tala pack is lucky that the local Native American tribe shares the land with them. Their history of coexistence runs deep. My butt plops next to Sky's at the top of the hill. I'm out of shape. In Carson City, we rarely shift because of the condensed human population. Sky rubs her forehead over my chest, as we watch the wild horses trot through the valley.

*"Locals call this place Willow Creek Hill, but to us, it's just Willow Hill,"* Sable announces to Maya telepathically as they snuggle beside us. I gaze into the vast area. Instead of grey concrete and towering buildings, green spreads beyond the horizon and animals dot the valley below. This is my new home.

After witnessing Sable and Maya's engagement, I hold my ground as the alphas of the Tala pack, Frost and Raven, approach me. I'm familiar with their scent because my aunt's a Native American witch doctor. And in order to visit her, I need permission from these fur-dictators. They corner me, forcing me to retell my heart-wrenching tale of self-preservation and abuse at the hands of Spike.

"I don't condone what your alpha did, but he will get a shifter's farewell. He and his pack are of our bloodline and deserve respect," Frost commands. "We will take care of the arrangements immediately."

"Thank you," is all I can push out. They walk off, and I rub my neck as the news sinks in. None of my pack members survived. I ball my fists. In order to bring the General to his knees, I'm going to need some help. It's time I return to my roots.

Taking a drag from my cigarette, I watch as a girl skips towards the dusty gravel road. A school bus honks and opens its door for her to jump in. But before she climbs the stairs, she pauses then pivots. She waves to an older lady and the woman blows the girl a kiss. When the vehicle is out of sight, I stomp out the cancer stick and grind it into the ground with the tip of my boot. I shove my hands into my pockets and stride towards my target. Our eyes meet, and the smile she once held on her worn face falters. She rests her fists on her hips and shakes her head.

"Well, look what the wolf dragged in. It's about damn time you came to visit me. Come inside." She snatches my elbow and guides me to her home. Once the door shuts, the hairs on my neck stand up and I quickly dodge a frying pan.

"Hey! What is your deal, you old hag!" I grumble as the cookware collides against the wall. She pinches my ear. Then she drags me to her cellar. I could fight her off, but I'm used to her antics.

Debbie is my mom's sister and a great asset when it comes to carrying out my plans. She is the one who altered baby Maya's appearance and placed a temporary cloaking spell on her when my former alpha stole the she-wolf from Frost's pack shortly after the death of his brother.

When my father died, my mom went crazy and landed herself in a mental institution. That's when Debbie started playing *mommy*. Not that I'm complaining. She's guarded me from many of Spike's beatings because he was scared shitless of her. And she allowed him to be afraid, never reminding him that as she withers with age, so does her magic. And without a female offspring, her reign of terror will end when she does.

She tried to pass her witch traits to me, her only mentally and physically able relative, but that didn't work. Then she adopted a kid from the orphanage, hoping to instill her wisdom by transferring her soul into the child. But that failed too. I smirk at the thought of her adoptive daughter, Sara. She's melting my aunt's icy heart, but I'll never say it out loud, for fear I'll be turned into a frog.

"Drink this every day." She shoves a container of milky liquid into my chest. "Starting today."

I wrinkle my nose as I sniff the contents. "Hell no!"

Her boney hand smacks the backside of my head. "Nephew, do not argue with me. I'm being *dead* serious. You are in grave danger of being found out and executed."

"What do you mean, Deb?"

"The Guardian is on his way to judge the events of last night. The cards have spoken. If you can't properly defend yourself, your end is imminent."

I take a swig of the liquid, immediately crumble on the floor, and pull at my hair. The pain is an inferno, bright and consuming. "Shit! Why didn't you fucking warn me!"

"Because you would have questioned me. And I don't have time. When you consume it, concentrate on the memories you wish to conceal. When the Guardian reads your thoughts, he won't be able to see them. But… it won't fool him for long, nor will it last if he wants a second peek. So, make the first one believable."

I rub my temples as the embers smolder. "How long do I need to do this?"

"Until he reads your mind."

"What about Sky? Is the anklet still working?"

Debbie pulls out a chair for me. "The charm is functioning as it should. But it's just a matter of time before her mind clears and she questions your intentions. Don't leave her side. She's your only hope. Make her love you before the power runs dry."

"That's not a problem. She is latched on to me, even talking about starting a family."

"That's good news. Especially considering all the work we have put into this: making sure you are always around when she goes into heat and that you constantly keep an eye on her at the steakhouse. And since the restaurant is a business, her family couldn't demand that you stay away, so your scent mingled with the regular customers and employees."

I tilt my head. "Why can't I leave Sky's side?"

"Her future is hard to read. But from what I have seen, her child is destined to become the next Guardian. And that baby needs to be *yours*, to keep our secrets locked away."

I blink, unsure if I'm hearing her right. "What do you mean the next Guardian? I thought Luna created those beings?"

"She chooses the *souls* that can handle her powers and bestows her blessings on to them. They are all born the same as us and can be killed the same too. They are not immortal."

"My offspring could be the next all-powerful protector?" I whisper to myself. "But what about the General?"

Debbie releases a breath and her age shines through. "I'm afraid war is imminent. The government's jealousy of our powers is overshadowing their better judgement. Help them as little as possible and continue to forge your way into Frost's and Sky's good graces. Without their assistance, I'm afraid we have no hope of winning."

"What about Maya?" I ask, referencing the future alpha of the Tala pack. If something happens to Frost, I'll need her support too.

Debbie meets my gaze. "You *leave* her alone. Do not directly influence her, unless absolutely necessary."

Maya was raised in the same orphanage as Sara, so the girls have a strong relationship. An unbreakable bond. If I mess with one, the other will strike. "Is this because you are afraid of the consequences it would have on your precious child?"

"Freddy, it's time for you to leave before we regret the threats that will inevitably spill out." She nods with finality and leads me out without another word. I bite my tongue and exit the small home with my potion in tow. I attempt to rein in my anger and not plot Sara's death. If she were a wolf, I could bring her to the General and let him have her. Maybe then my aunt would regain her ferocity and actually fight our enemies, instead of hiding from them and kissing their asses. Why do children have that impact on people? Maya did that with Spike. And now Sara is doing it with Debbie.

With this in mind, I vow to stay true to my proposal of world domination, even after I become a father.

# Sky

# Handyman

"**S**top biting your nails."

I pause mid-nibble and tug my claw out from between my teeth. "Freddy was supposed to call me an hour ago."

Carly rolls her eyes as she sets fresh silverware on a cleared table. I know I should keep calm, but something is off. I felt it last night when he aggressively fucked me. The whole situation with Spike's pack messed him up and I'm questioning if he might be broken beyond repair.

Carly claps her hands. "Earth to Sky." I give her my best sad wolf eyes in reply. She lets out a sigh and drops the menus she's holding on the bench to hug me. "Hey, it'll be okay. *If* he is telling the truth, the police will get his statement and release him, right? Didn't you say that?"

I can only nod. I hate keeping things from Carly. She is so important to me. So why can't I open up to her? Explain the Fangs awful past? Or the fact that Freddy just about raped me last night.

Carly snatches my chin. "I love you, Sky Bear, and that's all that matters."

She squishes my cheeks, giving me fish lips, before she pecks my mouth. A smile spreads across my face. She's such a goofball. The bell above the entrance signals the large party arriving for their reservation. Straightening my back, I approach the local hockey team, here to celebrate their latest victory on the ice, and smile. Once they are settled, Carly waves towards me and points to a small corner booth. I follow her direction, making my way through the dinner rush, and slide in next to its pale occupant.

I place my palm on his sweaty forehead. "Freddy, why didn't you call or text? Are you feeling all right?"

"It was a rough interrogation, between the cops and the Guardian questioning me. I felt guilty just being in the same room with them as they glared and analyzed my every move." The poor guy looks like he is going to throw up.

"But it's over with, right?"

Freddy runs his calloused thumb over mine. "Listen, about last night... I'm sorry if I hurt you or made you feel uncomfortable. I was looking to escape this bullshit, and buried inside you is the safest place I know."

His words wash over me, and my heart warms. "Things will get better. I promise. Just be patient and let this blow over. You'll see."

A plate clangs on the table. Carly narrows her eyes. "I didn't order this," Freddy barks.

"You look like shit and are scaring away the *paying* customers," she hisses.

I drop my hand from Freddy's forehead and rub my temples. Can't she just pretend to like him? For me? "Carly, thank you for the food. But table two is waving you over."

She gives Freddy one more glare before tossing her hair and

sauntering over to the table of college students, all begging for a closer look at the gorgeous goddess in human form.

Freddy pops a fry into his mouth. "She's right. I can't pay for this. Even if they are scraps meant for a dog."

I blink at his defeated form. "Hey, you listen to me. You will get through this." He snorts, but I continue. "You can work for me until you get on your feet. I'm in need of a handyman to fix some odds and ends, and I happen to know how amazing you are with your hands." I bump his shoulder and wait for his response. When none comes, I sigh. "Tell me what's really going on in that head of yours."

"The pack will *never* trust me. I'll be an outcast, or worse, a pitied charity case."

The interrogation must not have gone well. If that's the case, he is right. They won't welcome him with open paws. Especially around their impressionable pups. At least until they can trust him. An idea hits me and I blurt it out, "Then you'll have to prove yourself. And while you do that, you can live with me." The words spewing from my mouth surprise even me. Do I want Freddy to *live* with me? The look on his face mirrors mine. "There's a place near the restaurant that I was planning on renting. You can help with the bills and build your credit back up with the pack."

"Don't you think we'll just end up killing each other?"

I can't help the grin that graces my lips at his sudden mood change. "Oh, most definitely. But there is a pretty big backyard, and I can bury you easily." I wave the idea in the air.

"Oh, can you?" He leans on his elbows. "You do realize bigger men have tried and *failed*?"

I lean forward to meet his challenge. "That's because they weren't me."

We stare at each other for a minute before he clutches another potato stick. "Okay. Let's move in together. But I'm going to find a job. I won't take your pity employment offer."

I straighten my pencil skirt as I stand. "You *will* work for me until you find a better paying employer. Because I will not be supporting your lazy ass."

He salutes. "All right, boss."

"Finish your meal, servant. Then fix the dishwasher." I stalk off before he can argue. I can't help the grin burning my cheeks. He will build up honest revenue while showing the other shifters he is committed.

After I clear a few tables, I stride to my office to catch up on paperwork and hire him officially. Excitement bubbles up in my throat at the thought of living with him and potentially starting a family. I can't wait! Who knows? Maybe this time next year I will be cradling a tiny bundle of joy in my arms. Images of little fingers and little toes play in my mind as I lower myself into my chair and click in my password on my computer. I know I am getting ahead of things, but I really want this. I email the landlord and transfer the money to get us into the rental property. The ache in my heart grows as I rub my empty stomach. Even if he proves to *not* be the greatest choice, at least I'll have a consolation prize.

A knock pulls me out of my daydream. Oh shit. The look on my bestie's face as she leans against the closed door lets me know she's met my recent hire. She taps a painted talon on her arm, and I can see figurative steam drifting from her ears.

"Carly, I can explain…"

She pushes off the exit and stomps towards my safe haven. "You mean, you are going to explain *how* you forgot to consult me, your partner, on the decision to hire a thug to be *our* handyman."

"He needs a job so he can help pay rent when we move into the house on Peach Ave."

Carly slaps her chest. "You… you two are moving in together?" she screeches. "He murdered people and kidnapped you!"

I stand and hush her high-pitched accusations. "The cops talked to him about what happened. And if they cleared him, shouldn't we? Doesn't everyone deserve a second chance?"

Carly snatches my wrists like a lifeline. "What the actual fuck, Sky? You are so much better than this. What has he done to you? Maybe he's using some voodoo magic?"

I pull my hands away as if she's burned me. "Why do you think something is wrong with me?"

"You have never moved in with a *boyfriend.*" Her lip quivers.

Her tears have nothing to do with Freddy. And everything to do with Carly and me. "It's a two-bedroom house. Why don't you move in with us? It can be like the old days." When she doesn't say anything, I continue. "I'm sorry I didn't talk to you about this. But you know I want a child and my pack will never approve of…" I almost say *us* but decide to reword it, in order to soften the blow. "My situation."

"You know *he* won't allow that. I thought *our* relationship meant more to you than whatever *this* is?" She waves her hands in the air. "I thought we were sisters… best friends. Closer than your shifter buddies!" Carly swipes at her cheeks. "I can't believe how low I rate in your life. That you would choose that scumbag over me."

I can't breathe. Words won't form. My world is crumbling, and I can't say anything as she slams the office door. I drop into my chair and my head falls into my hands. I've somehow lost my best friend, business partner, and best employee. All in one swift move. I should chase her and beg for forgiveness. I shake my head.

She's always been a tad dramatic. She'll return… I hope.

# Freddy

# Dirty Deeds

"**S**tupid piece of shit!" I scramble to turn the wrench, as water vomits into my face.

My life is a filthy mess. The interrogation at the police station didn't go as easily as I thought it would. I'm on probation, but they didn't seem to buy my "sweet and innocent" story. And the Guardian was on to me from the moment he strutted into that room. I blame Maya. She must have warned him about our time together in Carson City. Because even with the aid of my aunt's potion, he was questioning every word that came from my mouth. But I survived, and that's all that matters. Plus, I have Sky eating out of the palm of my hand.

Satisfied with my repair of the dishwasher, as well as the status of my current predicament, I stand to replace the tool and wipe my face. My wolf senses tingle before I dodge a projectile. It splinters into a thousand pieces as it connects with the wall. Why does everyone throw shit at me?

My eyes lock on to the devil herself. "I guess Sky told you about *us*?"

"Leave the kitchen," Carly barks at the few remaining employees strewn around the area. "*Now*." The woman radiates power, control, and sex with every torturously appealing (but painfully off-limits) heeled step. Too bad she's human and only good enough to act as the occasional chew toy. "Break this off!"

"You mean *you* couldn't convince Sky to leave *me* so she could service your pussy? Weird." I collect my instruments, trying to hide the smile that won't leave my face. I know I'm playing with fire, but she needs to tie her own noose so I can separate the two BFFs, to keep Sky under *my* control. I hear the item whizz through the air, but I demand my legs to stay in their path. The plate smashes into the back of my head and throws off my balance.

Carly slaps my chest. "I *know* what you are doing, you piece of shit. Sky may not see it, but when she does, she will come back to me."

Fur erupts along my arms. I'd love to show her my full strength. But I leash him for now. I smell my target audience approaching. I wink at Carly before laying it on thick. "What hurts more, sweetheart? That she chose me over you? Or that you aren't good enough to hold on to her because you're a pitiful human?"

Before she can answer, the kitchen door is thrown open. "I'm sorry, Car…" The words float to the ground as Sky looks between us. I bring my hand to the back of my head and stare at the crimson liquid coating my fingertips. Sky covers my wound with a towel. "Are you okay?" Carly's mouth drops before she marches out with a middle finger waving in the air. Sky guides me to a chair and dabs my gash. "I'm so sorry. I knew she would be upset, but I figured she'd calm down and apologize. I never thought she'd outright attack you."

"I should press charges. That's the only way she'll learn a lesson."

"She's not normally like this—you know that." Sky leads me towards the exit. "Why don't you rest in my car while I finish up some paperwork? Then we can head back to my parents' house to pack."

"Are you sure?"

"Yes. I called the landlord and sent her our first and last month's rent as well as our deposit. Since the home is vacant, we can move in right away. Unless you've changed your mind."

I wrap an arm around her waist and kiss the top of her head. Sky leans into me and lets out a breath. "I'm ready whenever you are." As we walk out of the restaurant and towards her car, I know I've won. And it feels damn good. I have a job, a roof over my head, and Sky's pack to keep my enemies at bay.

"I'll be back as soon as I can. Here are the keys, if you want to listen to the radio or turn on the air."

I settle inside the luxury vehicle as Sky returns to the Wolves' Den. I rest my hands behind my head and melt into the leather seats. Life is finally looking up. It's not world domination yet, but I'll get there. One step at a time. Spike is dead and I'm mingling with powerful shifters, and that's a good start. I swallow the lump constricting my throat. I just wish my mate was by my side.

My phone pings but I ignore the General's needy demands. He's lucky I didn't have any useable information on his unit, otherwise I would have buried his ass at the precinct. Movement from the corner of my eye causes me to pivot. Carly's stomping to her vehicle, hips swaying, locks bouncing.

"That's right, sweet cheeks. Move along." I wiggle my fingers at her.

Once she drives off, the hairs on the back of my neck stand up and I sniff the air. The Guardian is nearby. I exit the car to meet him before his paws can leave the forest floor.

"What brings you here, Luna's *pet*?" I lean against a pine tree and pretend to pick my fangs. Even though I can't see him, I know he's waiting to pounce. The leaves shuffle and a large wolf emerges, his eyes glittering, though they never leave mine. "I would shift and play mind games with you again, but I have an injury and don't want to aggravate it during the transition." I rub the mark Carly left on my scalp. I'm not sure he buys into the excuse. But either way, he shifts to two legs and his human form towers in front of me. His silence scares me more than I want to admit. Did my aunt's protective magic not work? She's getting older and has admitted her skills are fading. "Are you just going to stand there, or do you have something to say?" I prod.

"When I'm in your presence, I feel as if something is amiss, Frederick."

"Nobody calls me that."

"That is the name your kin gave you, is it not?"

I snort at his phrasing. "*My kin* is almost extinct. They have no say in who I am anymore."

"Then how about we agree to call each other by the names *we've* chosen."

I can't help but swallow. This shifter is all power. Yet belongs to no pack. He's a free agent, doing Luna's will, while keeping peace between the humans and the shifters. If someone steps out of line, it's his job to deliver the punishment. And although I have never seen his weapon firsthand, I've heard the stories. They say electricity runs through his veins. That he can't stay long in any pack's territory because the alpha waves roll off him enough to steal every unclaimed female in the vicinity.

"And what is your chosen name?" I prompt.

"Azure."

I quirk a brow. "What brings you over here, Azure?"

He tastes the air. "I was curious."

"About what exactly?"

"Your memories weren't very clear. But I could have sworn I saw a familiar woman in them."

Is he talking about Sky? Like hell is he sinking his fangs into her. I own her. "The shifter you may have seen is my fiancée," I fib. "We are actually moving in together and starting a family."

Azure's eyes snap to mine, and I know he is testing the truth of my words on the tip of his tongue. But I never falter. I breathe a sigh of relief when he pivots from the establishment and returns to the trees. "Stay out of trouble. Because the next time we meet, I won't be so lenient."

The man transforms into a massive beast and snarls to concrete his threat, then gallops towards the lowering sun. I stay long enough to see his blur follow the setting globe. Then I return to the car and slump into the soft interior. I grin at my reflection in the rearview mirror.

Because nothing can stop me now.

# Azure

# Blurry

When I reached Cold Creek, I developed migraines and muscle aches. It's maddening. Almost as if this place is cursed. I managed to question the lone survivor of the Fangs pack, but his memories were a blur. And the police were no help. They were frightened of something more powerful than me. Most of them were literally shaking in their boots.

"Here you go. Hot tea with a splash of honey."

"Thank you." I sip it, in hopes of easing my tension. When I dissected Freddy's past, I saw glimpses of a shifter I've been dreaming about. I clench the mug. But he informed me that she is *taken*. How can that be? Maybe she isn't who I thought she was? But I was so close! And her scent! A shiver rattles my tense form. It's an aphrodisiac. But she belongs to *him*. The cup explodes in my palm at the thought. "I'm so sorry."

"Don't worry about it, dear." Celeste, the Canis family matriarch, grabs another ceramic dish. "Living with wolves teaches you a few life lessons. Including making sure you have extra glassware." She slides over a fresh mug. "Anything you want to talk about?"

I pivot from the glorious hues of red and orange reflected through the wall of windows and offer her a smile. "No. I'm sure everything will resolve itself in the end."

She pats my shoulder. "That's a great mindset to have."

I breathe in the harmonious scents of the Canis family. "Tell me more about your children?" I tap on a glass frame resting on the counter—the image is of a little girl in a pink tutu and tiara.

Celeste's eyes twinkle as she places a photo album in my lap. The first pages are of her and her husband when they were married. Then she flips through those of when she had her first pup. "This is Sable. You've met him already. He has a tough exterior, but he has a heart of gold. He'll give you the shirt off his back without hesitation. Our second child is a force to be reckoned with." Her laugh warms the air. "Skylar is our little princess."

"She's beautiful."

Celeste clutches the memories as she nibbles her lip. "She is, isn't she? But she's the one I worry about the most. I question if our love has spoiled her." She lets out a sigh. "Sky is impatient and, at times, hardheaded."

When she doesn't continue, I ask, "Are you referring to her relationship with the rebel shifter?"

"Maybe." She rubs her wrinkled forehead. "But it's her life. Her choice."

"But you are her mother, and she trusts your judgement." I pat her hand.

"I've spoken to her countless times about waiting for her mate, but she doesn't want to hear it."

My mind wanders to my twin sister and her newborn. Parenting is not an effortless undertaking. "I'm sure it's not easy to feel ignored by your offspring."

She swipes her cheeks and forces out a laugh. "What's done is done." She points to another photo. "This is our youngest pup, Aspen. He is the most sensitive of the three and easily distracted. One time he was cooking chili and left it on the stove unattended all day. When I came home, the house was smoky, and the pot had to be thrown out. I hope he grows out of it." She closes the book and meets my gaze. "Thank you for what you did for Sable's mate," she praises.

"I didn't do much."

"You cleared Maya of her alleged disloyalty to Spike and made my son the happiest man on this planet." She sips her beverage. "Now they can have their happily ever after."

Absolving Maya was easy. Her memories were crystal clear, just like her innocence. But that tale is hers to tell. If only all the shifters' details were so effortless to see. Sable and Maya found each other again against all odds. They never gave up on true love. I drain the contents of my liquid refreshment. "Thank you for the hospitality."

"Anytime, Guardian."

I stand and breathe in the cool night air. I love traveling within the darkness. Everything is peaceful. Comforting. "Please call me Azure."

"Thank you, Azure. Come by whenever you're in town. You are always welcome."

Hopefully I won't be needed here in the near future, but the hairs on the back of my neck tell me otherwise. Something is brewing in Cold Creek, and I plan on keeping tabs on its residents. Fur erupts from my pores as I prepare myself for my long journey. My limbs stretch as I gallop into the forest, the wind tickles my ears, and the leaves crunch under the weight of my claws. But the farther I go, the more my heart screams for us to return. I mute it. Too much has happened in Carson City. I need to consult with the other Guardians in order to determine our next steps.

# Sky

# Fur-in-law

"I never want to see another box in my life," I grumble.

Maya laughs as she slides a box cutter over one of my cardboard nemeses. I can't help but smile as I watch her dig into the kitchen utensils. I must admit I was jealous of their relationship at first. Sable is my best friend and brother, all wrapped into one. Then, when his mate returned, he was devoted to her, pushing me aside. But now that the fear of being separated from his love again has ebbed, he is spending more time with me. And although we didn't get along at first, Maya is slowly becoming a delightful fur-in-law. As she places a pile of dinner plates in the cabinet, I can't help but recall how insecure she was when I first met her. But now that she is married and surrounded by loved ones, her confidence *blinds* me. Maybe it's all that alpha blood she has coursing through her veins…

"Where's Freddy?"

"The freezer is making a high-pitched sound, so he's checking it out." I watch as Maya reaches towards the top shelf to put up the wine glasses. I can see the thoughts running through her head, as clearly as if they were tangible. "Go ahead and say it," I urge her.

"What do you *think* I'm going to say?"

"That I'm moving too fast with him. I *know* you still don't trust him."

Maya's fingertips tighten over a mug. "Did I say I didn't trust him?"

"I know you two have a complicated history with Spike's pack."

Maya snatches my wrist, and our eyes meet. "Wouldn't you rather *wait* to settle down? You know. When you find your mate?"

"I appreciate your concern. But I'm happy." I shrug her off and relocate the plates. "Besides, I'm the captain of my own vessel. Luna can kiss my furry ass. I'm not going to wait until I'm an old lady to have pups."

"You're as stubborn as your brother. Just you wait. When your man comes into your life, you are going to regret moving in with this dumbass."

I nibble my bottom lip. "Hey, Maya?"

"Yeah?" She stretches on her tiptoes to place a serving platter on the top shelf.

Carly still hasn't spoken to me. I miss her so much. "Do you think Luna would allow a female to have a female mate?"

Maya slips and the dish explodes at my feet. "Oh no, I'm so sorry." She bends, collecting the pieces while refusing to meet my gaze.

I move to help her. "Forget I asked."

"You just caught me off guard—that's all." She rubs her neck. "I'm still new to all this wolf stuff, Sky. But if you want my opinion as an alpha, I think Luna assigns us mates in order to procreate."

I can only nod through my disappointment. Maya and Sable are the future leaders of our pack. Once her parents retire, she will step into their massive paw prints. And if she feels the way they do about same-sex partners, there's no hope. Warmth on my arm pulls me out of my despair.

"Hey, let me research it, okay? As your honorary sister, I'm totally on your side. Love is love and I honestly think Luna wants her people happy. And if *anybody* finds their happiness with a member of the same sex, then who the fuck cares!"

The front door shuts and our noses take in the scent of a supreme stuffed-crust pizza. "*Who's* having sex with whom now?" Sable questions.

I snatch the food from my brother. "Where the hell have you been? We're starving!"

Maya pecks her husband on the cheek. "Nobody is having sex with anybody. Not yet anyway." She throws me a grin.

We dig into the saucy goodness until we're ready to burst. "This would be a hell of a lot easier if your *boyfriend* were here to help," Sable growls.

"I'm sure he'll be back soon," I reply.

"You two shouldn't be moving in together until you are married," he lectures before Maya elbows him in the side. "I'm serious!"

"So, you're saying I should marry him as soon as possible?" I bat my lashes.

"Hell no! That is *not* what I am fucking saying!" My brother leans forward. "Listen… if you want to move in with us, you are more than welcome. We're staying near Frost and there are plenty of vacant caves in the area."

"Sable, are you recommending I pack up *again*?"

"Yes."

"I moved out to be on my *own* and have some personal space.

Plus, this rental is closer to work."

"If you want to be on your own, why is Freddy living here?" He gives me a pointed stare.

"Because I want him *here*."

"And where does Carly fit into this? I thought you were all about *hoes before bros*?"

The silence could be cut with a knife. I grind my jaw. He knows damn well that I'm walking on thin ice when it comes to Carly. She still pops into the restaurant, since she owns part of it, and I always lay it on thick and do my best to reconnect with her, but she never says more than a few words before she leaves. I must have really hurt her with my actions. Her stubbornness matches mine head-on; however, if I could just have a good conversation with her and apologize, we could work past this.

When I ignore Mr. Alpha's question, he tries a new tactic. "He's not worth risking your friendship with her. Are you even planning on marrying him?"

"No."

"So what's the point of you two living together?"

"Because we get to have all the *sex*." I grin, done with this conversation while knowing how to end it.

Sable lifts a hand. "Just wrap it before you tap it." Maya and I burst into a fit of giggles until we are wiping tears from the corners of our eyes. "Hey, I'm dead-ass serious! You don't want any STDs. And I bet that man is crawling with them."

The door slams behind us, and we turn to see the wolf in question. "Do you want to say that to my face, jackass? Or just continue to talk shit behind my back?"

Sable narrows his eyes and bumps chests with my irate boyfriend. "I *said* you like to sleep around so your limp dick is covered in diseases."

I stand between the two idiots. "Enough."

Maya grabs Sable's wrist. "I need to get back to the cave and finish some schoolwork. I'll see you tomorrow at the restaurant, Sky." She loosens her grip on my brother to hug me.

"Thanks again for helping out at the steakhouse."

"No problem. I need the extra cash for schoolbooks anyway." My brother's jaw ticks at her comment. He told me about Maya's insistence to finish college on her own... costs and all. Even though her new husband is loaded. "Bye, guys." Maya shuts the door before her mate can go off on her about working for me and going to school at the same time.

I pivot to Mr. Moody. "Were you really going to *hit* my brother?"

"No. Because he would have submitted to me."

I aim to move away from this topic. "What took you so long?"

Freddy peels off his shirt and tosses it on the couch. Then he stomps to the fridge and pulls out a beer before planting himself in front of the TV to watch a wrestling match.

With my hands on my hips, I stand in front of his entertainment. "These boxes are not going to magically unpack themselves."

Freddy snatches my wrist, tugging me on top of him. I squeal, but he quickly turns it into a moan as he nips my ear and nuzzles my neck. Our lips meet in a frenzy of teeth and tongues. This week has been so crazy. Our schedules have been separating us, and by the time the evening rolls around, we pass out—*exhausted from the day's activities*. He rubs my nub and I arch my hips against the friction, regretting the fabric between us.

"What were you saying?"

The words can't form in my mouth as my blood is redirected. He isn't playing fair, as usual. But at this point, I don't give a damn.

"Would you rather I unpack or continue to make you wet?"

Maybe I'll just hire someone. My little brother might want the extra money. But the thought of a relative touching my intimates turns me off to the idea. Freddy's finger sneaks below my waistband and all thoughts flutter from my mind and into the air. Our clothes are tossed aside in a flurry of colors. I situate myself above him before slamming his rod inside my molten core. My breathing hitches as he pinches my nipples. This is what I need. To forget everything and just *feel*. Freddy withdraws himself before he drops to his knees and devours my dripping center.

"We taste delicious. The perfect blend of sweet and salty." He circles my clit, teasing me. It's driving me insane as I buck my hips to get him closer.

"Fuck the boxes," I hiss. His chuckle rings out before he nips my swollen bits, and I explode all over his cheeks.

# Freddy

# Back to the Grind

*Four years later…*

The rain descends in buckets off the restaurant's roof, while the ember of my lit cigarette illuminates my pursed lips. It's been almost four *years* since the fall of the Fangs. Since I lost my mate and assimilated to this new way of life. With the Canis family and the Tala pack. And not a day goes by that I don't see Angelica's face. Or hear her voice beckoning me to rescue her before it's too late.

Sky and I have fallen into a routine of working and fucking. I crush the butt into the cement, extinguishing it with the tip of my boot. But she isn't any closer to marrying me like Aunt Debbie demands. Not that I want *that*. The princess also hasn't gotten pregnant either. I'm questioning if Luna is purposely thwarting my plans, or if it's really just our luck. Maya is graduating from the university soon. Then she and Sable will be attempting to create a fur-demon too. I'll be damned if they beat us to it. A figure running across the parking lot drags my attention from my self-pity.

*What the fuck is she doing?*

I reenter the kitchen and return to my tinkering with the temperamental stove. It took some getting used to, but I think I'm a damn good handyman.

"Yeah, I heard she's *officially* back."

"After all this time?"

"Who called whom?"

My fingers still as I listen to the servers' gossip. Another thing I've learned about working in the food biz is that you're surrounded by big mouths. They never stop talking shit.

"Ladies, I believe you have customers waiting for their meals." They scurry out at Sky's command. She saunters over and smirks. "You aren't done with that yet?"

"Does it look like I'm done with it?" I snip.

"Well, why don't you take a break? I have some news to tell you."

"No need to have a heart-to-heart over Carly's return. I knew she'd weasel her way back into your life. Just keep that bitch away from me."

Sky narrows her eyes before stomping out, and I arch a brow at her adult temper tantrum. She usually takes my gruff in stride. An hour later, I straighten my sore back and test out the control panel. When it turns on, I pack up my tools, eager to get more nicotine in my system. This job has been keeping me out of trouble, but to be honest, I'd rather be carrying a weapon and doing some sort of security detail.

The kitchen entrance swings open and the goddess herself graces me with her presence. "Sky is asking for you in the dining room, table seventeen."

"So she sent her loyal bitch to fetch me? Did you miss me?"

"Nobody misses the *shit* under their boots." Carly saunters off with a toss of her locks. I clench my fists, aching to bend her over my knee, before striding towards my destination. I freeze at the figure seated across from Sky.

*This can't be happening.*

"Freddy, you never told me you used to work for the government," Sky sings.

I nod towards the man in the suit. "Because I didn't. They tried recruiting me and I declined."

"He's just being modest. He collaborated with us on a few occasions." The General's smile boils my blood. "Why don't you join me and your girlfriend, Freddy? We were just about to order."

"Sky, Carly is asking for you," I lie. "Why don't you go check on her, while I catch up with my *old* pal."

Sky rises from her seat and extends a palm. "It was nice meeting you. I'll see you around."

"Yes, you will." The General never removes his eyes from mine. "And I look forward to our next exchange."

Once Sky is out of earshot, I lower myself onto the chair. "What the fuck do you want?"

"I want what was *promised* to me."

"Well, since you killed the man who made those promises, it's *your* fault they were left unfulfilled."

"I didn't kill anyone. Didn't you see what happened?" He pats his lips with his napkin. "It was horrible. The Fangs were taken down by the Tala shifters." The General sips his beer.

This man has balls of steel. He's lucky I don't tear him limb from limb. I slam my fist on the table. "Don't fuck with me. I know your so-called *men* didn't even step in during that bloodbath! They turned their backs on us. Allowed everyone to perish, including my mate."

"Now, Freddy, is this any way a *father* should be acting? What kind of example are you providing for your offspring?" He *tsks* his tongue.

I expected various retorts. But this one steals my breath away. "What are you talking about?"

"Oh, she didn't tell you? Well, from what my sources say, Skylar is pregnant. And I assume the fleabag belongs to you." Is that what she was trying to tell me? Shit. And I blew her off. "Interesting. Well. It seems you need to work on your communication skills, *dog*." The General chugs the remainder of his alcohol, then leans on his elbows. "If you care at all for her or your pup, you'll answer when I tug on your leash. Because my patience is *gone*. And my trigger finger is itching." He nods towards a figure, and the man lifts his shirt to reveal a gun holster. "Do we have an understanding, pooch?"

My pulse quickens as I try to figure my way out of this mess. My aunt's words repeat in my head: *War is imminent.* Which side do I want to be on? I glance at the man with the weapon, then to the General. "What do you need me to do?"

The fucker grins before gripping my shoulder. "That's a *good* boy!" He shakes his head at the other man and we watch as he leaves the restaurant. "I want the shifters Spike promised me." He slides a piece of paper across the table. "My men will be at these coordinates to collect them on these dates and times. Be there or the bullets will rain down on your pitiful life."

"Why can't I just bring them to you?"

"Because I don't trust a backstabber. We are doing this my way."

"And Sky and the baby will be left alone?"

"Yes, as long as you deliver."

"How many are we talking?"

The General shrugs. "As many as it takes to clone their abilities and transfer them to my super soldiers."

I let out a hearty laugh. "That's *never* going to work. Luna only *bestows* these powers on select bloodlines. Humans can't handle shifting. Their weak bodies are not equipped to produce fur and claws," I rehearse what my mom always said on the subject.

The lightbulb clicks. "Then I'll breed enough *dogs* to make my own loyal K-9 unit."

I clamp my jaw shut. His plan could have continued to fail, but I had to open my big mouth and now I've dropped the solution right into his lap.

# Sky

# Fetch the Stick

*Earlier that day…*

I kick my office door shut and scream into my hands. "This can't be happening." I crash into my chair. The phone blares, and I snatch it from its base, suck in air, and answer the call. "Wolves' Den Steakhouse, Skylar speaking. How may I direct your call?"

The silence on the other line grinds at my nerves.

"This is the third time you've called. Stop harassing my business." I bite my lip, to change my misery into pain. "I've had a shit week and I'm not dealing with this bullshit too." I clamp a hand over my mouth. This could be a business call. What the hell is wrong with me? I've been overly emotional, exhausted, and feeling like crap. "I'm sorry. That language was uncalled for. But please stop calling if all you are going to do is listen to me talk to myself. Thank you and have a wonderful day." I slam the phone back on its base and clench my fists when the ringing starts again. I answer on the second ring. "Hello!"

"So this is how you are answering business calls?" Carly purrs. That honey-laced voice. I can't control the sob that escapes. "Woah, Sky. What's wrong?"

"I think I'm pregnant," I choke out.

"Give me five minutes."

The line goes dead. I bring my knees to my chest, and I rock. This is what I wanted, right? Why am I so terrified? I run my hands through my hair. Because the reality of the situation is hitting me head-on. I'm *not* with my mate. Which means that if I ever find him, it will complicate this pup's life. I sit upright and laugh at my hysterics. I'm 100% sure I'm just late. I mean, it's been stressful around here. Yeah. Okay, maybe more like *90%* sure...

Plastic smacks me in the face. I blink and stare at the projectile. Then I look up at the woman I've been desperately trying to get to forgive me for years. Her hands are on her hips, her eyes are bloodshot, and dried tears decorate her cheeks. "Piss on the damn stick, so we can see how much shit we're in."

I leap out of my chair and into her arms. "I'm so sorry. I'm a horrible best friend."

"Shh. We've both been shitty friends. But don't worry, I'll help you dig the grave for whichever loser decided to knock you up."

"Wait. You don't know who I'm with?"

"*Wait.* Don't tell me... Are you and that douchebag really still together?"

"Yes."

"Funny. I didn't have to even *say* his name and you knew who I was talking about."

"Why are you here?" I pull away. "You never give me the time of day unless it's work-related. Why did you decide to make amends today?"

She shoves her phone in my face. I skim the text message from an unknown number saying: *Skylar needs your assistance. Call her.*

I try to call the number, but it goes to an indistinct voicemail. "What the hell?" I question.

"I don't care *who* it was. My concern is for you."

"Why are you choosing to care about me now?" I don't let her answer before I add, "Well, don't worry because I'm fine."

"I've always cared! That's the problem! I've cared too much. And you so easily pushed me aside to be with *him*."

"I said I'm sorry a hundred times!"

"So prove it and leave him already!" The silence is deafening. "And that's *why* we always end up here, like this. Are you really that desperate for the one thing I can't provide you, that you're willing to deal with his abuse? Why can't I be enough for you?" She doesn't wait for an answer, and she turns to leave.

I grab her wrist. "Don't go." I'm done being strong. "I need my best friend."

"Well, I'm sure as hell not holding the stick for you."

My eyes land on the pregnancy tests on the desk, and I laugh. "But don't you want to help me aim?"

Her lips twitch. "I missed that humor, Sky Bear." She runs a hand over my arm. "Listen, I'm sorry I've been so distant. Can you forgive me?"

"Only if you promise to give Freddy a chance. And I mean a *real* chance."

She snorts. "If he passes my test, I will."

"What test? Oh no. Not *that*!"

Carly shoves me towards the bathroom. "That's the deal, chica. Take it or leave it. Now go find out if I'm gonna be an aunt."

I've missed her so much. And I'm sure Freddy will pass the test. He won't fail. Not like my ex. But I'll worry about that later. There is a piece of plastic eager for my attention.

Carly squeezes my thigh as the doctor lectures me on the *dos and don'ts* of pregnancy. I've been frozen ever since the stick hit the counter. I attempted to tell Freddy, but he blew me off because he heard Carly was around again. I tried to work and ignore the issue, but I was having a hard time keeping my emotions intact. *Thank Luna* Carly called Mom and explained our situation. Mom was able to pull some strings and get me an appointment.

"Here is a prescription for prenatal vitamins and make sure you adjust your diet to include extra iron. We've found that shifters require more of the mineral when they are with child."

Carly accepts the blue piece of paper. "Thank you again for seeing us on short notice."

"Of course. Tell Celeste I said congratulations."

My desperate gaze falls on my bestie as she guides me to the parking lot. "I'm pregnant." They're the first words I've been able to stutter out.

"Now you need to decide what you are going to do about it."

"What do you mean?"

"Are you gonna tell Freddy? He isn't exactly daddy material."

"Freddy may have a tough exterior, but he is a good guy. And he has been so helpful at the restaurant."

Carly pats my hand like I've lost my mind. "We'll see." She buckles me into the car.

"Thank you for taking me to this appointment."

Her eyes mist and she kisses the top of my head. Then she makes the executive decision to drive me to my parents' house. At first, I'm upset. But then I realize how much I *needed* to return to my roots. I stretch my arms wide and welcome the forest like an old friend. The familiarity brings tears to my cheeks. I breathe in the fresh country air and my muscles relax. A bird zooms into a tree before lowering into a nest. My fingertips graze my belly. It's going to take a village to raise this pup.

"Skylar!" Mom picks me up and twirls. "Oh, my Luna! I can't believe it!"

"Mom, hush. I don't want everyone to know until I tell Freddy."

"Well, just your dad, okay? Because I'm going to burst if I can't talk to somebody about this!" Once she sets me on the ground, she grins at Carly and embraces her too. "I almost forgot how beautiful that smile is, my dear. Next time you have a scuffle with Sky, don't take it out on us. We're family after all."

Carly returns the hug. "I promise I'm not going anywhere."

"Good. Now why don't we go inside. I'll make chocolate chip cookies and we can have some good old-fashioned girl talk." We discuss boys, clothes, and anything *but* baby stuff. Especially when Aspen shows up questioning our get-together. Which is fine with me. I have nine months to focus on everything baby-related.

"Are you sure you don't want me to go with you?"

"I appreciate all you've done today, but I've got this."

"I should move in with you," Carly blurts out. "I can help with your prenatal care."

I squeeze her wrist. "I want to live by Sable. With the Tala pack, on the reservation."

"Wait. Don't shut me out of your life. I wasted years because I was too damn stubborn. But I won't let that happen again. You're stuck with my furless ass. I'll just move in with you and pretend to be a bitch. I won't shave and I'll walk around naked. It'll be fun."

"I'm grateful you're in my life. And trust me, I won't *let* you leave again. Except for right now, because I need to deal with Freddy, and you need to work your magic with the restaurant."

She places her palms on my cheeks. "You're going to be an amazing mother." Her lips graze mine, then tremble.

I kiss her softly, stilling her movements. "*We* will be amazing mothers." I guide her hand to my belly. "Together we'll raise one kick-ass kid."

She laughs. "Maybe we should swear less often."

We hug one more time before going our separate ways. She returns to the Wolves' Den to make sure everything is running smoothly. And I go home, to tell Freddy he's going to be a daddy.

My hand stills on the knob. *You can do this!* I stand straight and push open the door.

# Freddy

# The Collection

I pace the living room as my hand tugs at my hair. What the fuck am I going to do? The General knew Sky was pregnant before I did! He must have spies everywhere. I kick the recycling bin and plastic flies across the room. I need to figure out what to do before he destroys *everything*. My wolf claws at my subconscious, begging to rip apart something, *anything*.

Just as the front door swings open, I shed to fur and bullet down the road as fast as my four feet can move. All I see is red. I crave the sensation of blood dripping over my fangs. Images of Angelica's mangled body haunt me. Then those of Sky and our unborn pup are added to the menagerie of gore. The General will be destroyed. But the only way to do it is from the *inside*. Get him to trust me and I'll poison his organization. My tongue lulls and my chest heaves as my beast conquers the forest. Once my muscles fail, I slump on to the dead leaves.

I miss this. Doing *what* I want. *When* I want. Not like the fucking domestic hound that I've become. My ears stand at attention and my hackles rise as the ground vibrates beneath my paws. Her scent makes my fluff settle. When she turns the corner, our eyes meet. The she-devil's emotions vibrate through our telepathic connection. She's scared. Her ears flatten and she cowers to the ground. Then inches forward and nuzzles my neck.

This mess is not Sky's fault.

I lick her muzzle and we stare out into the night air, hoping Luna will provide us the answers we are searching for. We lie under the moonlight, lost in our thoughts. The cool breeze intertwines our fur before it drifts over the hills.

A twig snaps and a rabbit leaps for its burrow. We grin at each other before springing into action. Together we corner the mammal. Taking the lead, I snap it's neck and shake it out of existence. Crimson oozes and eases my troubles. Damn, I've missed this. Sky tugs the other end until the corpse splits in two.

A howl rips through the territory, and our heads snap to the sound breaking through the darkness. Sitting on top of the hill is Tala's beta, Jackson. He leaps into the valley, landing in front of us with a booming thud. Then he shifts to his human form. "Why are you hunting *here*?" His voice surges with authority, but I stand tall as I shift.

"We are a part of the pack, are we not?" I question. "We are allowed to hunt within *our* boundaries."

"Rabbit season has passed, and we have moved on to deer. What? You couldn't handle *that* kill?"

A growl rips through my throat. I've always hated him. He's a pompous know-it-all. A very naked Sky stands at my side. She places a hand on my arm before turning to hug her wolf friend. This does nothing to ease my fury. I don't like others touching my toys. "Jackson, it has been too long," she purrs into his neck.

"That is entirely your fault, Skylar."

I collect Sky and shove her behind me. "We did nothing wrong.

And I do not appreciate the third degree."

"My alpha sent me to collect the two of you. He noticed you were near and asked that you join us around the fire tonight."

Does he know something?

"Why are you sweating, Freddy? Do you have something you want to admit?"

I charge the smug fleabag, but Sky snatches my wrist before I make contact. "We would be honored to join the pack gathering. Thank you." Jackson relaxes as Sky passes me to grasp his arm. "How is your son doing?" she asks, steering the conversation towards more neutral territory.

"Growing like a weed! He'll be so happy to see you." Jackson shoots me a glare before turning his attention to my girl again. Their words are muffled as I follow behind them, wondering how I'm going to stay under the alpha's radar.

"Aren't the fires beautiful?" Sky sighs as she sprawls out, the light dancing across her skin.

"When can we go home?"

"Stop being a party pooper, wolfman. This is fun. We have danced, ate, and now we are watching the fire crackle. Can't you just relax?"

I wait as some pups pass us while chasing their tails. One of those fluffballs belongs to Jackson. "Why haven't you told me?" I growl into her ear.

The embers flicker behind her eyes for a few minutes before I open my mouth to repeat myself, but she pushes out, "I want my child to grow up with their family and around our ancestral grounds. Here."

"You mean *our* pup," I grind my jaw. "The same kid you've yet to tell me about."

"So how did you find out?"

Oh shit. I can't admit that the General told me without raising her suspicions. "Everyone at the restaurant has big mouths." She purses her lips but accepts the answer with a nod. "It is *ours*, right?"

She rolls her eyes. "Yes."

I turn my attention to the sparks as her words sink in. Living with the main pack will be safer than staying at our place. Afterall, there is strength in numbers.

"Freddy?"

I blink but still see the inferno consuming the logs and nothing past it. "Yeah."

"Are you happy about the pup?"

"I'm scared shitless."

She bursts out laughing. "Oh, thank Luna. So am I!" Her amusement is contagious and we both chuckle until we're crying.

"What's so funny?" Maya asks as she and Sable sit next to us while they sip their drinks.

Sky shakes her head, then relaxes into my arms. "Just life."

"Don't be a stranger." Sable collects his sister into a bear hug. "It was nice hanging out with you again. Just like the old days."

I can't ignore the pointed glare he aims in my direction. Sky's time has been limited and shared between her career and me. *Well, get used to it, pretty boy.* Because soon there will be a baby to contend with, and everybody else is fucked.

"I'll be back tomorrow with some of our things. Can you talk to Frost about what I asked you?"

Sable grumbles, "You are better off asking Maya or Jackson about Carly, sis."

My ears perk. What did I miss when I took a piss?

"She's a big part of my life and I want her to be welcome here." She gives her brother her best pouty lips.

"Fine, but no promises."

"I love you."

"Wow. Are you crying?" Sable blinks.

Sky swipes at her cheek. "I'm just exhausted."

I snatch her waist. "Say goodnight, so you can get some rest," I command.

"Goodnight." She waves as I tug her along. The night air is cool against our heated bodies and the crickets' symphony serenades us. "You know what would help me unwind?" She pulls me off the beaten path and through the dark woods.

After a few minutes, I question her sanity, until she slams me against a tree and bites my bottom lip. I growl as the pain shoots straight to my cock. I dig my nails into her hips and position her in front of my rod. I'm rewarded with a moan. She grinds against my hard-on and soon her breath is nothing more than a series of gasps.

I hold her still while I devour her mouth. Her whimper almost makes me combust. My knees meet the rough earth, and I lick my lips as I examine her dripping pussy. She becomes impatient and rubs herself against my nose. My tongue massages her core, swallowing her nectar. Her legs get weak and she shivers. I circle her clit until she quivers on the edge of her escape. Then I stand.

Her eyes pop open and desire is reflected back into mine. I would love to shove her against the bark until her back bleeds. But I remind myself that she doesn't take it rough. Although every now and then she will humor me and attempt to appease my darker urges, Sky isn't Angelica.

I spin her and push her back down. Her juicy ass is on full display. It takes everything in me not to service that hole. One day…

I line up my dick, and instead of my normal pounding, I tease her as I inch in and out. She attempts to adjust her hips to meet mine, but I hold her still. "When were you planning on *asking* if Carly could move into our cave?"

Sky moans as I continue at a snail's crawl. But she never answers. I slam into her. I know she is close. I tug my cock out.

"I didn't want to mention it until I knew the pack would allow her onto the territory. She is human and it's their decision."

My dick is throbbing as it begs to return to her wet hole, but I need answers. "Why do you want her there?"

Sky pivots. Then she shoves at my chest. I stumble and trip over a rock. I fall onto my back and the air is knocked out of me. I stare at the night sky as my spine screams. Like a wild animal, Sky pounces and rides my dick. I want more responses, but this is hot. Her breasts bounce, and she gasps for oxygen. Then she bites her lip as she increases her tempo. Her hands rub circles over her nipples before she tugs on them and cries her release to the woodland gods, and I grip her hips to my own beat until I release my load.

Once we're home, I tuck a very satisfied Sky under the covers. I'd love to lie beside her, but I'm already late to my meeting with the furless dictator.

As the crickets continue to lull the rest of the world to sleep, I trudge to my gathering. A deer soars out of my path and my mind drifts to my child. Sky spoke to the Tala pack, and they welcomed her back with open paws. Me, on the other hand... I'll remain under close watch. We haven't told anybody about the child yet. But I could see the questioning glances they were throwing us. I know Jackson smelled the hormones in his wolf form, just as I did. But he didn't say anything. At least not to me.

After we left the campfire, we agreed to begin filling our new home. It is a cave house by the lake. I know once word gets out, her parents will move closer to us. They love their children and want to be a part of their grandpups' lives. Plus, I can count on them to watch over Sky while I keep the General busy. I glare at the coordinates and stomp my foot. Where the hell is he?

Headlights approach. I shield my eyes from the brightness. Once the vehicle stops, the man himself and three armed lackeys slip out. "Shouldn't you and your bitch be celebrating?"

"If you want my assistance, you will keep her name out of your mouth."

He throws a folder at my chest like a frisbee. "I need three males and three females by next month."

"I can't accomplish this in a month. It will raise too much suspicion if you take from a single pack, and traveling to others will take time."

"So, you propose we take from multiple areas?"

"Yes, starting with the ones farthest away, so they don't catch on locally and shut us down." I point to a map. "These should be good. And they are large enough that the missing members could go unnoticed for some time. Enough time for us to sneak out."

He snatches the file and shoves it into the chest of the man next to him. "Take notes of the locations and set up rendezvous points and times."

I light a cigarette and take a drag. The glow flickers off my features, giving me a hellish appearance. The smoke billows around the General's face, mutating him into the devil. I chew the filter. "Why do you hate shifters?"

"Listen, mutt, just shut up. Keep your end of the bargain, and your family will remain intact. That's all *you* need to know."

"When will I be free of *you*?"

"When you fulfill the quota your deceased leader promised me."

"Do I have your word that the hostages won't be harmed?"

"Don't worry. They will have clean water and kibble. And they'll make a great addition to my collection."

My blood runs cold. His *collection*? Who does he have? Is anyone missing from Cold Creek?

"Aren't you afraid they will be sniffed out?" I attempt to squeeze the location out of him again.

"The drugs we inject them with help conceal their presence." A soldier flicks a piece of paper at me with rendezvous points, and the General nods to his team. "Let's move out. Don't disappoint me, mutt. Or I'll burn your world to the ground."

# Sky

# Loyalties

"You're pregnant! You should be able to eat whatever you want!" Carly yells.

"I'm only six *weeks* pregnant."

My bestie whips eggs in a bowl, while shutting the fridge with her foot. And I lean back on my barstool, enjoying the show.

"Still, what's the whole point of being pregnant if you are not able to use it as an excuse to get what you want?"

"I have everything I want."

From across the counter, our eyes meet, and she grins. "Where did you say asshole was?"

I reread the text. "He said he went to see his mom and would be away for a week."

"Didn't his mom go crazy and end up in the loony bin?"

"Carly, that's insensitive. But, yes. When his father died, she fell ill." I shudder at the memory of my mom explaining how the poor woman went on a killing spree. Anybody in arm's length was torn to shreds. Then she curled up in the carnage and slept as if nothing had happened. It's sweet that he went to see her, especially after finding out I was pregnant. It sounds like he wants some parental advice. Although I'm not sure what kind of support she can offer.

"Why does he need a week for that?"

"I'm sure visiting her will throw him through an emotional loop. So he is taking time to resettle himself before returning home."

Carly slides a plate of bacon, eggs, and biscuits across the counter. Then she wraps her arms around me. "So, does that mean you'll be left alone, *exposed,* and up for the taking?" She nuzzles the soft spot behind my ear, causing goose bumps to crawl up my arm. "What if someone were to sneak into your bed?"

"As much as my hormone-filled body would love that, I haven't talked to Freddy about our situation," I say delicately. "I promise, when he comes home, I will find a way to brooch the topic."

Carly's fingertips dance up my leg. "What he doesn't know... can't hurt him."

I bite my lip. "He is the father of this child and I want to make this work with him."

She rubs circles over my thin underwear. "We don't need him. I mean, you have the pup. We can raise it together."

I arch my hips to increase the pressure. "I'll text him."

"When?" she whispers against my lobe before she nips it.

"Now." The message is short and sweet, asking him if it would be considered cheating if I were to have relations with a woman. I try to word it as if I'm curious. "He said he is the only one to service me. No substitutions." I pout.

"Are you really going to listen to him?"

I start on the breakfast she made. "When he returns, I'll have a nice *long* conversation about what I need if our relationship is meant to continue." My phone dings and I anxiously check it, hoping it's my boyfriend changing his mind.

"I have to get to work. Eat your food, then meet me there, okay?" She kisses my cheek before she collects her things.

"I may be running a little late. That message was from Jackson. He said he's on his way to talk."

"Oh, *the* Jackson?" Carly wiggles her brows. "The one I have been begging you to set me up with?"

"He only has eyes for shifters—*sorry*." I wave her out the door. "I'll see you soon."

"Bye, Sky Bear."

I stir the eggs around. It's been nice to have Carly living with me again. I've never realized how lonely it's been with just Freddy. It's like a piece of my soul was missing. I clear my plate just as a knock sounds on the door.

"It's open," I shout as I scrub the dishes. One downfall of living in a cheaper area: there's no dishwasher. And Carly hates doing the dishes because it messes up her nails. I flex my claws. There's no point in getting mine professionally polished when every time I shift, the fake attachments pop off.

"See, this is what I'm talking about. We need more fur-woman like *you*." Jackson settles on the couch. "Barefoot, pregnant, and washing the dishes." I hurl a soapy sponge at his head. He dodges it and smirks. "Your aim has gotten worse."

"As much as I love you criticizing me, why don't you tell me why you are here?" I dry my hands and lower myself onto the chair next to him.

"Well, Frost wanted me to come by and speak to you about an issue."

"Okay," I draw out. "Just hurry up and tell me. I need to get to work."

"He has denied Carly access to the territory."

I didn't expect this response. The pack *knows* Carly is like a sister to me. Like a daughter to my mom and dad. Surely, that gains her some benefits. "Why did he say no?"

"For one thing, she is *human*. We can't trust that she won't exploit us and our ways. Or worse, what if she is attacked by a new shifter and the Guardians get involved? There are so many reasons. I'm sorry."

I've known Jackson my whole life. He handles a lot of the alpha's more *undesirable* chores and he's not afraid to get his paws dirty. Something's up. "If that was all that was said, you wouldn't be so squirmy. So out with it already. What else did his *highness* say."

"Hey, watch your mouth. He is the alpha and his word is law."

"What else did he say?" I press again, my voice nearly a hiss this time.

"Apparently, the rumor is that you have more than a friendship with the girl, and Frost doesn't want any of the pups to think that that is an option for their future." He holds his hands up as I leap to my feet. "You know I see no problem with it. But he is our leader, and he has to think about the future of the entire pack."

"Then maybe I don't want to be a member of his fucking judgmental pack!"

"Calm down."

"Fuck you! Carly is closer to me than a sister ever could be." I sniffle. "And I need her!" I throw my hands up in defeat. I dash into my room and slam the door. The rules are bullshit. I bury my face into my pillow and breathe in her scent. Since Freddy is out of town, Carly sleeps next to me and the bedding smells like her floral shampoo. Jackson's words wash over me. Would my bestie be in danger? Would the other pack members reject her or attempt to hurt her because she has no fur? Maybe we can make her an honorary pack member, or liaison, like we've done for the Native Americans who share the reserve with us?

Jackson taps on the doorframe. "I know you are upset, and I wish I could say something to make you feel better. But I suck at this shit." My silence is deafening. He approaches the bed and pats my foot. "Are you going to move next to your brother or not?"

"I've tried living without her, and I can't. I won't," I whisper. "If they won't welcome Carly, then no."

"If you change your mind, your cave home will always be there waiting for you." When I don't meet his gaze, he strides out of the room.

"Jackson?"

"Yeah?"

"Is it really worth it? I mean, waiting for your mate?"

A sad smile crosses his face, and I know he is reminiscing about his deceased wife. He runs a hand through his hair and leans on the wall as if the weight of the world has fallen on his shoulders. "Yes, it is worth the wait."

I rub my belly. "Do you think Luna made a mistake by allowing this pregnancy?"

The bed dips as he sits beside me. "Luna gives us freewill. You had unprotected sex and got pregnant. That was *your* choice."

"So I made a mistake?"

"No child is a mistake. They're a *new* beginning."

I know he is thinking about the son his mate left behind when she passed. In his grief, he gave his child to another pack member who couldn't have kids. The boy still calls Jackson *Dad*, and they spend a lot of time together, but I'm sure the choice haunts him. "They'll help us raise our pup, right? Even if we decide to stay here."

"You know what they say: *it takes a village to raise a kid.* And, sweetie, we have something stronger: a damn wolf pack." He kisses my forehead. "I'll tell Frost you won't be moving in. If you change your mind, let me know." Jackson wipes my cheeks with his thumb. "Chin up. Things will get better. You'll see." He exits the room, and I can't help but assess his sculpted body. He is older, but still smoking hot. I'm glad he keeps by the alpha's side because I don't think he'd be safe here with Carly on the prowl.

"What do you mean *we aren't moving*?" Carly waves her palm over the cardboard she dragged inside.

"I don't want to move again," I groan. "Plus, this place is big enough."

Carly arches a brow as she pretends to look around the two-bedroom house. "*Who* are you trying to fool?"

"Drop it. I've made my choice."

"What will your boyfriend say?"

He was pretty adamant about moving closer to the others. But I won't leave my bestie. And I'm not going to hurt her feelings by explaining the *real* reason I want to stay. I bite my lip. *But* I know she will find out sooner or later. And I'd rather she find out from a friend. I tug her to the couch. "The pack leader doesn't want you to get hurt, so he denied our request."

Carly looks like I've slapped her across the face as she rises to her feet. "What?"

I stare at my clasped hands. "I'm sorry… I really wanted this to work out."

"So, what now? You and Freddy are moving there after the baby is born and I'm stuck here?"

My head shoots up at her accusation. "*No*. I told Frost if you can't come, then neither can I."

"You would do that, for me?"

"I meant what I said. I *need* you." I rub my belly. "We need you."

"I won't let you guys down. And I'll do my best to get along with the sperm donor."

"Thank you."

"Now, let's move his shit out of the guest room and start on the nursery!" We walk hand in hand, eager to get our new journey started.

"You didn't have to do this."

"Are you kidding me? I *love* shopping!"

"Yes, but for baby stuff?"

Carly ruffles through her bags and pulls out a lacey strapless gown. "Not *everything* is baby-related."

I roll my eyes. She's gearing up for another mercy mission. A married man was sending dick pictures to her, and she's collecting all the evidence to give to his partner. Including a meetup at his home. "Oh no. Not *him* again." I avert my gaze.

Carly groans. "Grown-ass men should not be in costumes unless they're strippers."

We watch a man pull on a bear head. He dances around the food court, offering samples of *beary* smoothies. He makes a beeline to our table. "No, thank you." I wave him off. "I'm more of a meat eater." I nod to my double cheeseburger.

But the idiot is persistent. "Are your ears clogged, Pooh Bear? We aren't interested." Carly tugs his mask off.

"Hey!" he yells.

She waves a twenty-dollar bill at a teenager. "Here, kid. Give Mr. Teddy some exercise." The teen takes off with the costume piece, and the headless bear runs after him screaming.

"You shouldn't have done that."

"It'll teach the jerk to listen when someone says stop." She grinds her teeth and stabs at her salad.

I wiggle my toes against her thigh. "Are you okay?"

"Yeah. I just had a moment." She doesn't need to say any more. I know when she was violated at the university, it really messed her up. I think that's why she stopped dating men in college and explored women. Every now and then, she has episodes of PTSD, and it takes a while for her to snap back. Hearing me say *no* must have taken her for a spin.

"Hey, ladies. I just wanted to tell you how awesome that was." We pivot to two young men in jeans and cut-off shirts. "Can we buy you dinner?"

I point to our half-eaten meal. "No, thank you."

"Well, how about we treat you to a movie?" The blond leans towards us. "It'll be fun."

"How about a round of beers on *me,* handsome?" Carly tugs a business card out of her cleavage and hands it to them.

"Wolves' Den?"

"Yes, it's a delicious steakhouse right by the university. You should take your friends and have a guys' night out."

"Will you be there?"

She grins. "I'm always there."

"Awesome. I'll give you a call tonight and set something up."

Carly whispers in his ear. He blinks, nods, and then stalks off with drool slithering down his chin.

"What did you tell those poor boys?" I smirk.

"That if they go, they should post pictures of their meals on their socials."

"*And*?"

"And, if he does, I'll send him boob pics." She returns to her food. I chuckle and devour my burger. I'm not sure if she's kidding or not, but either way, I'm amazed by and a little scared of her marketing skills.

# Freddy

# The Test

It's been a long fucking week. Not only did I travel over three hundred miles, but I came up empty-handed. It's harder than I thought to lure wolves out of their dens. No matter how many beers I throw back or how much I chat about the weather. Plus, I'll be damned, but my conscious is eating me up. Trapping my own kind for the government's personal use is bullshit. But the General has me on a tight leash. I need to be done with him before Sky has our kid, because I won't let that bastard get his bloody hands on them. And I'm running out of time.

I burst through my front door and toss my duffle bag at the washing machine. One thing I don't miss about some of the other packs is their incessant need to *not* have indoor plumbing. And my clothes are raunchy. Thank Luna Frost engineered our pack's caves to accommodate electricity and running water. Most of the wolves in Cold Creek have those amenities, but outside of that… it can be prehistoric.

"Sky?"

The house is empty and too quiet. She must be at work. I tug the fridge door open and glare at the healthy shit inside. Where the hell is my alcohol? I rub my hands over my dusty face. Just because *she* can't drink doesn't mean I have to abide by those rules. I'm not growing a fetus.

I crane my neck and my lips pull back. Bingo.

She stashed the goods on top of the freezer. It's warm, but it'll do the trick. I snatch the fire whiskey and head towards the bathroom. After a few chugs, my mind is buzzing and the guilt dwindles. The warmth from the cascading shower seeps into my travel-worn bones. The grime swirls down the drain and I hope the scent of betrayal tags along with it. I clench my fist and pound the tile. What kind of punishment will Luna serve me? But is there *any* way out of it? When I leave the comfort of the steam, I guzzle a few more mouthfuls of the amber liquid. I don't bother to throw clothes on, and trudge to bed.

"I've missed you," I groan into the feather pillow. My body goes stiff. That isn't Sky's smell. I sniff again and snarl. Carly's been sleeping in *my* bed. That little bitch! I'm gone for a week, and she wiggles under the covers! I slurp at my nightcap and slam it on the bedside table.

Why does nobody respect me?

The front door opens and footsteps approach the threshold. My eyes narrow before the figure emerges. "Well, look what the cat dragged in."

"Get out of my house."

Carly slinks into the room and *tsks*. "No alcohol. It's not good for the baby." She glides her fingertips over my liquid sanity.

"Give me the bottle. Before I take it back by force."

She leans forward. "Try it, big guy. I dare you." What game is she playing? My gaze drifts to her outfit. A black pencil skirt, with a button-up blouse. And right now, there is enough cleavage to bury my fangs in. "Well, someone is being inappropriate," she purrs as she nods at my erection.

"You came into my room, wearing that... What did you expect to happen?"

"What do *you* expect to happen?"

"I expect you to get the fuck out."

"This has been my house for the last week." She cocks a hip. "And I don't plan on going anywhere."

My blood is boiling at her disrespectful attitude. I slide out of the bed and tower over her. "I'm only going to ask you nicely, one more time. Leave."

"But what will Sky say when I tell her you kicked me out?"

"I don't care. I pay half of everything here. So half of everything is mine." I grab her wrist and tug her to the exit. I'm tired, drunk, and done playing human games.

She digs in her heels and shoves me against the wall. Well, shit. The little peon is extending her claws. "You listen here, you big *idiot*. Sky can do so much *better* than you. But since you knocked her up and she feels obligated to stay with you, let me tell you something... you are stuck with me. Because I won't give her up."

My hard-on is painful as she assaults me. I missed this rough foreplay. And she's been the only one playing. My turn. I slam her against the wall, my hand on her throat. Her pulse quickens as it thumps against my fingertips. Fear permeates through her pores, and I buzz with power. "You forget, little *girl,* that you are just a pitiful human." I squeeze her collar. "I can break you in two in a blink of an eye, then bury your body so nobody will ever find you." I snort. "Not that anybody would search. Yeah, Sky told me about your pathetic family. How they all died, and you went from foster home to foster home your entire life."

She leans into my grip. "What are you waiting for?"

I narrow my eyes. "What are you hoping to accomplish right now?"

"A compromise." Her nails graze my thigh. I suck in a breath as she chokes my rod. It has been over a week since I've had any release. And her expert fingers are deliciously tempting.

"What *compromise*?"

She ceases her massage and reaches for the hem of her shirt. Then she slowly unbuttons it. The fabric glides off, revealing a red lacey bra. My palms ache to grab the round orbs as my mouth waters, demanding to take a bite.

"We both want the same thing, Freddy." She snatches my free wrist, placing it on her breast. "We want Sky and the baby healthy, loved, and happy."

I tighten my grip on her neck and she releases my hand and squeaks. "I don't share. They are *mine*." Carly surrenders and I release her. She rubs her neck. "It's time for you to leave," I growl out my command.

"I will be in Sky's life. I want to help her raise her child."

"So why don't you ask her to leave me for you?"

"Because she wants to do what's right for the child, and the pack isn't going to be much help."

My ears perk up. "What do you mean the pack won't help?"

"They don't like the fact that she has a human as a BFF."

My lips curl. This is the first I've heard of this. That means Sky won't have the protection of the pack after all. This isn't good. "What's in it for me, if I let you help with the child?" Her eyes light up, thinking she's won with her tactics, but I shoot her down fast. "I told you I don't share. You will never be intimate with Sky. Or I'll *kill* you. No questions asked." Carly slaps me. The sting doesn't compare to the shock. Does she have a death wish? I slam my open palms on each side of her head. "Are you asking for a knife in the back?"

"I know how you like it." She tugs a black tie from the depths of her bra. "I too have… darker desires sometimes. So here is my deal. Tie me up. Fuck me. Get your fill. When we are done, we don't tell Sky and you let me move in." She swings the silk tie as if further tempting me. This chick is unhinged. My cock pulsates at the thought. But is it worth the consequences?

"Have you lost your mind?"

"Sky is worth the risk." Her hand comes up to slap me again, but I'm ready this time. I snatch her waist and toss her on to the bed.

"You obviously know nothing about me. I'm not stupid enough to fall for your tricks. The second I bury myself inside your pussy, you'll rat me out to Sky, I'll lose her, and you can slip in." Her face pales. *Bingo.* I grab the tie from her hands and turn her around. She screams and tries to kick as I bind her wrists behind her back. I shove my erection against her spine and howl in her ear. "Your plan won't work on me, little slut." I twirl her and stare into her wide eyes. I grab the shirt that she discarded on the floor and finish securing her to the headboard. Then take in my masterpiece.

"Let me go, you monster!"

"Oh, no. Because when Sky comes home, she'll see what you tried to do. Then it'll be your ass she kicks out."

She pulls on her restraints. "This isn't going to work. I told her I was going to trick you. She already knows what I'm doing."

They are both manipulating me? My wolf claws at my insides, ready to destroy the backstabbers. I turn on my heels and sprint out the front door. This isn't the way this is going down. I go to shift, but I notice headlights pulling up.

"You're home." Sky runs over to hug me. "What's wrong?"

I snatch her elbow and yank her inside the house. Then I toss her into our room.

"What's going on in here?" she demands, the question directed at Carly. "I thought you were joking about testing him!" She runs to untie her friend.

"Don't touch that," I command.

She stops mid-stride and turns to me. "You can't leave her like that."

"Yes, I can."

"Come on, she was just testing you and you passed."

"I don't give a shit what she was *trying* to do."

Sky bites her lip as she looks between a very naked me and a half-naked Carly. I see the wheels turn in her head as she clenches her thighs together, and I smell her arousal. But I can't let her plan succeed. I won't be controlled. "What are you going to do to her?" Sky asks.

"She can rot there for all I care. I can still fit on the bed and sleep comfortably."

"Please, Freddy," she begs. "Let her go." Her pleas have my dick twitching. "What was her deal?"

"That I could fuck her once and then she could live with us."

"What if you get to watch us?" Sky points between herself and Carly.

"I won't share you, especially with *her*."

Sky drops to her knees and collects me in her mouth. I stumble with the sudden jolt of pleasure. My eyes fall back in my head, and I guide her over my shaft. Damn that mouth. She suckles before she pops me out. "Please let her stay with us and offer her the same protection you're giving me."

"She's not a shifter. I can't promise to protect her." These chicks are out of their minds. I stomp to Carly and release her. "Get the fuck out of my house. If you ever pull a stunt like that again, it will be your last."

Carly scurries to grab her discarded clothing. Then leaves with a backward glance at Sky. Her lip trembles and she mouths, "Sorry."

Once the front door shuts, Sky pivots to me with tears streaming down her cheeks. "I'm not letting her leave like that." She collects some clothes and shoves them into a backpack before striding out and slamming the door.

I stand in the empty home, hard as a rock, and wonder *what the fuck just happened*. I wouldn't cheat on her. Shouldn't that give me some brownie points? Sky will be back. There's no way she'll keep my child from me. Let Carly have this *one* win. Because in the end, I'll be the true victor.

# Sky

# The Plan

*F*reddy and Carly will never get along. What was I thinking? I rub the anklet he gave me and resist the urge to throw it into the woods. My toes dance in the cool water and ripples spread out to the middle of the pond. I flop into the lush grass and my eyes flutter shut. The serenade of forest creatures lulls me to sleep. A wet nose startles my dreams. I shove it aside before I turn towards Sable's fur suit. His tongue hangs out as his bushy tail creates a fresh breeze. I scratch his ears, then I bury my face into his mane. Things were easier before Freddy and Maya came into our lives. No complications. No drama. Sable nudges my belly.

"The *baby* is fine. It's everything else that's collapsing." He whimpers as he nips my shirt in response. "Freddy doesn't like Carly and they're always fighting." He vocalizes his displeasure. "I know you don't like him, but he is the child's father." I huff out a breath. "And Frost won't even *consider* letting Carly move on to the territory. I'm torn, big brother. Torn between having to pick between Freddy and Carly. When I am selfish and want them both."

I look into his eyes. "Why can't I have both?" He releases a puff of air. "I know. I'm spoiled. But I want what I want." I smirk. "It's really your fault, you know? You rarely tell me no."

Sable slumps on the ground. He's the best listener but he hates the drama that revolves around my life. His ears perk up as he spots a shadow approaching in the water. He crawls to the edge of the pond.

"Don't even *think* about it! I have my phone right…"

He leaps, sending droplets all over me, before he paddles to chase a Mallard around. It quacks and smacks its wings across its attacker's face.

"*There* he is!" Maya strides over. "Playing with his feathered friends again?" She hands me an iced tea while she sips hers. "Did you and Freddy break up?"

"No."

"Then why are you staying at your parents' house?"

"Freddy is out of town *again* and I don't want to be alone."

"What about Carly?"

I clench my cup. "Freddy doesn't want us staying over each other's houses."

"So what? He's not your boss."

I twirl my straw. "It's complicated."

Sable prances over with the duck speared on his fangs.

"That bird isn't going to feed us all." Maya giggles.

My brother shakes the wetness from his coat, causing us to raise our palms in defense. He drops the corpse at my feet, then shifts to two legs. He scoops his mate in his arms. "It's for *Sky,* not us."

"Can you eat duck while you're pregnant?" Maya questions. I

shrug as I poke the feathers with my toe.

"Hey, it'll work out, sis. Because your big brother will help. Do you want me to bury Freddy? Hide Carly in our closet until Frost goes to bed?"

"No," I whine.

He releases Maya to sit next to me, smacking my knee until I meet his gaze. "Stop fucking pouting. You are a *Canis*." He cringes as Maya swats him. "And a member of the *Tala* pack. You can do this. You are strong, caring, and we love you."

"Dinner is done!" my dad yells from the cave door.

Sable helps me stand and wraps an arm around my neck. Then drapes the other over his wife. "Let's feast, ladies!"

I fork my venison steak. I would have seasoned it differently. It's not *bad*, just a little gamey. The conversation surrounds me while we sit at the kitchen table. Sable and Maya talk about their *plan*... They are waiting a while before they pop out pups.

Aspen laughs until tears kiss his cheeks. "You actually believe you have that much *control*? Give me a break." He snorts at my belly. "It's not going to work."

"I just want to be established in my profession before we have kids. If we can stick to our strategy, that would be great. But if Luna alters it, we will be okay with that too." Maya runs her thumb over Sable's palm.

And his eyes twinkle. "Shit. We can start right now if you want, babe?"

Mom clears her throat. "The fire is lit outside if everyone's ready for s'mores!"

"Nice save, Ma." Aspen scurries out the door.

Maya and Sable push back their chairs, eager to reacquaint themselves with the night air.

"Are you coming too, honey?" My mom runs a hand through my hair. "I bought your favorite dark chocolate candy bar."

"They have a *plan…*" I mumble to myself.

"Sweetie, every family is different. Don't worry about it. I guarantee that this so-called plan of theirs will not work. It never does. Trust me." She rubs my back. "You'll see. Luna rarely gives us exactly what we ask for. Now, come on, before all the marshmallows disappear." She guides me into the starry evening. The silence soothes my jealousy. She's right. You can't predict the future.

We sit crossed-legged around the embers. The flames lick the moon and add a fantasy-like atmosphere to the gathering. We tell ghost stories and eat sweets until well past midnight. After consuming too many s'mores, I lay my head on Mom's shoulder. Her soft voice lulls me into a comforting trance. She's an amazing mother. How does she do it?

Sable stirs the logs and a red ember flies to my hand. I shake out my wrist and narrow my eyes at him. "Stop playing with it."

"Oh, stop being a baby." He reaches for my arm. "Want me to kiss the little booboo for you, baby sister?"

I kick him. "Just set your stick down and walk away from the fire before you set your wife ablaze."

"Sorry I'm late to the party!"

I beam at the visitor. "Carly? What are you doing here?"

"Sable invited me. So here I am."

My mom stands and stretches. "Well, this old lady is heading to bed. Come on, dear." She spanks my dad before grabbing his hand.

They stroll towards the cave. "Good night, kids."

Carly settles in next to me and Aspen hands her a s'more. She bites into it and cream oozes from the sides. "Nothing beats a good charred marshmallow."

"I'm hitting the hay too. Night, guys." My younger brother yawns and stalks off.

Carly strokes the blister forming on my hand. "Are you okay?"

"Yeah, it's nothing. Sable just attempted to set me on fire."

My big brother rolls his eyes and flips me off. Carly kisses the injury and cradles it. "I'm sorry. Do you want me to get some ice from the kitchen?"

"It's okay. I'm just glad you're here because I know *you* won't try to kill me." I stick my tongue out at Mr. Fire-Starter, before I rub my face and lean into my best friend. From the corner of my eye, I see Maya passed out and drooling on my brother's shoulder. But he doesn't even notice as he pokes at the inferno again. "Your wife is getting you all wet."

He turns slowly, so as not to wake her. "I should get my sleeping beauty to bed." He collects her in his arms.

"I'm *not* sleeping," Maya mumbles into his chest.

"Good night, girls." he mutters.

"Night." Maya attempts to wave but she looks like she's swatting a mosquito. My heart clenches as the night swallows their figures. I wish I had *that* with my child's father. Maybe once the baby is born, he'll be more protective. Hold me tight like that. Whisper sweet nothings into my ear.

"I'm sorry I screwed everything up with you and Freddy."

"He'll forgive you."

"When?" Carly snorts out. "Hopefully before the baby turns

eighteen."

"I told you we will work it out. You guys can have split custody." I smirk. "I'll stay with you half the week, then Freddy during the other half."

"Just *leave* him. Please. I know I sound like a broken record, but trust me on this. I've dealt with men like him a lot." At my silence, she stands and shoves her fingers into her jean pockets. "It's getting late. I'll see you at work tomorrow." When her footsteps can't be heard anymore, I drop my face into my hands and cry. Stupid hormones. I'm so *weak*. That's probably why Freddy couldn't care less about what I want. A sudden, sharp pain in my stomach has me bending over. I take in a deep breath, and it passes.

I hope Sable is right… that everything will work out.

"No, I said it goes to table *three,* Dale!" I holler at the clueless server as I expedite the other meals.

"When are you going to fire him?" John mutters as he flips a steak on the grill.

"Dale has a family to support. His wife stays at home to take care of their special needs kid." I check the next order. "Just give him another chance." I swipe my brow before bracing myself on the counter.

"Hey, boss, are you okay?" John shuffles to my side.

I hold up a hand. "I'm fine. And I'll be even better when I have the meat for table seven."

He backpedals. "Twenty more seconds."

Carly shoves through the kitchen door. When our eyes meet, she scowls and stomps over. She snatches my forearm. "I told you it's too hot for you in the kitchen." She pulls me from the line and tosses our chef a glare. "Where the fuck is Jimmy?"

"He called out, *again*," John throws over his shoulder as he plops the steak on a plate. "Order up."

"That's three times this week. He is *fired*," Carly snarls.

"But he is a foster dad," I whine. "What will happen to the children?"

"I'm co-owner of this place, am I not?"

"Yes, but…"

"No *buts*! I know you're all maternal at the moment, but you can't be a doormat. Jimmy is fired—end of discussion. And if you don't sit your ass down and chug water, Dale will be next." I slump in my office chair, and she slaps a bottle in my hand. "Drink. I'll expedite dinner service until Monica comes in. Then I'll check on you."

"Stop worrying about me."

"Well, *someone* has to," she mutters as she rushes to the dining room.

Why did I ever want to own a restaurant? It is not easy finding employees who take the job seriously. They always call out or come in stoned. My phone buzzes and I see a text from Jackson, demanding my presence for a mandatory pack meeting. I rub my chin. It's rare to be commanded to attend anything, especially when my rank is probably just above the pups. I shrug it off. They know I'm a busy businesswoman. I grab the picture frame sitting next to my computer monitor. I glide my finger over the ultrasound of our baby boy. Yes, *boy*. My mom is beyond happy. She even made duplicates for the family.

I'm trying to be patient with Freddy. But he has been traveling a lot lately. I suppose it has something to do with his old government buddy I met a few months ago, but I'm not sure. Freddy never talks about it. I itch my ankle where the anklet he gave me rests. He still despises Carly. But I visit her at her house and we see each other at work. I'll take what I can get.

My internal angst pauses as my phone screams. I groan at Jackson's caller ID and let him go to voicemail. Then my work telephone blares. He is being persistent. "Mental institution, Queen Nut here. How may I direct your call?"

"Why aren't you answering your phone?"

"You know, Jackson, not all of us can stay at home and *not* work for a living."

He snorts. "You are more than set financially. You don't *need* to work. You choose to."

"It's called contributing to society. You should really try it."

"See, what I do is *more* important. It's called protecting and guiding a pack. You should try it too."

"Sounds boring. No thanks. I'd rather be my own boss, not someone's bitch—whoops, I mean *beta*."

"Well, from one bitch to another, Frost needs you to come to the meeting room."

"Wait, you call me a bitch, then you expect me to follow your orders?"

"Aren't you a female wolf?"

"How badly does the alpha want me there?"

"He demands it. Even if I have to collect you myself."

I twirl in my office chair. "Is there any way I can play the pregnancy card to get out of it?"

"Nope. But if it makes you feel any better, your whole family will be there too."

Dread tickles at the base of my spine. "Why?"

"Come and find out." The line clicks.

I chew my bottom lip as I debate whether Jackson is serious or not. Then I question what Frost could do if I didn't show up. A knock on my office door pulls me out of my reflections. "I came to see if you wanted a ride." My mom enters. "I think you might be getting a little niece or nephew soon," she sings.

I release a breath. "Really?" I grab my purse. "Do you think that's why Frost is gathering us?"

"I hope so!"

I laugh at my mom's baby-crazed mindset. "But why would he order us there to tell us *that*? Isn't that a simple phone call?"

"Well, it is his daughter, our future alpha, who is pregnant." She puts her hand on the small of my back and guides me out the door. "There's only one way to find out."

# Freddy

# Mistakes

"Get the fuck off me!" A fist slams into the shifter's face, silencing him for the duration of his transport to the facility.

"You didn't have to do that," I growl. "He was bound."

The soldiers laugh as they toss their captive into the back of their van. "But then we have to hear him bitch the entire way. And we don't get paid enough for that."

I light a cigarette. That makes five shifters I've stalked for the General. Only one more female, then I'm off the hook—as long as the slimy bastard doesn't slit my throat to keep his secrets buried. But that idiot has another thing coming to him if he thinks I didn't cover my tracks. If I'm killed, everything goes to Sky and my son. Including a safety deposit box containing all the evidence needed to put that fucker behind bars. I take a drag on the cancer stick before exhaling my doubts. The smoke dances in the wind as if reaching out to the full moon.

"Here's the next pickup location." The soldier shoves a piece of paper under my nose. "Don't be late."

I snatch the document from his hand and resist the urge to shove it down his throat. The General still hasn't allowed me access to the compound where they are keeping the wolves. He loves his secrets. I stomp out the cigarette, then put the used filter in my pocket to toss out once we've distanced ourselves from the crime scene. The last shifters I grabbed were from Robert's pack. And he'll be on the hunt. So I can't risk shifting and leaving my fur scent here either.

I trudge to my motorcycle and soon the engine roars to life between my legs. I rev it and allow the hum of the motor to shake my thighs before I screech the tires. I bullet down the deserted road towards the highway that will take me home. Once I pull into the driveway, I stride into the dark house. I let out a breath, glad to be able to clean up without the third degree from her hormonal highness. Ever since I refused to let her play her games with Carly, she's been in a mood. Demanding. Nagging. The typical girlfriend bullshit. But the pregnancy makes things worse.

As I strip off my clothes, the bathroom door swings open. "Where were *you*?" And the interrogation begins.

"Sky, I'm exhausted."

"I tried calling your cell a hundred times."

"I told you I leave my phone on silent."

"You couldn't take two seconds to send me a quick text to let me know you were okay?"

*Not when I'm corralling creatures with sensitive hearing.* I slide into the shower stall and settle under the cascading hot water. It scalds my skin and burns off all evidence of my traitorous acts.

"Don't you even *want* to know how my appointment went?"

"How did it go?" I say between scrubbing.

"They said everything looks good. So I guess the cramping was just from stretching."

"That's good," I mumble in reply as I continue to rinse off the day's events.

"I'll meet you in bed," she huffs. Women are nothing but trouble. Huge headaches.

When I wake up in the morning, Sky is already gone. She leaves a note reminding me to pay my half of the rent by Friday. I crumble it up and toss it in the trash. I haven't been able to work as much as I need to because I've been so focused on getting the wolves. I don't have the cash. And I know this will cause conflict. But I don't care. After today's pickup, I can finally be rid of this huge weight and look forward to the birth of my son.

My motorcycle tears down the street and the wind whips my hair. I park it on the side of the road and climb to the coordinates. A whistle from across the woods catches my attention and I detour to see what's going on. I hide my steps and stick to the shadows, squinting through the foliage to take in a group of men. They are definitely from the General. I step out to introduce myself, but stop in my tracks. My nose twitches against the breeze. Shit. Why are *they* so far away from the pack? I blend into the tall grass and grind my jaw. There's a splash and I peek as a familiar male wades in the water.

*Oh no.*

The group of soldiers moves in on the oblivious shifter, their tranquilizers aimed at his paddling form. Damn it. *Run, Sable!* I know Maya isn't too far behind her mate. If they grab them, it'll be over for the General, because the pack will not rest until they find the duo. Especially after they just got Maya back into their lives and she's next in line to be alpha.

The idiots shoot, then leap into the pond. They wrestle with Sable, until the wolf is bloodied and subdued, then drag his limp figure to the muddy shore before they lift him into the vehicle and peel off.

The heart-wrenching scream breaks my concentration. I twist to see Maya chasing her mate's abductors. I squeeze my lids closed, in an attempt to drown out her sorrow, as images flash through my mind of the day I lost Angelica. At least the men were smart enough to leave Maya behind. I start the trek back to my motorcycle, to get the hell out of here before Frost comes to track down the kidnappers. I push the bike before kick-starting it and taking off. Once I'm a good bit away from yet another crime scene, I park at a small diner and snatch my phone out of my pocket.

"You need to put that wolf back!" I shout the moment the man answers.

The General's laughter chills my bones. "You are just jealous because my guys found one *without* you."

"Those idiots don't know who they grabbed! That male is next in line to become alpha! They will search for him."

"Then he is even more valuable. Alpha blood will ensure his offspring are untouchable."

I run a hand through my hair as I kick the side of the building. "Fucking *listen* to me!"

"No. You listen to me! You'll bring me the female you promised, or I'm taking your bitch! And call it a bonus, seeing as she's already pregnant." The line goes dead. And a roar rips through my throat while I slam my fist into the brick exterior. This can't be happening! The pulsating in my bloodied knuckles dulls my nerves.

*One* more shifter. Then this nightmare is over. I meander around the small town, racking my brain for a new plan. They may have Sable, but that doesn't mean *game over* for me. If the pack does hunt him down, I'll be nowhere in sight. Which means they can't blame me. And, technically, I just locate the wolves. I don't ever capture them. Then again, if I do get arrested, will the General help me? I scoff at the thought. If anything, he'd torture me and throw me into his program.

I scratch my stubble. From what I've been able to gather from his goons, his operation is small. He may not have as much power as he likes to suggest or that many higher-ups backing him. So I could roll over on him, spill what little information I have, and ask for a plea bargain, reminding them of the fact that I was protecting my family.

"Well, well, well. You are pretty far from your territory."

I blink at my darkening surroundings. How long have I been strolling? I stare at the gorgeous blonde in front of me. Her shifter gaze takes in my leather jacket, jeans, and riding boots before she cocks her hip and licks her lips.

"I thought that was you, Freddy."

"Bridgett. It's been a while."

"Yes, it has. What brings you to our neck of the woods?"

I take a closer look at the area and curse. I walked into Robert's territory without even realizing it. This is dangerous, because he was the last pack I singled out for the General. I catch a scent drifting in the night air. Bingo. Here's my perfect *alibi*. I give her my best bad boy grin. She's in heat. "Well, I knew my services could be of some use. If they are welcomed, that is."

Bridgett bites her lip. "Robert doesn't want outsiders wandering too close, honey."

I trail a fingertip down her cheek. "You can't blame a wolf for trying."

She runs her nose along my neck, collecting my musk, before she glides her tongue over my stubble to taste my sweat. "What Robert doesn't know won't hurt him."

She slams me against the nearest office building and smashes her mouth onto mine. I groan into her teeth. I miss *this* passion. This ravenous sensation. My erection presses along her stomach, and she coos before reaching down to rub me through my pants.

"Touch me," she commands.

I fist her dress and locate her drenched panties. I rip them aside and pump two fingers into her core. She leans into the pressure, begging for more. I shove two more into her center. She moves her hips to my merciless rhythm before exploding into euphoria. Her juices drip over my wrist. Nothing beats the taste of an unclaimed bitch ovulating. I lick the sweet honey off each knuckle.

"I'm going to mouth-fuck you into oblivion." She tugs me to a fire escape. "Why don't you stay the night?" She nods at the rusty stairs. "I'm on the third floor." She sashays towards the building's main entrance. "I'll unlock the window for you, Romeo."

I look around the vacant alley. Bridgett saw me, so my alibi is concrete. If I leave now, I can make it back home before Sky returns from work. But she'll be nagging and demand to know why I can't pay my half of the rent. I glance up the metal staircase. *Decisions, decisions.*

My phone's ringing pulls me out of my fantasy. "What?" I growl.

"We have a problem. We need to meet up and create a game plan." The line goes dead. Fuck. My choice has been made for me. I have to visit my aunt. She must have had a vision. I pout at the window before trudging back to my bike.

I readjust myself, settle on the seat, rev the motor, and pray for some good news.

# Sky

# Gone

Mom's practically bouncing when we enter the meeting room. Usually only the alphas gather around the table with the higher-ups of the pack. When a nobody is invited, it's because they are in trouble. But I've been so busy I know it can't be me. My mother squeezes my wrist. I haven't seen her *this* happy in a long time. She deserves it. She works so hard serving others.

We all get situated and stare expectantly at Frost, the energy surrounding him buzzing with power. The door swings open and Maya and Jackson tumble into the space. Mom grabs Maya's hands. "Your dad said you needed to tell us something. Has it finally happened? Are you and Sable expecting?"

The atmosphere shifts as Maya embraces Mom and whispers, "I wish it were that simple, Celeste."

My pulse stutters. My neck snaps to Jackson. He can't even look at us.

"Why don't we all have a seat?" Frost commands, then nods to his daughter.

Maya's lip trembles. "Robert came to us seeking our assistance to help track some missing pack members." My mind goes a million miles a minute. How could shifters go missing? We are excellent trackers and have a built-in GPS system. "Dad told Robert that we couldn't risk leaving the safety of the territory to find them, but Sable and I didn't agree." Tears plop on the table. "I knew if I could just hunt down the Guardian, we could find the wolves. But when I finally got the Guardian's scent, we were exhausted and had to stop to rest."

My head tilts left, then right, as I look for my older brother. My hands shake so severely I have to grip the table to steady them. "Stop," I whisper my demand. This can't be happening. "Please."

"We wanted to wash off the trip's grime, but I forgot..." She sobs and it takes her a minute to continue. "I forgot the soap. So I turned back to grab it, and Sable went to the ravine. While he was swimming, some men attacked him. I tried to chase them, but I was too slow..."

Mom covers her mouth. "My baby boy. Please tell me it's not true."

Frost whispers, "I'm sorry. We have teams of our best trackers out there searching for him, but they haven't found any leads. I had hoped to give you better news..." His sentiments are drowned out by my mother's cries.

She tumbles her chair to the ground and dashes out of the room. My heart breaks. I can't even *look* at Maya. How could she drag my brother with her, knowing how dangerous the situation was? Who the hell does she think she is? She knows damn well she can't disobey an alpha's command. And yet, she did. And being daddy's little pet, she's probably not going to get into any trouble. This is bullshit. I stomp out with Aspen in tow.

We huddle under the protection of the large oak trees. Our misfit family. Sable was a part of it, but now he is either missing or dead. I know the drill. They'll send out hunting parties and we'll pray for the best. But hope doesn't mean much lately.

Grass crunches behind us as Jackson leads Maya towards her cave. I narrow my glare in her direction. That *bitch.* She's dead in my eyes for dragging my brother into this. Dad follows my sight line and swipes at his eyes. "Come on, baby girl." He guides me along. "Let's get you home."

A sharp pain radiates in my gut as if an imaginary knife has jabbed me in the stomach. I bend and hold my side.

"Sky?" Mom snaps out of her grief. "Are you all right?"

"I'm just tired," I push out. "Can I sleep in my room at the old house?" I don't want to be anywhere near *her.* I want to relive my puphood, where I grew up. Where Sable loved to snuggle under the covers and read *Little Red Riding Hood.* He made the best wolf voices, while I did Red and Grandma.

"Of course, dear."

We drive in silence, lost in our misery. Once we arrive at our cave, my feet have a mind of their own. They drag me to my big brother's room. I glide my hands over his comforter. The fabric beckons my weary soul. I burrow under the covers. His faint scent lulls me into a sense of comfort and gives me hope that he'll be found as memories flood my mind. Us, playing hide and seek. Him, helping me with algebra homework and sneaking me extra cookies. The mattress dips and a warm arm drapes over my belly. Mom's body quakes with grief and I join her, sharing my own heartbreak.

"Wake up, honey."

Do I have food poisoning? I hold my abdomen. Or maybe the flu? Dad lifts me into his arms, like he used to do when I was a little girl. But my anklet is snagged on the sheet. He jerks my foot free but breaks the charm into two pieces. That's when I notice Sable's bed is stained with crimson. I pinch my eyes closed as the pain radiates from my back.

"I called Carly and Freddy. Is there anyone else?" Aspen squeezes my wrist gently.

While I fight the urge to vomit from the smell of latex and rubbing alcohol, I stare at the IV sticking out of my hand. The doctor's words replay over and over in my mind. I'm losing my baby and there's nothing they can do to prevent it. Warm tears glide down my cheeks. They say it's rare, that only about three percent of pregnancies that pass the twenty-week mark result in late-term miscarriages. *Lucky* me.

"I can call Maya if you want?" my brother offers.

I'm about to attack his statement when Carly runs in and crushes me. "What can I do? I feel so helpless?" she whispers into my hair. "Where is the dead-beat dad?" she hisses, examining the room. "He is *never* around when you actually need him."

My brain is foggy, but her words ring truer than ever.

"I called him, but he didn't answer." Aspen runs a hand through his hair. "I'm going to call Maya."

"No."

"But she's your sister-in-law."

"I said *no*." I know he doesn't agree, but I'm done caring about what everyone else wants.

"Okay, what about Frost?"

"Why? He wouldn't even listen to me when I wanted to move back to the family cave. Fuck him." The room is filled with familiar faces, all with pity in their eyes. And I'm done playing the victim. I just want to find peace again. "Get out. *Everyone.*" I roll away from them and pull the sheet up to my chin. It takes a minute, but they finally shuffle out, leaving me with soft words of encouragement that fall on deaf ears.

My parents bring me to their cave to take care of me, where I promptly fall into an abyss of self-loathing. Days fade into weeks. The search for Sable comes back empty-handed. The missing person's report has the same results. We plan and execute his funeral—having accepted his death as the only possible scenario—and following the ceremony, the fact that my brother is truly gone is burned into my soul.

My son is gone too. No matter how hard my mom tries, I refuse to suffer through another memorial. I can't stomach saying goodbye again so soon.

My fingertips grip the hem of my shirt, and in a rage-induced fit, I shred it, kicking and screaming until exhaustion brings me to a heap on the floor. The dust flitters in the air, moisture covers my cheeks, and the cold surface cradles my face. Damn these worthless tears. No amount of crying will bring him back or change the fact that I'm a horrible mother.

"Sky?" My mom's voice hardly registers before she lifts me into her arms and rocks me. She lays me under the cool covers again.

"I failed him," I mutter the one truth that sits heavy in my heart.

She strokes my hair. "Oh Luna, if only I could take away your pain. If only I could... It's not fair." She's right. Life's a bitch.

"Rest, dear." The command soothes my guilt-ridden body. I don't deserve to sleep. Nonetheless, the darkness swallows me.

"Get out of my house this instant! She has been through enough, without having to deal with *you*!"

The door slamming finally pulls me out of my restless slumber. What day is it?

"Mom?" I ask, unsure if I'm dreaming.

"Sorry, honey. Go back to sleep."

"Who were you yelling at?"

"Freddy."

That's a name I haven't heard in a while. After I locked myself away, I cut off all communication with the world. I scoot to the edge of the bed and head to the shower. I slump over the bathroom counter. I've been a mess as I grieve my lost family members. I lift my chin and meet my reflection. Who's this red-eyed beast? Mom draws me a bath with her signature mix of lavender and chamomile oils and holds my hand while I lower myself into the fragrant water.

"The lawyer called and said he has an interested buyer."

The liquid envelops me as it creeps over my chilled body. I talked to our family lawyer and informed him I wanted to sell my share of the Wolves' Den, because I'm in no state of mind to pull my own weight over there. I'm glad there's somebody able to buy my share and help Carly.

"Are you sure you want to sell, honey? You can take some time to think about it. There is no rush. Everyone can pitch in until you get back on your feet."

"I told you I'm done. With the stress, the heavy workload, the worthless employees."

"Not all of them are like that."

I know she's right. But I need to put distance between me and the memories of Sable. "Mom, I want to travel the world. Or settle down and become a spinster," I mumble the last bit. "Either way, the restaurant feels like a ball and chain when it comes to achieving any of my goals. I mean, what would I have done when the baby was born?" My lip quivers. "I can't take care of a child and work eighty hours a week." She helps me wash in silence. I know she has more opinions to share, but she doesn't have a chance because the doorbell rings. "Go ahead and answer it. I'll be fine."

"No, it's okay. If they're important, they have a key to let themselves in." She runs a pumice stone over my heels. "We should go to the spa and get deep-tissue massages. You know, have a girls' night out. What do you think?" I turn towards the sound as the doorbell screams for the millionth time. She squeezes her eyes shut. "If it's that damn man again, I'm going to rip him to shreds!"

I chuckle as her protective mama wolf seeps through and fur pokes free from her pores. I place my hand on hers and our eyes meet. "Thank you for taking such good care of me. You are the best mother a girl could have."

Her lip quivers and she hands me a towel. "The time will come when you too will be a great mother, Sky. Just be patient. Luna has a plan for you." She kisses my hair and strides out.

I hug the fabric around my frame, unable to accept this as a fact. I had my chance, and I failed. I hear shouting and I decide to take matters into my own paws and see what the fuss is all about. "Mom, just let them in." I fall onto the couch, clutching my towel. Whoever is banging down the door obviously needs to say their piece.

"Why are you ignoring me?" Freddy snarls. His gaze travels over my body and his scowl turns into a frown. For once, concern wrinkles his forehead.

"*Where* were you when I needed you?"

"I was with my aunt on the reservation."

"Why?"

"Family issues. I came as soon as I could. And when I did, you wouldn't let me explain what happened." He glares at my mom. "Everybody is forgetting that it was my kid too."

"You were just the sperm donor."

He blinks at my new resolve and backbone. "What?"

"Don't bullshit me. You were always gone, never provided a stable income, and constantly returned to our home smelling like another pack."

He backpedals, spewing out more shit-filled lies.

I hold up a palm and say what I should have in the very beginning. "Shut. The. Fuck up. I will not be your cuddle buddy any longer. The rent is paid for the month. So stay there if you need to. Obviously, you know you are fired, since you haven't even bothered to show up to work in months." I turn away from him, ending this meaningless conversation.

Dad places a hand on Freddy's shoulder. "It's time for you to leave." The rogue wolf watches me for a minute before he stomps out, slamming the door on our happily ever after.

# Freddy

## Oversights

A sapling splinters beneath the force of my knuckles. The crunching of wood covers the sound of my yell. No matter how much I struggled to keep Sky and my son safe, I've failed. And all my secrecy and underhandedness with the General has been for nothing.

Fuck!

My aunt warned me that there was a shift in her card readings, and it wasn't good. And on top of all that, her magical veil isn't working because her abilities have finally dried up. She can't protect us anymore. Then the old bat informed me that she is done helping *me*! And that she is going to kiss Maya's ass in hopes of getting in her good graces. So that the next alpha will trust her. She even had the balls to demand that I stay away from her house, so she can protect her darling adoptive prick of a child, Sara.

Now I really am on my own. Even at Sable's funeral, I was an outcast. No one noticed me.

My phone vibrates as I receive a text from Bridgett. She's asking if I'm attending the art gallery on the reservation tonight. My nostrils flare as I recognize the influx of new scents mingling in the air. This can be my chance to grab the last shifter and be free of the General. I skim the tree line and remain in the shadows while I observe my target. I was wrong when I thought the pack would drop everything and look for Sable. They gave up too easily. Let's see if *her* disappearance brings the same results. Once she's out of reach of her family, I step out from the darkness.

"It sure does feel like old times, huh? Debbie told me she let my secret slip about helping Spike conceal you all those years... I hope you are mature enough to let it go." I walk past the tree she is leaning on and into a dark grove, hoping Maya takes the bait.

"Why didn't you tell me yourself?"

"Why? So you could hate me *more*? And cause more stress to Sky? Maybe kill *another* baby, or heck, why not another husband? I hear Aspen is still on the market."

"See? This is the Freddy I know: harsh, cruel, and a complete jackass. But you hide it well, don't you? Around everybody else. But you can't fool me."

I crush her against a tree with my body. "You just won't let me forget my past, will you?" Even with her dark history, she's so quick to judge others. Everybody loves her and her sins are so effortlessly forgiven. "Good. It'll make *this* a lot easier."

She flinches as I jab a needle into her skin. One wonderful thing about working with the devil is I now have access to all the toys in his arsenal. Including a quick sedative formulated to help wolves take a nap. Her shocked expression makes this especially worth it. "What did you do?" She drifts into my arms.

"It looks like you've had too much to drink. Why don't I take you somewhere safe?" I toss her over my shoulder. Then I skip into the forest with my prize. It's a long walk but well worth the trek to have my leash removed for good. I bang on the compound door while juggling Maya's motionless frame. The General never showed me the location, but I'm not an idiot. I've listened to the men gripe about it being in the middle of nowhere. Then I smelled the air when they were near before scouring the forest for the identical scent. "Open up!"

They crack the entrance and I shoulder my way through until I arrive at the nearest cell. "You're not authorized to be here. How did you find this place?" a soldier demands.

"I'm not as ignorant as your leader thinks. Now contain her before she wakes up."

The guy snorts as he injects Maya with a green substance. "Don't worry, errand boy. We drug them so they can't shift."

How the hell do they have this technology? "Just tell the General I brought him a female. Judging by her scent, she's already in heat and we are on a time crunch with her cycle."

"Where...?" She blinks up at us.

"Did you have a nice nap?" I can't help but slap that smug look off her face. "Welcome to your new home."

Maya takes in her surroundings, gasping when she notices the other females in her midst. "They're from Robert's pack! *You* stole them!"

"No, I just hinted as to where they could be found."

"But why?"

"Because they are trying to replicate our abilities."

"Who?"

"Our military higher-ups. Our government." Shit. I don't even know how high this goes. However, Maya doesn't need to know that.

"But why would you help them hurt your kind?"

"Because after that bloodbath at the warehouse, I had to do *something* to stay out of prison."

"You are a fucking coward. A traitor."

"And you are my *final* offering. A female who can breed immediately. I'll make sure your funeral is as beautiful as your husband's. Now that I'm free from them, I don't have to look over my shoulder."

"Wait. Just tell me this one thing. Did you even love Sky?"

"What I have with Sky is real."

"She doesn't even know the *real* you."

Her words barrel through my last ounce of sanity. I pivot on my heel, a blade clenched in my grip, and slice its edge across her skin. She collapses to the cold floor. My labored breaths echo in the concrete prison as crimson seeps into her dress. "I need to make sure your dad doesn't send out a search party." I shred the fabric from her body and use my toe to shove her backward. The thud of her pitiful frame hitting the ground for a second time is music to my ears. I'm *free*. "Goodbye, *Scarlett*," I taunt her with her orphan name. "I would stick around to watch the free porn, but I have a party to join." I bow to her highness in a sign of mock respect.

The once mighty future alpha of the Tala pack is now crying at my feet. And damn does it feel good. I stride out and slam the door, leaving her—and my past—behind me. I look forward to watching the world burn, suddenly realizing I have nothing and no one to lose.

I'm eager to show my face at the art gallery before they notice Maya is missing. I drag her bloody gown over the ground to remove my scent and add hers to the trail. Now that I am free of the General's threats and Sky wants nothing to do with me, shit is about to hit the motherfucking fan. The shifters will follow the path and find Maya in the compound. Then destroy the General's operation. And by the time Maya reveals my participation, I'll be long gone.

Frost and Raven hang on my every word. The social event is quickly closed, and they assemble their fur-army, itching for revenge. As they come together, I hightail it out of town.

Once the wind is whipping through my hair, the taste of freedom doesn't feel so great. What is wrong with me? My heart tugs me back to Cold Creek. I finally got what I wanted, but guilt weighs heavily in my stomach. Before I can register what's happening, I'm parking my motorcycle and marching to Skylar's window for a final goodbye. I jiggle the glass and grin. She left it unlocked, just like our old booty-call days. I squeeze past the panels and inside her room. Once my eyes adjust to the darkness, I see her form nestled under the covers.

"I told you to *leave*."

"I don't take directions well."

"What do you want?"

Good question. What *do* I want? I guess I feel like I owe it to my deceased son to make an effort to apologize to his mother, for causing her so much distress that her body aborted a piece of our souls. Guilt is a bitch, and I'll be damned if it ruins my well-deserved withdrawal from my self-imposed restraints.

The hairs on the back of my neck rise and I sniff the air. I stumble out Sky's window, never speaking a word in response, as my mind's too hyper-focused on the shifters in our midst. What are *they* doing here?

# Azure

# Protector

"**W**olves' Den Steakhouse, Skylar speaking. How may I direct your call?" Her voice strums the very chords that piece my soul together. Just hearing the gentle melody lulls my wolf into a state of contentment.

"This is the *third* time you've called. Stop harassing my business." The angel's voice cracks. "I've had a shit week and I'm not dealing with this bullshit too." I pinch my eyes shut as her agony takes my breath away. Damn it. Why did she choose *him*? All I want to do is tell her everything will be all right. That I'll always be in the shadows protecting, guarding, and loving her. "I'm sorry. That language was uncalled for. But please stop calling if all you are going to do is listen to me talk to myself. Thank you and have a wonderful day."

The dial tone resounds in my ear. I clutch the device. I may not be able to be there for Sky, but I know someone who can be. I send a quick text to the woman who co-owns the restaurant and ask Luna to deliver it urgently.

My cell vibrates, but I ignore Sky as she attempts to track me down. Freddy's parting words slam into my gut: *The shifter you may have seen is my fiancée. We are actually moving in together and starting a family.*

I won't be a homewrecker. If the situation were different… I shake my head of the forbidden fantasies playing out in my subconscious. I love her enough to let her have the life she desperately wants.

"Who was that?" my twin questions as she walks over. "Don't tell me you're leaving already!"

I snap on my rainbow triangular *happy birthday* hat and blow my noisemaker in her ear. "I wouldn't miss Hunter's birthday." I snatch the preschooler into my arms. "We still have a cake and presents to demolish!"

He squeals and hugs me tight. "I missed you, Uncle Azure."

"I'm sorry, buddy. Adulting is a sick joke—trust me on this one. Don't get any older."

"Did you get me what I wanted?" His dark eyes sparkle with the question.

"Hunter!" Lily scolds. "Just having him here is enough, right?"

The boy side-glances his mother before opening his hand, and I pull the trinket from my pocket. His eyes grow wide as he releases me, and I place the gift in his tiny palm. "Is this really it?" he whispers in disbelief.

I ruffle his jet-black hair. "It is, big guy. You're old enough to have it now. Just promise me you'll be careful."

"Azure," Lily grinds out. "You cannot give a five-year-old a pocketknife."

"His fangs and claws are sharper than that old thing. And it's not just a knife. It's a family heirloom that Dad gave to me when I was his age."

"Ouch!" Blood drips from Hunter's pointer finger and he pops the digit in his mouth.

"You see!" Lily rushes to the rescue.

"Mom, I'm fine!" He continues to suck on his injury. "Stop babying me." He tugs away from her and runs off.

"But what about your cake?" my sister yells to his back.

"Just let him lick his wounds, sis." I pat her shoulder.

"Every time he lashes out like that..." Her lip quivers. "Some days I think he hates me."

"Hey, don't say that. You're doing a damn good job!" I spin her to face me. "Stop doubting yourself. You're an amazing mother."

"Am I? I don't feel that way." She plops down on the picnic bench and watches Hunter as he sits near the pond by himself. "I'm trying so hard to do everything *right* that I'm doing everything wrong. Look at him! It's his birthday and he just wants to be alone."

"There's nothing wrong with that."

"The shifters here are all older. There're no pups for him to play with and he's learning to be okay with this solitary lifestyle."

"Do you want me to find another location? I can even help you move."

She scoffs. "You are busier than ever with your hero work. Not that I blame you, but I don't want to relocate him until after you settle down with a pack."

"That might not happen."

"Then we'll live and die in these woods." She leans her head on my shoulder.

"Why don't you search for your mate?" I urge her.

"Yes, let me do that, between raising and homeschooling a child.

I'm so exhausted that most days I pass out while reading him his bedtime stories."

Why did Luna have to give me these abilities? I should be a better brother. I'll stay a few months and assist my sister with my nephew. I can take him camping, hunting, and teach him the ropes. Man to man. *Wolf to wolf.* Maybe he'll open up to me?

"It won't always be like this. Eventually things will calm down and we will each have our happily ever after," I encourage her.

"You're *too* confident."

"No, I'm just confident enough."

She relaxes into me, and we both watch the orange and red hues touch the horizon. I'll never have that ending. But I can assist Lily in finding hers. I'm eager to witness her tale unfold when she's ready to leap into it.

*"Stop! Don't hurt him! Sable!"*

I jolt out of my dream and hold my throbbing head.

"Uncle?" Hunter rubs his lids.

"Shh, everything's fine. Go back to sleep."

He yawns and stretches. "Did you have a bad dream?"

"I think it was a vision." I massage my temples. It's been a while.

"Does that mean you have to leave?"

I rise from the dew-slick grass and peer down at him. "I'm afraid so."

"Can I go with you this time? Please? Mom doesn't let me do

anything fun. She's always afraid I'll get hurt."

"Sorry. Not this time." I frown at his growl. "How about I show you how to set some more snares and we can catch breakfast together?"

He morphs into his fur suit and his tail goes a mile a minute as he dances circles around my ankles. These last few months have been remarkable. I think I've really connected with my nephew. I scratch behind his ears, shift to my wolf form, and we gallop deeper into the woods.

But Maya's screams echo in my subconscious, reminding me that death is approaching.

After I drop Hunter and our rabbits off with Lily, I bullet through the trees as fast as my four legs can move. The wind and leaves batter my body but I can't slow my pace. A shifter is in danger. I call upon my Luna-given powers and zap my paws to energize them into traveling quicker. I can't let her die.

I skid to a halt and sniff the air. She's not far... I scratch the earth, bury my nose into the sand, and taste the granules. It's her blood. I'd recognize it anywhere. There was something unique about the girl from the moment I met her—Luna placed her in my path for a reason. My ears pivot. Voices. My claws rip through the weeds until I finally reach my destination. There's an old rundown building in the middle of the vegetation. I lean the side of my head against the metal entrance.

"I have all the power. So why don't you show me *more* respect?" a human booms.

"That's all the *respect* you deserve. You took us from our families. Then you drugged us so we couldn't defend ourselves. Fuck you," Maya growls, but her words are laced with pain and uncertainty.

Humans poisoned her? I hear others inside and wonder how many are being held captive. The hairs on the back of my neck tingle and I know I'll have to wait for my answers.

A man snarls before a gun cocks. I instantly transform to two feet and summon my electric energy. I aim for the object that's blocking my view. The hinges splinter as the door explodes, sending shards across the concrete floor. Once the dust settles, I spot a small group of shifters. They're surrounded by soldiers—all with their weapons drawn.

"Now, everyone!" Sable coughs. "Run!"

"Can you stand?" Maya croaks to her mate.

"Go with the others. Get to safety. Hurry."

"My life is meaningless without you." She huddles beside him.

"Stubborn to the bitter end, huh?"

"Azure?" When our eyes meet, I lift my palms and blue lightning bolts sizzle along the tips of my fingers before striking out at the armed soldiers. The guards twitch wildly before crumbling to the ground. Once they are subdued, Maya releases a breath, leaning her forehead on Sable's chest before chuckling my way. "Well, it's about damn time you showed up."

I help the duo to their feet. "I caught your scent and knew there would be trouble in your midst. I'm glad I checked it out."

"Sable is injured. Can you help him?"

I lift her mate and clear them past the debris. As soon as I'm certain that the captives are safe, I collect the soldiers and prepare them for questioning. Maya raises a dirt-caked brow and I explain, "I'm staying here for the time being. I need to get to the bottom of this operation, so no one else is taken."

"Will you be safe?"

"Yes, and when my job is complete, I will seek you out and update you."

She embraces me. "Thank you for saving us."

"Your packs must be worried. Return home. I'll see you soon."

She raises her chin and sets her gaze on the distance. She's a wolf on a mission. I watch until the shifters are hidden by the tree line, then narrow my eyes at their abusers. I kneel in front of the leader. "You're going to tell me everything I need to know."

He spits insults in my direction. "Fuck you, you *freak*! I'm not telling you shit."

I let the spittle roll over my grin. "That's amusing. You actually *think* you have an option." Before he can comprehend my meaning, I slap a hand on his temple and suck out every memory locked away in his underdeveloped brain. The violence, abuse, and torture play out like a film reel in my head. His screams do nothing to alleviate the rage fueling me forward. After he passes out, I stride to the next simpering soldier. Until they are all sobbing in the fetal position, begging for death in hopes of prematurely ending their misery.

I need to contact the other Guardians as well as the numerous pack leaders.

My fists clench. My jaw ticks. We've been *deceived*. Zaps of brightness illuminate my dark skin as my blue veins shimmer. I can't wait to wrap my hands around the traitor and feel him squirm. Then I'll demand that he release *my* mate from his bloodthirsty hold... or greet his maker, should he refuse.

## Sky

# WTF!

**M**y bedroom door smashes against the wall, disturbing picture frames and knickknacks, moments before my alpha plows into my room and searches—wild-eyed—until his gaze lands on my open window. The same window Freddy just leapt from. His snarl vibrates my spine and I shrink under the safety of my covers. He curses, then hauls ass into the night air.

I blink, letting the night's events sink in... What the fuck? I throw my blankets off. Has everyone lost their minds?

"What the hell is going on? Frost just barged into my room without even *knocking,* and Fred..." My knees weaken and I melt to the floor. My fingers shake as they touch the ghost in my living room. "Oh, thank Luna! It's really you!"

Sable squeezes the air from my lungs while I bury my face into his chest. I'll never take our sibling bond for granted again. He might be a gruffy jerk to others, but to me he's a cinnamon roll. He's always there when I need him and I'm glad he puts up with me. "It's okay, Sky. I'm here."

His words soothe some of my heart-wrenching grief. He strokes my hair and I know, eventually, everything is going to be fine now that I have my big protective brother back. Once I've collected my emotions, I pull away to wipe my tears. Mom rubs my hand as she too swipes at her cheeks. That's when I notice Maya nestled beside him. Dried blood paints her skin and bruises litter her frame. She was *never* my enemy, and yet I treated her like one.

"I'm so sorry I blamed you, Maya."

She rubs my arm. "It's okay, Sky. And I'm sorry you lost the baby."

"I've missed so much around here." Sable scratches his scruffy beard and ash sprinkles his lap. "Can I see pictures of my nephew?"

Mom patches up my brother's wounds while I leaf through the baby's ultrasound photos. It's hard showing my brother, but in a way, it helps me remember the love I have for my angel. My son isn't truly gone. He's waiting with Luna until I join him.

"You know what?" Maya clears her throat. "We are going to get matching tattoos in memory of your son."

"A tattoo of what exactly?" I ask.

She waves around the ultrasound of his two tiny feet. "This. It will remind us to always move forward no matter how muddy life gets."

"That's a wonderful idea." I smile, and for once, it's sincere. She's always been super sweet to me. Why I treated her so poorly, I'll never know. But I'll make it up to her.

We leap up from the couch as the front door flies open, and Freddy is hurled at our feet. "Frost, what the hell is wrong with you," I hiss as I kneel next to my ex, quickly checking for a pulse. If anyone is killing him, it's *me*.

"Get away from him," Dad demands.

I blink. My dad *never* yells at me. My gaze refocuses on Freddy. "*What* have you done?"

"I did what I had to, to survive. To be able to stay with you."

Maya steps towards him. "You had a second chance, and you fucking blew it. You sold out our kind. Betrayed us all."

Frost pulls Freddy up by his shirt before zip-tying his hands. "Go ahead and shift like this. I'd love to watch your arms dislocate," he hisses. "You are going to be under lock and key until the Guardian arrives to deal with you."

Frost shoves the rogue wolf out the door. But my ex-boyfriend's eyes never leave mine as they beg me to help him. "I don't understand. What did Freddy do that was so wrong?" My traitorous lip quivers as I question the actions of the alpha as he drags my ex out the door.

"Come sit next to me, sis, and I'll explain everything," Sable soothes.

The entrance is slammed open again as Aspen huffs inside. "Frost just *shoved* Freddy into his trunk and drove off." He clamps his mouth shut as his eyes fall on our long-lost brother. "Forget Freddy! What are you doing here?"

"I was just about to explain everything to Sky. Why don't you join us, brother?" Sable collects his mate in his lap as he describes his resurrection. He begins by explaining how he was attacked when he and Maya searched for Robert's missing pack members. When he woke up, he was in a compound, behind bars, and unable to shift.

Then Maya showed up and helped him and the other wolves escape. But, unfortunately, when they reached the exit, they were cornered with nowhere to go—all guns aimed at the escapees.

Everyone is leaning in on the edge of their seats as the tale progresses. Sable takes a breath, describing how all hope was lost, before the Guardian burst the door right off its hinges and saved the day with his lightning bolts. He stayed back at the scene to further investigate but promised to update the packs as information became available.

I gulp. What if, somehow, *I* missed some sign? Would the Guardian punish me too?

"I have an idea." Maya collects my hand and squeezes me out of my despair. "How about I clean up and take you to the family tree? We marked it during Sable's funeral service, but now maybe we can dedicate it to your baby boy."

I don't want to say goodbye. I panic and meet my mom's gaze, looking for motherly advice. She pats my back. "Why don't you girls go ahead while I finish tending to your brother? We'll meet you soon."

I can only nod as Maya guides me to my room. She talks to me as she cleans herself up, but the words fall on deaf ears as anxiety shrouds me in darkness.

We walk, hand in hand, into the warm night towards the rows of candles that lead to the large oak tree. I place my palm over the thick trunk as I gaze up into its forest of branches. The Native Americans believe that its roots grow to the center of the earth, which allows us to communicate with our loved ones in the beyond. When a pack member passes from our world into the next, we mark its trunk and guide the spirits with candlelight.

"Is that Jackson? With *your* Carly?" Maya points to two figures in the distance.

I follow her extended finger and gawk as Carly embraces Jackson. In my depressive state, I pushed her away and she has every right to hate me and fall into his arms. She looks happy and healthy. She deserves that and more. And since Jackson lost his mate, he is free to mingle with whomever he wants without the possibility of being ripped apart when he finds his significant other.

"Carly!" Maya hollers.

She pulls away from Jackson and runs towards us. I can't stop my feet as they pound the ground to meet her halfway. She tugs me into a tight hug, and my knees go weak as I sob. I've missed her. Once I regain my balance, I look into her eyes. She takes a step back while pressing her hands against my shoulders, putting distance between us, as confusion swims in her eyes.

"Bitch! How could you? You *ignore* my calls and texts. Then you don't even *mention* you are selling our restaurant!"

Did she just call me a bitch after everything that has happened? She has some nerve!

"I just *lost* my child! What do you expect from me?"

"I expect you to at least call back your best friend!" Tears wet her cheeks. "You promised you wouldn't leave me again!" She chokes on a sob. "I love *you*! But you couldn't give two shits about me! Just like everyone else in my life!"

"Carly, that's not true. I love you enough to stay the hell *away* from you before I fuck something else up and end up killing you too."

"What? Is that really how you feel? Sky Bear, that's so far from the truth." Carly snatches me up again. She rubs my back, then gently kisses my tears away. "This was *not* your fault. Do you hear me?"

I can't meet her gaze. I am a complete failure. That's why she deserves better. Just look at the Wolves' Den—it's *thriving* without me. Jackson's proximity also proves she can do better without me interfering in her life. Carly snatches my chin, expecting an answer that I cannot give her.

"I don't know how to do this," I whisper.

"Do what, baby?"

"How to do *life*."

Carly's laugh rings out and I blink my confusion. I just poured my heart out to her and she is giggling? Before I can smack her, she leans her forehead on mine and we share a breath. "No one knows what the fuck they're doing. We are just as confused as you are. The only difference is some of us hide it better than others."

The silence is deafening as her words sink in and burrow into my soul. *Nobody* knows what they are doing? Is that really true? A clap echoes in the distance, and I soon realize the whole pack has gathered around us. My face turns red when the crowd of onlookers start applauding together with little whistles sprinkled in. Maybe she is right? Carly winks at me before she bows and waves at her audience. I can't stop the laugh that bubbles out. She is one in a million, and I can't navigate this fucked-up world without her.

## Freddy

# Lessons Learned

I pound on the metal door of my holding cell. "Let me out! I have rights, you know!"

My complaints land on deaf ears as I pace the windowless concrete chamber like some unwanted dog at the pound. I fucked up by going to check on Sky. I should've just left town. I kick the wall. Sky's father, Phoenix, and Frost were both quick to pounce on me when I escaped. For old men, they have power left in their punches. I massage my swollen jaw. They are pissed. And I know they are not the *only* ones looking to beat the shit out of me. I slump in the metallic chair before running my hands through my hair. The door swings open, and I blink up at the massive shadow darkening the doorway. My only exit clicks shut and the beastly figure corners me.

"How were you able to hide your *true* memories?" The Guardian snarls as electricity sizzles from his fingertips.

"How about you release me, and I'll consider discussing it?"

The creature slams his hands on the table. "Lives are at stake! You *will* tell me! Freely or by *force*." He removes his palms. I side-glance the prints indented on the bent table before my eyes meet his again. I open my mouth to spit out a nasty retort, but he quickly knocks me against the concrete wall, his grip wrapped around my throat. "What *she* sees in you, I will never understand." He squeezes. "She deserves so much more than *you*."

"Why do you give a shit now? Where have you been this whole time, O' Great Protector? While shifters were being abducted and experimented on?" I squeak past my closing airway. "You have *failed* us, and now you're looking for somebody to pin *your* sins on. But they were going missing well before I was yanked into it."

Electricity shoots up my arm and through my memories. I howl but it's soundless as I feel him digging through my dark secrets while I'm forced to relive them. Everything Spike put me through... Walking home to find my mother surrounded by gore and blood, acting as if it's the most normal thing in the world... The first time I saw my son...

I kick and roar, trying to free myself from his grip and the agony of my own mind. "Stop!" The hardest events to endure are next. And there isn't a damn thing I can do about it.

Angelica's blood soaking my clothes as it drips to my feet... The moment I found out she was gone... The reminder of the bond we once shared... It breaks my stone-cold heart.

Finally, he steps back. Releasing me from my own personal hell.

"There's no justification for your behavior. But I see where you came from, and the suffering that led you on this dark path. So my plan of execution will have to be put off. But..." He stabs a finger into my chest. "If you ever lay a hand on Skylar again, you will be six feet under, where you belong. Do you understand me?"

When I remain silent, I'm jolted back by a spark of electricity against my spine. My breath is stolen as I spasm from the pain. A man clears his throat before he waves to my captor. The Guardian strides out without a backward glance. *Prick.* He has no idea how brutal life is. I massage my temples. In all those memories, I don't recall seeing my aunt's actions revealed. Maybe her magic *is* still working?

The lights flicker twice before they extinguish, and the sudden darkness hums all around me. Great, the blue bastard shorted the building with his powers. The door slams open, but I can't see a damn thing. I morph into fur, to activate my night vision, and yelp when hands grip my paws and tug. I kick and bite against anything and everything within reach. A metal object slams into my face, my eyes roll back, and darkness takes over.

Knuckles crush into my stomach, jarring me awake and returning me to my present hell.

"Well, look what I found at the pound." Another jab. I force my eyes open and glare at the punk presently using me as his personal punching bag, while my hands are tied behind my back. "I'd be hiding if I were you. The Guardian is hunting you down as we speak."

The General throws his head back and laughs. "How could he be? You don't even know who I am."

I clench my teeth. "I brought you the wolves you required. Even a female in heat! It was *your* fault they escaped!"

The vein in his neck seems to protrude and pulse. "That little setback has ruined *years* of research and you are going to help rectify it!"

Now it's my turn to laugh. "I'm not helping you do *shit*! Do what you want with me. I'm not letting anybody leash *me* again. I'm no one's bitch."

He grinds his jaw, pivoting before he waves his hand in the air. "I don't have time for this bullshit. I want his end to be painful—drag it out for *days*. Unless he changes his mind. Then chain him up with the rest."

His men take turns beating the life out of me. My vision darkens again and I welcome the escape like an old friend.

I've learned a valuable lesson: Never betray your kind, especially for *humans*. They are the real monsters.

SKY'S TAIL

# Luna's Laws

*H*aving my pillar of support is Luna-sent. We've fallen into a nice flow of things. I'm teaching Carly office management tasks and she's learning at her own pace.

"And which button do I push now?"

I lean towards the screen. "This one."

"I'm never going to get it!" she moans. "Are you sure you don't want to buy out Jackson?"

It still makes me laugh that *Jackson*, of all shifters, bought my share of the steakhouse. He doesn't have an entrepreneurial bone in his body.

"You know I was doing everything to get this business up and running. I never took time to just be an adult. Or even a wolf. Don't look at me like that. You know what I mean. Right out of college, I jumped into *this*. Where was my self-exploration time? My formative years were spent locked behind these walls—*I don't mean it like that!*" I grab her wrist as Carly goes to storm out. "I love every second that we spend together. Including the many, many hours here. But, Carly, I need this. I'm taking time off to rediscover who I am."

She places my hand over her heart. "You can find yourself here."

All I can do is hug my best friend. My wolf instincts have been suppressed for too long because of all my human responsibilities. It's time I discover *balance* for the two. I pray to Luna that my mate—wherever he is—understands how much I need my bestie. She may make questionable choices, but she has a heart of gold. And anybody would be incredibly lucky to have her in their life. "This search is about more than…"

Carly cuts me off. "Don't tell me you are letting your snobby alpha dictate who you have sex with? We don't need his permission to be together. You know what? I'm going to go *tell* him just that!"

I snatch her waist for a second time. "I told you this decision has nothing to do with their rules. I *want* to have what Maya and my mom have. I want to find my mate."

She doesn't let me explain that she's still going to be a priority, even after I discover my fur-partner.

"I'm going to make my rounds, ensure the lunch rush is successful." Hurt is etched into her features as she walks out of our office.

Even though she's acting like the subject is dropped, I know all too well my best friend hasn't let it go. She has anarchy written all over her pretty face. I'll have to warn Maya. Because, as future leader of the pack, she will inevitably have to deal with my rebellious furless work wife. Additionally, I'm no longer fighting Luna. I've had enough bad luck trying to make relationships stick. I'm going to see if she can do better.

Wherever my mate is, I'll wait for him. If I'm too old to have kids, then I will adopt or become a crazy cat lady.

My alarm blares and I leap out of bed. I was so nervous I couldn't sleep a wink, so I took a sleep aid and now I'm late.

To help narrow down my options for a mate, I need to travel through the packs. But because of the recent wolf kidnappings, territories require permission from the alphas as well as an escort. Although everybody in *our* area was returned, their abductions were facilitated with the help from a member of the Tala pack. So we're not on the best of terms with some of the shifters now questioning if there are any more rogue members in our group. A lump forms in the back of my throat at the thought. Freddy betrayed us, and I was his bed buddy. Shit, he was the father of my child. How did I not realize what he was doing? I shake my head. Stop. He was a great manipulator and I was blinded by his tricks.

I jiggle my tense limbs. "You can do this. It's just like riding a bike. A bike you haven't ridden in months."

I place my dress in my mouth and urge my fur to push past my skin. I shake my floppy ears before scratching behind them, and I quickly lose my balance and fall to my side. I wince but stand on all fours. Birds flutter past, chirping their amusement at my obvious clumsiness. I nip at their feathery tails. Once they retreat to the treetops, I relax, my nose twitches, and my talons wiggle. The earth is warm beneath my paws. I bullet through the forest, enjoying the breeze as it tickles my coat. I run at full speed, extending my limbs as far as they can go. The freedom lulls my tongue out and I taste the air.

It isn't long before I skid to a halt and nod to the shifter guarding our boundary line. I morph into two feet, glide my dress over my body, and fluff my hair. I tug leaves and twigs out of my mane and flick them aside. This gathering with the alpha is important. I should look reasonably presentable. I take a breath, shove the door open, and recite my apology to the shadows, "I'm so sorry. I didn't mean to keep you all waiting."

My mouth clamps shut as I stare at the group. Did I get the location wrong? I take inventory of the guests. There's Frost sitting at the front of the table with Jackson by his side. Then my gaze stops on Carly. She's standing next to them, addressing the crowd. Is she in trouble?

Frost slides his chair back, the scrape of metal against wood permeating the silence. "*Your* friend was just explaining how wrong Luna's mate law is."

Oh no... As I try to gather my wits, Carly sends a glare to the alpha. "That's what you got, out of my entire speech? This is a new millennium! Men and women should decide who they want to be with!"

Sable stands and rubs Carly's arm, trying his best to apply his new alpha-in-training techniques. "The pack laws are what drives our wolf instincts." Frost smirks at Carly, but it soon melts into a frown as Sable continues, "*But* I have scoured the documents and I've found nowhere in which it states that same gender unions are prohibited." He aims his glare at Frost. "I know it has been a tradition to ban such things, but I vote to *allow* it from here on out."

My brother sits but the rest of the room erupts into a mixture of shouts and praises. My vision blurs. I'm so proud of him. He's returned home stronger and wiser. The chaos in the room is deafening as older generations talk down to the more carefree youths.

I steal a glance at Frost, and he is staring daggers at his next in line. His wife, Raven, grabs his wrist and squeezes. Their eyes meet and he calms. Then she gracefully stands. The room falls silent. It's rare for the alpha's wife to assert herself. She's normally maternal, soft-spoken, and allows others to lead. So, when she does speak, everyone respects what she has to say.

"Family, please take a moment to reflect on this situation *without* judgement." Everyone lowers themselves into their chairs. Some grumble while they sip on their water. Others rub their chins in thought. She raises her palms skyward and lowers her lids. "Luna, as your humble children, we beg your guidance. We understand and respect your laws, but we would also like to venture out to find our true loves, our predestined mates, even if they are of the same sex. If this decision does not please you, let us know through your Guardians. Or smite me down right here and now." Giggles wave through the crowd at her conclusion, but other than that, the room remains silent. Seeing as no lightning falls from the sky, Raven drops her hands. "Well, I'm still alive, so I guess that is a good sign."

Frost leaps up. "You aren't taking this *seriously*."

Ignoring her husband's outrage, Raven turns to the pack members. "Without punishment, who here has ever had sexual relations with the same gender?"

Over half of the room raises their hands, though some reluctantly. Frost sputters as he pivots and his eyes land on his wife's telling palm. His face goes red. "You too?"

Raven pats him on the arm. "I'll give you all the details later, dear. But, for now, do you see? If Luna really disapproved, don't you think she would have made her will known by now?"

The alpha plops down in his chair, not meeting anyone's eyes. "Fine. But when this blows up, let the record show *I* was against it."

The room erupts in applause and Carly collects me in an embrace. "Now you don't have to leave your home. *We* can be mates!" she squeals.

I blink past her and stare at Jackson as he too cringes at her misunderstanding. "Car," I push out. "That's *not* how it works."

"What do you mean?" she asks.

Maya smirks at my brother. "Apparently, when you meet your mate, you kiss and *come* in your pants."

Sable's mouth falls open. "Hey! Don't share personal shit like that with everyone."

"Like how when you…" Maya's mouth is clamped shut, my brother's hand firmly in place, and she's carried out by her mate.

I clear my throat and return my attention to my friend. "It's hard to explain." I rub my neck, trying to recall how my mother explained it to me. "Your mate is someone who you can't be without, and it feels like a piece of your soul is missing when they aren't near." I hold up a palm to stop her before she can insert her guilt trip. "And to test that bond, you must kiss them. When your lips touch, a spark ignites inside you and it illuminates the rest of your life."

Tears pool in Carly's eyes. "But I did all of *this*, for you, and you're telling me you…" She chokes on a sob and runs out the door. Her words shatter my heart. Doesn't she know how much I love her? That fur doesn't mean shit to me. I dash after her, but something tugs my elbow back.

"Don't worry, Sky. You talk to Frost about traveling. I'll try to explain things to Carly." Jackson sighs. "She'll be okay."

I snatch his wrist before he can turn. "Please don't hurt her feelings. I know she seems like a hard-ass, but she puts up a good front. She's fragile."

"I'll be patient with her. I promise."

At his tone, I cock a brow. "What happened between you two?" When his face pinkens, I blurt out, "Did you sleep together?" The question comes out louder than I anticipated. The whole room hushes while they lean into our conversation. Male shifters rarely seek human affection because nothing can come of it. Only two shifters can create a pup. And that's what are animal instincts demand.

Jackson's voice echoes with his beta position. "Carly has proven that she cares for our wellbeing. Frost asked that I keep watch over her, to guide her as she became our pack's human liaison."

"I didn't know that was a position?"

"The Guardian is investigating Sable and Maya's abduction still, but we have a sneaking suspicion that war is brewing. And now, more than ever, we need to strengthen our connections with our two-legged counterparts." Jackson slips out before I can question him further. But something tells me he and Carly have bonded, and she is in good hands. The beta is a great guy, though I'm not sure how our alpha feels about a human being BFFs with his beta. But that's tomorrow's problem and another tale left unwritten.

I shoot Carly a text, letting her know I'm here for her. I remind her that I love her, that she'll always be my best friend, and now an honorary wolf sister.

My brother returns without Maya. I lift a questioning brow. "Her backside is a little sore." He smirks but quickly changes tone as Frost approaches us.

"*Sable* will babysit you as you travel through the packs," the alpha interjects.

"What? I just returned!" my brother roars in response. I can't help the flutter in my heart. I'm looking forward to spending some time with him.

"I've had enough anarchy for one day. Sable, you are recovering from your injuries and have been advised not to shift. So this is a wonderful opportunity for you to heal and *drive* your *sister* around. It's only a few hours out of your day. Then you can return to smothering my daughter. Plus, it'll help solidify your future status as alpha and give the other leaders a chance to get to know you better. Especially if war is nipping at our heels."

I tug my neck side to side, loosening the muscles. Let the search begin.

He slides his warm hand down my face before cupping my chin.

227

We stare into each other's eyes, both praying this is it. He lowers his pillowy-soft lips to mine, and although he tastes amazing, there is no spark. No tingle. *Nothing.* I allow his tongue entrance and we kiss until we are breathless, though we're each left unsatisfied by the results.

"I was really hoping this was it," he says huskily. "You are an amazing woman, Skylar."

I let out a disappointed sigh. Then I turn on my heels to open the door and wave him out. "We will find our mates, eventually. Sorry you wasted your time coming here," I apologize with a small smile.

"You know, we could just release some pent-up frustrations together?" His disarming charm piques my interest, but I know better than to let my desires guide my direction.

"I appreciate the offer, but no thank you."

"Well, you know where to find me if you change your mind." He walks out, and shortly after, Sable saunters in.

"How many more are we going to have to see?" he grumbles.

Over the last few months, I have kissed over forty shifters… and nothing. And yet my dear *brother* is the one complaining. I chuck a decorative pillow at his head. "Shut it. You have your mate already."

"You'll find him, Sky."

"You have said that every single time, yet I still fail."

"And every time, I mean what I say. You are not a failure. Now, can we wrap this up, so I can go home to my wife?"

I sigh and nod. He leaps to his feet and quickly gathers our things before practically prancing out the exit. I text a message to Carly, catching her up on another no-go. She sends her sympathies and tells me she'd switch me any day. We agree to meet up later, then I walk out to the car with my brother.

I toss my stuff aside as I pass the threshold of my etched-in-stone cave home. It's located towards the rear of the territory and has an amazing view of the crystal-clear lake. And when I leave the windows open, the breeze holds a hint of dew.

My phone rings and I groan at the caller ID. "Yes, John"

The former cook, now store manager, whines, "The safe is sticking and Carly isn't answering. I'm sorry to bother you, but what was the trick again?"

"You have to jiggle the lock as you pull the handle."

I hear jiggling, then a click. "Thank you."

"How are you guys doing?"

"Good. I finally found a new hostess. And she actually shows up!"

"That's great. Do you need me to come in to help with the inventory again?"

"No, you relax and enjoy your much-deserved vacation. We are fine." He hangs up, leaving me frowning. We told everyone at the Wolves' Den that I was vacationing, so we didn't have to explain why I was traveling so much. Jackson insisted I buy back the steakhouse. Which I gladly did, and then immediately hired help so I wouldn't need to go in every day. It's not perfect, and it's a huge pay cut. But I'm not paying rent now or saving for five years' worth of diapers and wipes, so it's working out so far. And every now and then, I slip into the establishment and bust their balls.

A bird flies to the water's edge and pecks at the liquid before throwing its head back and swallowing. It's stunning, with its vibrant blue feathers. Out of habit, I rub my ankle where Freddy's jewelry once rested. I kind of miss wearing it. Maybe I'll hint at a white gold anklet with a dazzling blue charm from my parents for Lunamas—the wonderful holiday that mirrors the human's Christmas. Suddenly my feathered companion tenses and flutters to its nest.

Sable whoops from my front door. "I have been cleared to shift again! Let's celebrate!"

"I'm really not in the…"

He snatches my wrist and tugs me through the open door. He is acting like a little pup going on his first hunt. I smile at Maya as she laughs at her husband. "Are you sure you are ready for this? We can wait a little longer," she questions her mate.

"Mom checked my injuries and they are healed, and there's no sign of the serum in my blood. So I'm *more* than ready." Sable takes a deep breath, and turns to fur. He's shaky on all fours but his tail wags up a dust storm.

"Does your tattoo itch?" I question my sister-in-law as I rub my new ink.

"Yeah, a little." She glances at her matching design before returning her attention to Sable as he busts his ass over a stump.

I run a single nail over my son's tiny footprints and send him a little prayer. *I miss you, baby boy. More than you'll ever know.*

"Come on, slowpokes!" Aspen shifts mid-leap and chases his older sibling.

We smirk at each other, then follow his lead. We roll in the meadow and chase rodents, until we are panting. Maya's nose stabs the air. She bullets into the forest, howling a greeting as she goes. I lift my muzzle to the sun to catch the identity of the incoming guest, but the scent's not familiar. Sable limps after his mate and Aspen follows their heels.

I've reached my exercise limit for the day. I collapse in the field of wildflowers. Butterflies scatter under my intrusion, creating a kaleidoscope of colors in the clear blue sky. The pollen tickles my snout as I breathe in the floral arrangement. I roll side to side, crushing their petals and stealing their aroma with my fur. Who needs expensive perfume when you have *Flora De Meadow* under your paws?

The sun makes its descent and encases the world in a peaceful darkness. As I listen to my surroundings settle, I make a pact with myself. I am going to *stop* searching for my mate and allow Luna to present him to me. I've enjoyed the precious time I've spent with my brother, but I can't keep stealing him from Maya, especially now that he's allowed to shift and do more of his alpha-in-training duties.

My ears swivel as the alpha's call echoes in the valley. There is a party going on and every fur, feathered, and skin-clad friend is invited. I prance on all fours. Finally! Dancing and tons of food! With a newfound energy, I dart to my cave, morph into two legs, and change into a gorgeous ruby gown. Tonight, I'm going to party my tail off and look fabulous! I glide glittering eyeshadow over my lids and apply red gloss but pause mid-stroke as Carly barges in with Raven.

I can't contain my grin. "Hey, ladies. To what do I owe the pleasure?"

"See? And you were worried she wasn't going to come to this shindig." Carly smirks at Raven, then she kisses my cheek. "You look stunning." She grabs my wrist and spins me until my dress flutters and shimmers beneath the light.

"I deserve this. I'm letting my hair down and having fun."

"That's wonderful." Raven places her palm on my cheek. "Stand strong. Never give up." A knock on the open door tugs our attention to the newcomer. Raven smiles at her husband. "You look handsome." She adjusts his shirt. "Why the face?"

Frost crosses his arms over his chest. "Why didn't you tell me *our* daughter is pregnant."

My heart stops. Raven waves her hands around, shushing him. "You better act surprised when she announces it. She wants Sable to know first."

Frost snorts. "Are we sure it's *his* and not Jackson's?"

Raven shoves him outside. "Don't be ridiculous."

Carly blinks at the alpha's sudden departure. "Did Jackson and Maya *date*?" When she meets my gaze, she falters. "What's wrong?"

I tug out my earrings and throw them across the room. Tears ruin my makeup. I kick my heels off, shattering a picture frame of my family.

"What did I say?" Carly pulls me into her arms. "Take a breath. Talk to me."

The anger won't stop boiling beneath the surface of my limbs. I kick and pound my fists like a child. I worked so hard to find my mate and came up empty-handed. Sable found his by *accident*. I got pregnant and lost my son. But Maya is now pregnant and is going to have a healthy bundle.

"What the hell is going on in here?" Jackson pops his head in.

Carly tenses. "Get out!"

"What did I do?"

"You fucked Maya!" Carly snarls.

Jackson holds up his hands. "I *teased* her to drive Sable crazy, but

232

we've never had sex."

"Then why does Frost think she is pregnant with *your* child?"

"Woah, wait a minute. Maya isn't pregnant. Is she?"

Carly purses her lips and rocks me in her embrace. "We have more important matters to attend to."

He frowns and assesses the situation. He strokes my hair before passing me a tissue. "Skylar. I know once you calm down, your jealousy will dissolve into tears of happiness for your sister-in-law and brother. Plus, you are going to be the best aunt, spoiling this pup every chance you get." He pats my leg. "You'll get another opportunity to be a mom… I promise. Even if I have to take one for the team and become a father again."

I'm acting like a spoiled brat. I need to woman up. I swipe at my cheeks and right myself. "Fine. I'll go, but I'm wearing pajamas." I shove my legs into grey sweatpants with the words *Juicy* printed on the ass. Because I'm not in the mood to celebrate anymore. One day I'll be able to get past this loss and jealousy but not today.

Jackson opens his mouth to protest my outfit, but Carly sends him an icy glare. Then she fixes a smile on her face before locking arms with me. "You look great, Sky Bear."

She pulls me into the night air. Just in time to hear Frost's introduction of our guest. "Thank you for joining our celebration as we welcome back our pack members who were taken. We praise Luna for her protection over our loved ones during their time in captivity. And we honor our Guardian, who stepped in just in time to save them. Please, everybody, raise your glass. To Azure, Luna's mighty protector. To Azure!"

Everyone claps before chatting amongst themselves in the large field, a fire blazing in the center. I don't pay much attention to the dancing and laughter. I down my alcohol and plop on the ground near the embers as they crackle and shoot golden sparks into the starry sky. I imagine those sparks floating to the moon, beckoning to the holy one who *forgot* about me.

My keen senses pick up my older brother's whining. "I thought you were going to tell *me* before anybody else?"

"My mother guessed, and I only confirmed her suspicions. Then my dad with his large wolf ears heard everything. Are you disappointed? I know we had a plan and I wanted to be working."

"I'm the happiest I have ever been. Thank you."

"Thought you could use this." Carly hands me a plastic cup with another serving of liquid courage. Then she nods towards my family. "You'll probably hurt Sable's feelings if you don't congratulate them."

I chug the liquor and my head spins. "Fine. But after my performance, I'm going home."

"Aw, you old fur-lady!" Carly pouts. "Why don't you dance with me first?" She's tipsy and on a mission of her own.

I trudge towards the celebrating couple. "Maya, congratulations."

"Sky, I'm so sorry." She frowns as she takes in my forced smile.

"Silly! Don't be sorry! This is a great gift!" I hug her to hide my twinkling eyes. "And I will be the best aunt ever." I repeat Jackson's promise and hope she believes it. Someone clears their throat from behind us.

"Azure, are you enjoying your party?" Maya sings.

"Yes, thank you. And I heard congratulations are in order."

"Thank you. Oh, have you met my sister-in-law Sky yet?"

I greedily eye-fuck every inch of the beast's enormous brooding frame. He's tall, dark, and handsome with blue streaks running across his skin that glitter in the firelight. My core throbs and I step away from the hunky brute, knowing full well he's *off*-limits. Afterall, he is our protector and not my personal plaything. Azure extends his hand to me. Oh boy, those thick fingers. Our eyes meet, and a zing spirals to my toes when I touch his palm.

"It's nice to meet you." I have to get out of here before my body gets any crazy dry-humping ideas. "Excuse me. I need to check on my little brother. He was hitting on Robert's daughter last I saw him," I fib. Does Robert even *have* a daughter?

I dash away from the sexy fur-god. *Where did he come from?* I hiccup. Probably from Luna's voluptuous breasts. I admit I don't know much about the Guardians, except that they make sure we play nice with the humans and vice versa. Speaking of fine specimens, Carly waves at me, drawing me from the main group of shifters. I observe her swaying her hips to the music of the night. She's drunk and will regret everything tomorrow. But for now, she is as free as ever... with her hands in the air and her breasts bouncing. She tugs me to her chest. "Dance with me, beautiful!"

I grab fistfuls of her ass and she squeals in delight. "Just one dance." One turns to two, then two into three. Until Jackson demands a spin with my goddess. Carly's grin tells me she's eager to get some dick tonight. I wink at her before kissing her cheek and whispering, "Good luck." I play bow to the beta, knowing my girl is in good hands.

I slip to the quiet of the river's edge to collect my breath. The crickets sing me a sweet lullaby and I close my lids and let them serenade me. The air electrifies around me and shocks my center. I lick my lips, tasting the space. The blue beast has found me.

"May I?" His deep voice sends a shiver down my spine, while his warmth radiates off him and beckons me closer as he lowers himself beside me. My fingers twitch as they fight their urge to run over his bulging biceps. *That's it. No more drinking.* "I'm sorry."

"The hero of the evening is apologizing? For what?"

The insects' music is deafening as I wait for his response, and we eye-fuck each other through the tension. Just when I'm about to repeat myself, thinking he didn't hear me, he answers, "I saw *his* memories."

I swallow, but my throat is too tight.

"Who?" I push out, already knowing the answer but needing to hear him say it anyway.

"Freddy."

I can't look at him. Can't even breathe. If he saw his memories, that means he witnessed everything *we* did. Including our most intimate exchanges. Is that why he's here? To pity me? "So what?" I hiss out. "What do *you* have to be sorry about?"

Heat envelops my arm as he places his hand on my elbow. "I'm sorry for the loss of your child, Skylar. And for the loss of time you spent with that delinquent."

I bite my lip and stare at my feet, hating myself for needing to know. "Did Freddy love me?" Silence. I push to my feet and wobble. I may be drunk, but damn it, I still have my pride. "I don't need your pity or anyone else's. Good night, Guardian."

"Please. Call me Azure."

I ignore his request as I order my feet to move. It's hard. But I can't be surrounded by his sympathy. I need to sleep off this booze.

"Skylar, please wait." I don't look at the man meat as I continue my trek to my cave. "Please. Let me know what I did to upset you."

I shut my door, but he is too quick—*and stubborn*—to let me have my peace and stops me. I snarl and stab a finger into his chest. "Do you know how long it has been since I thought about that asshole? Then you come here and drag me down! With your intoxicating scent, and…" I swallow as my anger simmers. My fingers stretch flat on his chest. How long has it been since I've had a good fuck? I trace the bumps and ridges of his well-defined pecs. Damn. He lifts my wrist to his lips before kissing every inch of exposed flesh, sending tingles to my toes. My head falls back, and I moan. He must have more powers than I thought. Like seduction.

"The last thing I ever want to do is cause you *pain*. Unless that's what you desire."

What was the question? He's causing a pool of torturous wetness to form in all the right places. He twirls me so my back is against his chest as his nose glides over the nape of my neck. He runs his palms down my sides and rests them on my hips. This magic man is stirring my libido into a raging storm. I'm barely holding on as the winds of ecstasy ravage my frame. Am I allowed to be this close to Luna's chosen one? Is he allowed to fuck the beings he's sworn to protect? I moan as his erection digs into my ass. I guess I have some superpowers too. I grind my butt against him and I'm rewarded with a hiss.

"You are the most beautiful creature Luna has ever created."

"Then why don't you worship me as we fuck?" I whimper as my knees grow weak.

"Because I want to enjoy all of you. I want to savor your nectar and ravish your body." His lips dance a mere breath away from mine. "But I can't right now."

"Why not?"

"I need to find out who is behind these attacks."

"But you have Freddy behind bars. Isn't that enough?"

"He is not the mastermind. I need to track down the man they call the General."

I grind my teeth and rein in my hormones. He's playing around with me, just like my ex. "Then go already! What's stopping you?"

"I thought it was obvious. It's *you*."

"Well, I'm giving you permission! Leave!"

"You don't feel it? That *pull*? Skylar, we are *mates*." His words ring out, but I can't process them.

"But you are a Guardian."

"We are born just like every shifter. We are just blessed with abilities."

An idea springs to mind and I grin as I step towards him. "So, you are only a shifter with powers? Well, I have abilities too." I shimmy out of my pajamas. His gaze runs over my red lacey bra and thong, and his erection begs to be freed from his shorts. I slip past the doorway and into my bedroom. I lean over the covers and shake my ass so he can smell my arousal. "If we are mates, then let's finish the bonding."

He's hypnotized as he follows my teasing movements. His palm glides over each cheek in a sensual caress. "I'm not sure how long I'll be gone. And it wouldn't be fair to you, for me to complete the bond and leave."

I pivot. "I've been searching for you this whole time, and now that I find you, you want to leave? Oh no. You're taking me with you."

"It'll be too dangerous."

I corner him, his back pressing against the wall. He's making a lot of fuss about something he's not even one hundred percent sure of. My tongue wets my lips. There's only one way to find out if we are soul mates. I snatch a fistful of his hair and crash his mouth against mine. A spark shoots through my body and I melt. It's like he completed a recipe I didn't even know was missing an ingredient. We are all teeth and tongue as we grind our hot bodies together in a sensual dance.

He pushes me away gently. "I can't let you get hurt again. I have to protect you. And if you remain at my side, you won't be safe."

"You also have to love me and take care of me! How are you going to do that if you are miles away, fighting everyone else's battles?"

He rubs his temples. "I don't know. I've been trying to figure that out."

Now it's my turn to take a step back. "Wait. *What*? How long have you known we were mates?"

"Not long."

"How long?" I repeat the question.

"When I first came to see Maya. Your scent has been haunting my dreams ever since. And when you found out you were with child, I felt your anxiety. I would call your job, just to hear your voice."

My fuzzy mind takes a minute to process. "You were the prank caller from the restaurant?" My fist collides with his bicep. "You knew that whole time! What the fuck! How could you not tell me? Get out!" I shove him towards the door. "Now!"

The betrayal falls from my cheeks. He could have saved me from so much heartache if he would have just told me who he was.

"Freddy informed me you were carrying *his* child and that you two were engaged. What was I supposed to do? Split up your family?"

I pause on the doormat. Why would Freddy say that? He knew I wasn't going to marry him. I shake my head and return my focus to the blue idiot. "You should have *fought* that piece of shit for me, instead of acting like a little pussy and yielding to him. Am I not worth it? You know what? Don't answer that! Get the hell out. I want *nothing* to do with you! You are exactly like *him*! And what makes it worse, *Guardian*, is the fact that you protected everyone but me." I slam the door and instantly regret my outburst as my soul begs to forgive him so we can get dirty under the covers. I slide to the floor and wrap my arms around my knees, sobbing for the future

I'll never have because Luna has a sick sense of humor.

# Azure

# Escape

The slammed door echoes in the night air. I stare at it for an eternity while her pain soaks into my bones. I've been a nomad. Scouring the quadrant and taking care of the packs. My life was a smooth-moving routine. Until now.

Yes, Skylar is my mate. But I can't drag her into this mess. A Guardian's life is unpredictable at best. I run a hand over my face, then pause as I linger on the scent she left on my palm. It's floral, with a hint of spice. My tongue glides over my skin, trying to get a taste of her. The siren who has been beckoning me for the last five years. And here she is. Just five feet from me, and I'm ruining everything.

I take two steps into the nightscape, and my wolf screams to return to our mate. "I can't protect her from what's coming," I scold him. "She is safer with her pack when war breaks out."

No matter what I say, the ache and hunger won't die. I ground my teeth together as Freddy's memories pass through my subconscious. His rough touches. His words dragging her name down. Her screams of agony, while he came inside her. The electricity coursing through my body tingles my skin. It took everything in me to walk *away* from that fleabag at the precinct. I wanted to rip every limb from his body and shove them up his selfish ass! The miscreant took everything from her and gave nothing in return. Nothing except pain and suffering.

My phone vibrates and my attention is pulled away from the murderous thoughts. "We have a problem." My ears perk up as the chief of police reports that there was a blackout after I left the station. And only one prisoner is missing.

I clench my fists, knowing exactly which one. "Where is he?"

"We are working tirelessly to track him. But he literally just disappeared. I'm sorry for the delayed reporting but we are understaffed as it is, and it took some time to get full accountability in order to determine who was missing." His voice is shaky and filled with lies. Something is wrong but he can't tell me over the phone.

"I'm on my way. And have the surveillance videos ready for me." I hang up and resist the urge to crush my phone. I run through his memories, again. How can some of them be fuzzy? Who has altered them. And, more importantly, why? I scratch my stubble as I weigh my options.

"It's Freddy, isn't it?"

Her presence is so comfortable I didn't notice her standing by my side. Our eyes lock and the passion burning behind hers stirs my own fire.

She offers her palm. "Here." I blink at it, unsure of what she intends for me to do. "Take my memories. Every little bit can help, right?"

Why hadn't I thought of that? She has been by his side all of these years. Freddy may be able to cover his tracks, but she won't be. "I won't ask you to relive those painful times."

244

"You made Maya relive hers," she's quick to remind me as she shoves her hand on top of mine. "Just do it."

I caress her wrist, while taking in every curve of her body. As much as she wants me to believe she's okay, I know she isn't as strong as she presents herself to be. Her fear vibrates in the air and I smell her insecurities. "That was different. *You* are different."

"I'm just a worthless nobody. Now take what I am offering you before he gets away."

"Skylar, you are anything but worthless."

She shakes her head as she brushes past me to return to her cave.

"Where are you going?" I can't help the desperation in my voice, as I follow her like a lost puppy.

"I'm going with you."

"Like hell!"

She laughs at *me*. Actually laughs. I'm one of Luna's all-powerful Guardians. It has been a long time since anyone has challenged me like this. And, usually, the challengers are thugs and troublemakers. Not my soul mate. "Fuck you," she adds with a flick of her wrist.

The insult slams into my chest, causing me to step back. "*Excuse me?*"

"I sure as hell didn't stutter. Clear your ears out, wolfman." She snatches her purse off its hook before sauntering to the door.

I stand in front of it with my arms crossed while I give her my best alpha tone. "Absolutely not."

"Get out of my way, you little Smurf. Before I rub your nose into the ground and embarrass you."

"*Smurf?*"

"They are these little blue creatures who live in the forest."

"I've never seen these creatures."

She pushes past me. "They are from a cartoon show."

I make a mental note to look them up, so I can figure out if she is insulting me or not. "Where do you think *you* are going?"

"To the police station to find out how they lost Freddy." She pivots with her hands on her hips. "Are you coming?"

My desire to be close to her consumes me, and in two quick strides, I'm claiming her mouth as she melts in my arms. I let my lips linger over hers. "If this is going to work, you need to listen to my instructions and obey them."

"And if *you* want me, you need to learn to trust my judgement while accepting me for who I am."

A shiver runs down my spine as her breath tickles my cheek, and my wolf demands to meet her mouth again. "I do accept you, Skylar. But my need to protect you outweighs every rational thought. You have been hurt too much. And I don't want to add to that pain. You deserve better than that. Better than me."

She crushes her mouth against mine, and a fire ignites as the bond recognizes its other half again. We stand there, rubbing against each other, each begging for a more intimate position. Once we are breathless, she whispers, "Please, call me Sky."

I grin and let her take the lead. "Come, *Sky*. It's time we hunt down the bastard."

Her smirk makes my erection twitch. She's stunning. And she is all mine.

# Sky

# Gone But Not Forgotten

*T*he silence between us is comforting, but a little awkward. We know nothing about each other, yet we are destined to be together forever.

"Where are we meeting the police chief?"

Azure nods towards the back of the station as he pulls into a spot and turns off the engine. "Wait in the car. I'll return soon," he commands.

"What? Why?"

"Because I'm not sure who to trust in here, and I'm not about to rush inside with the most important thing in my life." He pushes open the car door and walks to my side. "Stay here," he orders for the second time. "If anyone comes near, hold down the horn."

"If you're not out here in twenty minutes, I'm coming in."

"I'll return as soon as I can. Now lock the doors."

As he disappears around the corner, I do exactly as he says, though only a few minutes pass before I'm yawning. It has been a long day. Successful but long. I shiver as I anticipate the bedtime activities that are sure to unfold following this slight detour. Azure is all muscle and charm. I can't wait to have his face between my legs, as I make good use of that impressive tongue. A rap on the glass pulls me from my daydream. Standing outside is a little girl, no older than five. Who the hell lets their daughter wander around Carson City? I roll the window down a crack.

"Are you lost, sweetie?"

She nods. I bite my lip as I glance back at the precinct. He told me to stay here with the door locked. But I doubt he meant for me to ignore a helpless child. Another knock brings me out of my thoughts. "Can you help me find my mommy?"

Her pouty lip pulls at my heartstrings. The least I could do is escort her inside where it's safer. Then I can get a sneak peek at what my man is up to. The grin quickly spreads across my face. *My* man. When I shut the car door, she tugs me in the opposite direction of the building.

"Let's go inside. Then we can call your mom."

"I think she is hurt! We have to hurry."

Was there an accident? Someone should have called emergency services. The girl pulls me into the woods and the hairs on my arm stand on end. I dig my feet into the dirt as fear clutches my heart. I release her wrist and reach for my phone. "I'm calling the authorities. They can help us find her."

The ground vibrates beneath us, and the trees shudder at the approaching figure. The beast breaks through the foliage, snarling in my direction. It's bigger than any shifter I've ever seen. His fur is jet black, with blue streaks mingled in its strands. I backpedal until he meets my eyes. The softness swirling in their depths calms my nerves. The wolf lowers so I can climb on. I scan the darkness for the girl, but she's gone. How drunk am I? Did I imagine her? I rub my arms with the sudden chill. A whimper draws my attention to my mate. "I'm safe." He growls into the woods, then leads me back to my car. And this time, I stay close to his side.

He shifts to two feet. "Are you hurt?"

"No."

He tugs me to his chest. "What were you doing in the woods?"

"There was a little girl. She said her mom was injured and that she needed help."

"Why didn't you call an ambulance?"

"She tugged me so fast I didn't have a moment to think. Then I felt... *uneasy*. But you came right on time."

"I knew something was off, so I rushed out here." His eyes scan the forest. "We need to meet with the pack so I can update everyone." He places his hand on the small of my back and guides me inside the vehicle.

Tingles prick my scalp and I pivot to the eerie darkness. Red orbs flash in the distance and a cold sweat seeps through my pores. Is that a pair of glowing eyes hiding amidst the bushes?

"Is Freddy still *free*?" Surely, he wouldn't be dumb enough to return. Memories choke me and my vision blurs.

"Calm down, Sky. It's going to be..."

# Azure

# Redemption

"**Y**ou have no right to take away the gift that *Luna* gave me!" My roar bounces off the hospital walls.

"Do not raise your voice at me. I'm only reiterating what the others and I have decided." She places a hand on my shoulder and sighs. "You know us and we do not take this lightly."

I shake her off. "Why are you doing this?"

"The shifters are questioning your abilities as their protector because of all these… *incidents*. Azure, don't look at me like that. You know it is odd too."

"What do they think I've been doing? I've been traveling the quadrant in search of answers!"

"And yet, you have *none*. Maybe your service to Luna has come to an end."

A whirlwind of a woman pushes past us and over to Sky's bed. "Sky Bear?" She kisses her hand. "Please be okay."

The beta of the Tala pack follows the emotional human. When he reaches our position, he stops short. "Sorry about her." He nods towards the figure weeping over my mate.

"Who is she?"

The woman in question straightens her spine before stomping towards the group. She presses her hands flat on my chest and shoves. "*Who* am *I*? Who am I! I'm her best friend! Her sister in arms!" She snarls. "That's who the fuck I am!"

"Calm down," Jackson coos.

"Fuck you!" she hollers at the beta. He purses his lips. Then she returns her scowl to me. "You're in her life for mere hours and then she ends up here! She has enough shit to deal with! She doesn't need your drama added to the mix!"

"What drama?"

"Don't play dumb! The whole hospital heard your argument!" She holds up a hand to stop my protests. "Shut up. I should have protected her from that asshat Freddy, but I didn't. So now I'm stepping up and telling you that if you hurt her, I'll castrate you and shove your balls down your throat as I watch you choke."

I assess the she-devil in jeans and a tank top. I'm unsure if I should be irritated by her outburst or proud that Sky has such an amazing companion. I've heard rumors of Carly. I even sent her an anonymous text when Skylar was hysterical after she found out she was pregnant. My mate stirs and the woman kneels at her bedside. Sky whispers softly before wiping her friend's tears away. Then the unthinkable happens. Carly presses her lips to Sky's. Jealousy boils up in the back of my throat and I stalk over to break up the embrace.

Jackson clasps a hand over my elbow. "Easy there, big boy." He chuckles. "Those two have a long and complicated history."

My neck snaps in his direction. Is he joking? But one look at him tells me he's serious. I take in the females. They are joyful as they laugh and touch foreheads. I let a breath out. If Carly makes my girl smile like this all the time, she's welcome to share Sky with me—if that's what they want. The only issue is the other woman is flesh and bone. It'll be hard to safeguard her. I return my focus to the girls, then back to Jackson. "Are same-gender relationships allowed in your pack?"

The beta crosses his arms over his chest as he sizes me up. "Why? Do you want me to kiss you?"

"Stop talking shit," Carly growls.

Jackson rubs her back in an attempt to calm her. "You two just took Azure by surprise—that's all. I was merely explaining what's been going on."

Sky's eyes widen as many emotions pass between us.

"Sky, my dear. I'm so glad you are up." My fellow Guardian steps out from the shadows.

I block her path. "Not now. She just woke up."

"What do you need?" Sky asks. The weakness laced in her words breaks my heart. I couldn't protect her. After watching the police security footage, or lack thereof, I called the other Guardians to update them on Freddy's escape. But they were already in the vicinity, doing their own research. When I returned to Sky's car to find it empty, I panicked. I smelled other wolves close by, and I knew she was in danger. I made it in time, but she started to talk nonsense, then passed out.

The Guardian pushes past me, pulling me out of my thoughts. "I wish to see your memories in hopes of bringing light to a few mysteries."

Sky bites her lip, her gaze bouncing between each of the members of the small crowd at her bedside. "Why are you against this, Azure?" she asks.

Hearing her whisper my name stirs something within me. An ache for closeness. A need to bury my seed inside her. Claim her as mine.

255

"I would rather you be fully rested." I sit on the edge of her bed. "Memory extracting is exhausting—mentally and physically."

Out of my peripheral, I see how Carly narrows her eyes at me while Jackson tries to gain control of her. "It can't be any worse than what *you* and Freddy have put her through!" she barks.

"Car," Sky soothes, as if trying to use her voice to lull the girl into complacency.

"No! Don't Carly me! I'm taking you *home* and locking you away in a fucking tower. No more of this fur-family bullshit."

She's trying to take my mate? Like hell! But it's Jackson who reacts first. "What? I thought you were moving into the territory too?"

The tension sizzles the atmosphere, but Carly waves him off. "Where have you been? Haven't you noticed that there has been nothing but blood and tears in your pack. I want nothing to do with it."

"Sky is a part of that *pack*!" Jackson hollers.

"You know what? There is too much testosterone in this room. Why don't you and Blue leave?" Carly glares my way, her gaze fierce and challenging. Jackson and I stand shoulder to shoulder and narrow our eyes.

"I agree with the human," the female Guardian announces as she steps between us. "We'll be able to focus better with you in the hallway," she commands, while guiding us to the door.

"What!" we answer in unison.

"Just go. We'll be fine," Sky coaxes, and the door closes in my face. I resist the urge to throw her over my shoulder like a caveman and drag her away.

Jackson shoves his hands through his hair while he paces, and I ask the question that's on everyone's mind, "What is Carly to you, exactly?"

"I'm not sure. All I know is that she drives me *crazy*."

"She definitely has that effect on others."

"What is Sky to you?"

"She's my mate."

We plop into the chairs positioned across from her door. "What happens now?" Jackson leans on his elbows.

"Once Sky is released, I'll bring her back to her cave and keep an eye on her."

"No, I mean when you lose your Guardianship powers?"

"I'm not sure. I'm hoping they will see reason and change their minds."

"Would *you* change your mind, if you were in their shoes and another protector was in your place?"

"If I were in their shoes, I'd examine *all* of the specifics before drawing such a hasty conclusion."

Jackson chews on my words. "Freddy escaped police custody and we aren't any closer to finding the man behind the main operation." He rubs his chin. "As the Talas' beta, it does make me question your abilities. Sorry, man." He pats my back. "Hey, don't worry about that now. You've found your mate and her crazy ex will be caught soon." He snorts as Carly strolls out. "Or at least one of them will be."

The human doesn't even look our way as she stomps off.

Jackson deflates as he sighs. "That being said, I'm not the only one questioning Luna's plans." He strides towards the girl but pauses. "I know I speak for the entire Tala pack when I say: you are always welcome among us. No matter what happens. We are all thankful for your protection and guidance. Especially our future alpha, Maya."

257

He saunters off and I can't help but recall the little she-wolf. Maya is a spirited individual, even though her beginnings were rough. When I read her memories, they seeped out in my tears. But through the ashes, she cultivated a new life with the Tala pack. And she always greets me with enthusiasm. However, I can't help but wonder if she will trust me after knowing that my powers are flaking. I stare at Sky's door and question the same thing about my mate.

Suddenly I'm attacked in a tight embrace. "Sorry about her." Sable smirks from my side.

Celeste pulls back and glares at her son. "He saved your sister and you. You should show some appreciation too." She straightens and dazzles me with a smile. "We are in your debt, Guardian." She half bows. "Thank you for blessing our family. We are forever grateful."

Sky hasn't told them that I'm her mate. *When would she have time?* my subconscious counters. I massage my neck. This has been the longest day.

Celeste doesn't wait for me to respond. She enters the hospital room with Phoenix in tow. "Sky, my sweet baby girl!"

"We'll give them a few minutes to themselves," Sable mumbles uncomfortably while Aspen nods in agreement. They lean against the wall and cross their arms at the same time, mirror images of each other.

"Sorry I'm late." Maya rushes over to me. "The other Guardians told me what happened. Are you okay?"

"What happened?" Sable questions.

Maya side-glances him before she turns to me. "I won't let them do this to you."

"I appreciate your confidence in me."

"You have done so much. One little mistake doesn't give them the right to do *this*."

"Do what?" Sable whines.

The female Guardian sneaks out of Sky's room, and I cringe as Maya narrows her eyes at her intended target. "Speaking of *them*..." She strides over. "We need to talk, now."

The Guardian raises a hand. "I have learned a great deal, thanks to Skylar, and I need to move quickly before we lose any more time. I require a meeting of the packs immediately."

Maya crosses her arms over her chest. "Not until you promise to leave Azure alone."

I am grateful I didn't lose her support.

The Guardian raises her brow, before she glances at me. "Due to recent information, you have been pardoned in my eyes. Although I need to report to the others, in order to finalize the decision." She pivots to Maya. "Please heed my warning: we must move quickly or we will lose the war."

Maya nods. "Let's go." She turns to her mate and gives him a kiss. "Send my love to Sky, and meet me back at the territory as soon as you can."

Sable shakes his head. "We are in this together." He places a hand on her belly. "Besides, who is going to keep you off your feet and make sure you take it easy?"

"I'll let Sky know what's going on," Aspen volunteers. "I know she'll understand. Plus, with Carly here, you'll hardly get a word in anyway. Go."

They march to the elevator. When the entrance slides open, Maya arches a brow at me. "Are you coming to save the world too?"

I glance at the hospital room, fighting the urge to be close to my mate. I swallow my wolf's desire. The shifter world is in disarray, and Sky is in good hands with her family. If I don't figure out what's going on, she might be in danger sooner rather than later. If I'm going to continue to save lives, I need to learn how to prioritize my time. And right now, the packs require my unique talents.

"Please inform Skylar that I love her, and I'll return as quickly as I can," I throw over my shoulder to Aspen, squeezing into the already full elevator, and watch the door close.

"Wait one damn second! You *love* Sky?" Sable narrows his eyes. "Since when?"

I smirk at his big brother moment. "I'll explain everything on the way."

# Sky

# Demands

*A few minutes prior…*

Azure and Jackson leave and it's just Carly, the other protector, and me. I arch a brow at my bestie. "Did you have to be so mean to the guys?"

"If they can't handle me, that's their problem." She kisses my hand. "Are you really going to be okay?"

"I just had a panic attack. The doctors say I'm fine. They are keeping me for observation because my overprotective mother demanded it. Why don't you pull up a chair? Then you can explain to me why you and Jackson came in together."

She purses her lips. "Why don't I grab you a coffee? Two creams and one sugar, right?"

"That's a wonderful idea." The Guardian smiles at Carly.

My best friend side-glances the other woman. "Are you sure we can *trust* her?"

I take in the muscled shifter. She looks like Azure, with red streaks in place of his blue. "Yes, we can. Now hurry so I can hear all the juicy details."

Carly kisses my forehead. "I'll be right back. Then you can tell me about your new boy toy. Starting with the one question that I've been dying to know: do those marks continue to his manhood? Oh, and can he use his powers to please you?" She grins at my scarlet cheeks before she heads out the door.

I clear my throat and turn to the Guardian. "You said you wanted to look through my memories? How does this mind-reading thing work?"

"Just relax and take a deep breath. What I see, you'll see. It may be uncomfortable, but you won't feel any physical pain."

"How is it possible for a Guardian to have a mate?" I blurt out.

"We are just as Luna created us, but with unique attributes. We are able to experience love, pain, and sympathy."

"Are *you* married?"

"Yes, my mate and I have three pups and have been together for over twenty-five years."

"Where is he now?"

"We settled with a local pack in my quadrant, where my family resides. I do my duty, then return to my loved ones."

"Don't you miss them when you're away?"

"I never plan on being away long, however, it does happen. I miss them all the time. But we stay in contact. Especially with the technology available nowadays. Video chatting, texting, smoke signals." She elbows me with a grin.

"I want a partner who can tuck our children in and hold me every night." I pout. "Is that not an option?"

"That is something to discuss with your mate, my dear. Knowing Azure, he'll have a hard time adjusting to that. But I know you two will be able to find a compromise."

I've finally found my significant other. Can't I just be happy with that? I rub my face. "I'm ready."

Her lids flutter as she inhales a long breath. The red lines adorning her frame shimmer and glow, before a warmth travels up my neck and spreads across my head. I'm sucked into my past as if I'm reliving it. Some memories are heartwarming, while others slide down my cheeks. Once she's finished, the Guardian leans back. Her eyes flicker open, but her gaze is far off. She massages her forehead and clears her throat. "Thank you, Skylar. I have learned a great deal. If you'll excuse me, I need to relay this information to the others."

"Wait! What did you find out?"

"Who the General is."

"Why is that important? I thought Azure freed all the shifters?"

"I hope he did, but we need to move quickly before the General realizes we're on to him. I can't allow him time to disappear so he can continue his mission elsewhere."

"Sky, my sweet baby girl!" My mom runs into the room and tugs me into a hug as she cries into my hair. "That's it! You are working in that restaurant and staying with us until you find a mate! I don't care what you say! You keep getting hurt! I need you safe."

My dad talks with the Guardian, before she excuses herself with a swift exit. Then he pulls my mom out of her death grip so I can breathe.

"I love you too, Mom. I'm sorry I scared you."

She pats her eyes. "I'm just glad Freddy is gone."

"Celeste," my dad warns.

"He's a nuisance! Now my Skylar can finally find her happily ever after."

"Funny you should mention *that*."

Aspen interrupts me as he barges in. "Dude, why did Azure ask me to tell you that he loves you?"

All eyes snap to me, as I wring the bedsheet in my hands. "He's… my mate."

"Wait… what?" Aspen pushes out. "But he's like Superman, right? Can he even have sex?"

"Aspen!" my mother chastises.

"It's a valid question! And if he can, does that mean all of his kids will have powers too?"

I blink at his logical question. Will our children have abilities?

"Either way, I'm thrilled to welcome him into this family," Mom sings. "He has done everything to protect my pups!"

Aspen shrugs. "Also, I guess I should mention that Maya and Sable had to go with the Guardians to attend an emergency pack meeting."

My ears perk up. "Did they say what they plan on doing?"

He shakes his head and I deflate against my pillow. *Of course, they wouldn't say.*

"Don't you worry, sweetie. Once things settle, we will perform the ceremony and you two can work on giving me more grandpups."

"Mom," I whine. "I'm not even sure we will work out."

"Well, of course you will! Luna ordained it!"

"I want a mate to be there for me, not me *and* the whole continent."

The door slams against the wall as Carly stomps into the room with coffee cups in her hand. She passes me one and sips from the other, as Jackson rushes in behind her. "We aren't done talking about this."

I've never seen him so mad. I smirk at my best friend. But that's what she does—the woman gets under your skin. My dad clears his throat and pulls Jackson out of his stare-off. Even though his jaw is still clenched, he makes an effort to be civil. "It's great to see everyone. If you'll excuse me, I need to return to the alpha."

Dad kisses my forehead. "I'm glad you are on the mend. I'm going to go with Jackson, to see if I can offer any assistance. I'll see you soon."

"Thanks, Daddy."

The two men stride out, leaving us girls and Aspen. "Can't I go with them?" he whines.

My mom smashes him to her chest. "You're staying with me."

"I'm an adult! Stop treating me like I'm five!"

Carly and I snicker at his muffled complaints. We glance at each other, knowing our girl talk will have to wait until everyone leaves.

# Azure

# Spellcaster

"Thank you all for seeing us on such short notice. My name is Dahlia. This is Christian, Franklin, and most of you already know Azure. We are here to assist in capturing the man responsible for stealing and experimenting on shifters. We've been able to narrow our search down to a possible suspect. He's a pawn in a military organization, attempting to create new soldiers. At first, they were using our blood to try to gain our abilities. When that failed, they switched to capturing adults with the intent of breeding them and stealing the *pups* after a certain age, so they can be leashed for battle. We know you must have many questions, but we are limited when it comes to time and need to move quickly."

"Dahlia, why do you need our assistance with collecting Captain Douchebag? You are basically gods." Maya snorts.

"Although we are familiar with these territories, your packs have been living here for generations. We are asking for your assistance in exploring those areas where we think he may be in hiding."

"How confident are you that he is this close?" Frost asks as he taps a map.

"We have read the minds of all those involved and have combined their experiences to pinpoint these coordinates."

"Surely you don't mean *everyone*?" Jackson stutters out. "There were children in that group." A collective gasp bounces off the conference room walls. Including mine. I didn't realize pups were among those rescued in the other territories. "The laws are extremely clear." Jackson balls his fists. "Because children cannot understand the process or agree to it knowingly, the Guardians are *not* allowed to infiltrate their minds."

"Under the circumstances…" Dahlia insists.

"Bullshit!" Maya slams her palms on the table. "You had *no* right to make that call!"

Rising from my chair, with all eyes on my towering figure, I speak out, "Everybody is weary from their travels as well as the magnitude of more recent events. Can we please stop the man who calls himself the General before anybody else is abducted?" I hold up a hand to Maya. "I promise we will reconvene once we have him in custody and discuss the severity of what's transpired." I narrow my eyes at my fellow protectors. They know what they did was wrong, especially deciding to break Luna's law on *my* turf. I understand time is of the essence, but we do not touch children's memories. It can be a traumatic experience for any shifter, but for a child, it can be devastating.

"We had no choice. They have seen the faces of their transgressors," Dahlia answers. "But I agree. We will never do this again. Now can we please move on and discuss the objectives?"

"Where are the children?" Jackson demands.

"They are safe."

The beta grinds his teeth. "*Where*?"

"We need to observe them for possible side effects, so their location is not to be disclosed for the time being."

My jaw drops. Another decision they excluded me from. Maya blows a fuse. "Let me get this straight… You say you rescued these innocent children, just to shove them in another cage, and call it *observation*?" Her head snaps to me. "Did you know about this?"

"I was never told *any* of this. Because if I had been, I would have *demanded* that any orphans be distributed to the packs for safekeeping. They need to know they are loved and a part of a lifelong family."

The Guardians stare, wide-eyed. Yeah, that's right. You want to cut me out and make me look like an idiot? That's fine. Because I said my piece, whether they like it or not. Maya nods. "All those in favor of fostering the pups?"

Dahlia straightens her spine. "We have no idea what these kids are capable of. Most of them have been experimented on—*they were born in captivity*. Their parents were forced to reproduce, the offspring stolen to be molded in to trained assassins."

"Correct me if I'm wrong. But you work for *us,* right? You are supposed to only interfere as *needed*. Well, we don't need you to interfere with the youngsters. We will take care of them. So, hand them over. Then we can discuss taking down the bad guy." Maya crosses her arms over her chest.

I place my hands on her shoulders and stare at my comrades. "I agree with Maya. The children will have a better life if they are surrounded by loving pack members. We can retrain them to use those skills for hunting. And we have plenty of doctors to monitor any possible physical or mental side effects."

Maya squeezes my wrist before turning back to the others. "Release them into our care so we can be on our way to whoop some ass."

Frost coughs on his water before standing. "Although my daughter is still training, as the *current* leader, I fully support what she is demanding—just maybe not entirely the way she verbalized it." He gives her a look. "The children should be released to the packs for foster care immediately." The other pack leaders nod in agreement.

Maya's eyes shine as she embraces her dad. He holds her tight and kisses her head. The interaction reminds me of how much time the she-wolf spent away from her family and how she ended up in Spike's pack, forced to have sex with the alpha just to have a warm bed and hot meal. But now, she is with her true family and thriving. Just like the orphaned furballs in question. I scratch my chin. When Sky has our pups, can I really expect my family to travel with me all over the quadrant? Or worse, leave them with her to raise alone? How will our relationship be if I'm always gone?

"The children will be released into the packs' care," Dahlia announces. "The alphas may follow me, and I'll escort them to the orphans' location. Then we can get back on track." Everyone gathers their belongings as we meet outside in the crisp air.

"Please feel free to roam the territory until we are ready to leave," Frost announces. "My mate is preparing a feast, and from the smell of it, it should be ready any minute. So if you are hungry, keep your ears open for her signal."

"Azure," Dahlia calls out. I stride to her and the others. "You will not be joining us to confront the General." She holds up her palm, stopping my objections. "Your emotions are unstable."

"I can help bring down the bastard," I demand.

"Then you may question our next witness. We have located the spellcaster," Franklin soothes. "It's imperative that we read her memories. She may hold the key to why we've been blind this whole time."

"I'll tag along." Maya pokes my shoulder. "Dad won't let me travel to collect the kids because of my current condition." She rubs her belly.

"The two of you go see what she knows, then call us. We're going to drop the children off, before traveling to the General's coordinates," Dahlia instructs.

"May Luna be with you on your journey."

"As with you."

Their shadows are swallowed by the foliage. The winds of change are blowing in. Only time will tell if we are doing the right thing. Depending on how far up this operation goes, the government could retaliate and crush our very existence. But what other choice do we have?

Maya elbows me. "Well, it looks like we will be in-laws soon!"

"Should we take your car?" I nod towards her growing abdomen, knowing it'd probably be uncomfortable to shift with the extra weight.

"I thought you'd be happier to be a part of my family."

"I'm thrilled, but I haven't had much time to wrap my head around everything. There has been so much going on." I drape an arm around her shoulder and guide her forward. "Hopefully this spellcaster gives us the answers we are searching for so we can celebrate our accomplishments soon."

"Maya!" A girl bounces over when we enter the home of the spellcaster. I squeeze past the threshold, and she skids to a stop as her gaze falls on my frame. Then she backpedals. I've tried to get used to this reaction from humans. They view me as an odd creation.

Maya pets my arm. "It's okay, Sara. This is my friend—Azure." The child takes in my muscled body lined with blue streaks, and she pales. Maya laughs as she embraces her friend, who hugs her in return, never taking her wide eyes off me. "Sorry for the quick visit, but we really need to speak to your mom. Is she home?"

"Yes, I'll go get her." Sara scurries around the corner.

"Don't worry about her. She'll come around."

I shrug. "Don't be upset with her reaction. It's normal."

"I'm surprised Dahlia suggested *you* come here," she says, smoothly changing the subject.

"Why do you say that?"

"Well, Debbie is *Freddy's* only sane living relative."

I cringe at the thought. Did they send me here as some sort of test? Or maybe they hoped that after I confront her, I could break the spell the witch has on my powers?

"What a pleasure," an older woman says as she enters the room. "Maya, you are looking absolutely radiant!" They embrace, before the human takes in my size. "And you must be one of the Guardians I have heard so much about." She extends a weathered hand. "It's an honor to meet one face to face. My ancestors will be envious." I shake her cold palm, and my wolf picks up on the fear radiating off her. She clears her throat and nods at her basement. "Let's go somewhere more private." She guides us towards the door, as she hollers down the hall, "Sara, make sure you brush your teeth and get ready for bed. I'll be in to say goodnight soon." She ushers us forward, without waiting for a response from the girl.

We descend into the underbelly of the home. The shelves are bursting with concoctions and odds and ends, like bird beaks and sheep brains. Things that would cause any normal human to shiver in their boots. I side-glance Maya to gauge her reaction, knowing she basically raised Sara during their time at the orphanage. This must be a shock to know her friend is living above this chaos. She trails her fingertip over the jars of limbs and dried plants. "You have quite the collection, Debbie. Did the Department of Human Services see these when they did the home inspection prior to Sara's arrival?"

No longer is Maya the carefree, relaxed woman I've come

to know—her mama wolf instincts are peeking through and she appears ready to pounce.

"They did not know of this room." Debbie lowers herself onto a chair and motions to the two other unoccupied seats. "And Sara has never been down here and never will be."

Maya clenches her fists. "If you hurt a hair on that child's head, I'll rip you to shreds!"

I lay a hand on her arm. "Take a breath."

She snarls, tugging out of my grasp. "Tell us what you did to protect that traitorous nephew of yours!"

"All I did was cloak some memories to keep my family safe."

"Did you realize that by concealing those events, you also hindered our abilities to narrow down where and who is responsible for stealing the shifters?" I question.

"No, that's not what I did," she pushes out. "Spike threatened my family and demanded I cloak Maya's appearance, so I did. Then I created a memory potion for Freddy to hide his actions, in order to protect us from the possible ramifications of hiding her because of the bloodshed it was sure to create. I had no ill intentions." She shoves her hand in mine. "I know your powers. Read my past and see that what I say is true!"

"How do I know you haven't cloaked your memories too?"

"My magic has extinguished. I can't use it anymore, even if I wanted to. And with no heirs to transfer my skills upon, it's all over."

"What about Freddy? Isn't he a relative?" Maya's eyebrow raises as she taps her arm.

"The males do not carry the gene. And my poor sister can't use her gifts while medicated at the institution."

"If it wasn't for you, Azure would have caught the culprits earlier!

Before Sable and I were captured!"

"The Guardian rescued you in time, did he not?"

"Yes, but…" Maya sputters out.

"My magic stopped a little after Sky lost her child, which allowed the Guardian to rescue you and the other shifters."

I take in her words. And she's right. I had sensed trouble when I picked up Maya's scent. Then the same thing happened when I was leaving the police department. I *felt* that Sky was in distress. "Maya, please calm down." I place a hand on her belly to silently remind her of the stress she's causing her unborn child. She pivots and strides out of the basement without a backward glance. I narrow my eyes at the older woman, and she visibly swallows. I clutch her wrist and clench my jaw. "Your nephew is gone."

The color drains from her face. "Freddy is *dead*?"

She really doesn't know, does she? I glance around the seemingly quiet room and tell her what the other Guardians divulged to me in private. "The General grabbed him from the precinct. He's as good as dead." I lean forward. "If, by chance, the fleabag is still breathing, do *not* attempt to cover up his tracks a second time. Because if that worthless mutt hurts Skylar again, I'll return to you."

"I… I understand." Her eyes flick towards the exit. "I know what I did was wrong, but please don't hurt my loved ones. I don't want Sara to end up back in the system." She bites her trembling lip, before she meets my gaze. "I love her. She is the child I was never blessed with. And she doesn't deserve any more pain. She has suffered so much in her short life."

Of course I don't want to orphan a child. Plus, Maya will have my ass if I do anything to hurt *her* Sara. They have been through a lot together. "Do I have permission to read your memories?"

Her nod is all I need. I direct my power through her frame, guiding it to the temporal lobe and just like a streaming service, I play through her memories. Debbie loved her family but she was secretly jealous that her younger sister, Willow, was gifted with the ability to shift into a wolf. It was rare amongst the spellcasters, so the girl was favored. They were best friends and did everything together, even when Willow married a shifter and left home. Their relationship was rock solid, until the murder of her brother-in-law. It splintered her sister's sanity, and she attacked innocent humans before being committed to an institution. This left Debbie with the task of raising a disobedient Freddy and dealing with many of his bad choices, including becoming Spike's beta. Debbie helped protect him from the alpha's abuse as much as she could. But with her powers fading, he was mostly on his own.

Once the events lead up to this present moment, I break the connection. The emotions swirl in my head. Her magic was conjured to aid in the safety of her family, but at what cost? And as a witch, her duty was to help the natives, not just herself. The consequences of her actions are now on her. Her nephew is in the enemy's hands and her magic is depleted.

Her sobs pull me out of my thoughts. I pat her hand and stand. "I will inform the Guardians of your actions, and it'll be up to them what punishment you receive."

"Wait! Please! At least tell me it won't mean my death!" Her eyes swim with unshed tears.

I don't inform her that the Guardians don't normally enact the punishments. They merely gather the accused and monitor their progress through the judicial system, to ensure they get a fair sentencing. "I do not think they will hurt you. Especially *if* you continue to stay away from spells and end your cloaking so we can take down the real enemy."

She holds up her hands. "I swear that's all over."

"I'll show myself out." As I exit the small home, I phone the information I collected to Dahlia.

"Thank you, Azure. We have the General in custody now."

"That was fast."

277

"The packs were eager to bring him down."

"Was Freddy with the General?"

"No. But we haven't dug up the graves or checked their industrial furnaces for remnants either."

"What did the leader's memories reveal?"

"The General ordered Freddy to join their cause or be killed."

The silence is thick. I want to be able to tell Sky that her attacker is gone for good. But that won't be today. "I'll let the others know of this success."

"I'm not sure how much of a success it is," she mutters under her breath.

"What do you mean?"

"I don't believe the General was working alone. It was too complex a mission and needed too many resources for one man to acquire. We are still investigating, but we fear his orders have been coming down from higher up in the chain."

Her words send a chill down my spine. Are the humans trying to collectively cage the shifters? What does this mean for our future? "What can I do to help?"

"You have done your part, Azure. We all need to take a breather and then reconvene when we have more information."

"Where is the General now?"

"The human authorities have him and the other soldiers in their possession."

I snort, wondering how long that'll be the case, considering the recent escape. I clench my fists, the electricity sparking at my fingertips. "How are we going to keep tabs on him?"

"They've agreed to allow us visiting rights."

"But what if there are others who take his place?"

"We will stay vigilant like we always do."

"We need somebody on the inside," I grind out. "A human who can keep their ears to the wall and provide us up-to-date information on the comings and goings of their government. Additionally, one of us should shadow them to provide extra muscle."

"I spoke with Frost, and they are training a human to liaison between us and the government."

"Do you think that will be enough?"

"It'll have to do for now. We cannot provoke a war."

I rub my hand over my face. She is right. Even with our shifting abilities, the humans outnumber us two to one. And the government could easily turn us into the world's enemy with one well-rehearsed press release and a handful of doctored images.

"Do not fret, my friend. Tomorrow is a new day. Be with your mate and celebrate this small victory."

"But..." I push out, not knowing how long we will be able to enjoy this false sense of peace.

"Azure, I'm sorry I questioned your abilities. Rest assured, we will bring justice to our people. But let's return to our families, take a breather, and regroup."

The line cuts out and I squeeze my phone, wishing I could crumble it to pieces and observe the remnants fluttering in the wind along with my worries.

"It's bad, isn't it?"

I wrap Maya in a hug. "The General is behind bars."

She tries to read my face, "But?"

Should I confide in her or let her enjoy this triumph? I glance at her belly before meeting her eyes again. "But we are afraid these events have been approved by officials higher than his position."

"No. That can't be."

"You are probably right. And for now, that's what we will believe. Because there is no sense in worrying without all the facts, right?"

"You are absolutely right." She rubs her stomach.

"Why don't we go home?" I guide her towards the vehicle but she turns and grins. "*What*?"

"You said why don't *we* go home."

I mirror her smile. "Yes, I guess I did." And I can't wait to curl up with my mate and make use of every second of peace we have been granted. I look forward to completing the bond and burying myself inside Sky. When we finally become one, it'll be carnal.

# Sky

# Claimed

"**M**om, I'm fine—*really*." She kisses my forehead as she tucks me into my bed. "Please don't cry."

She swipes at her cheek. "I'm allowed to be upset. I just got Sable back, then you end up in the hospital. It's been rough."

"Well, you better keep Aspen close." I smirk at my little brother as he taps on his phone.

He raises his head and gives me a death glare. "Why would you tell her that?"

Mother blubbers as she wraps her arms around my sibling, nearly squeezing the life out of him. While my mom's face is hidden, I stick my tongue out at my baby brother. He promptly raises a naughty finger.

"Sky is right! You will need to be vigilant, Aspen. I don't need you to get hurt next."

"Ma, I'm fine. Aw, Sky, don't cry. Are you in pain?" he quickly lies, his eyebrows drawing down in my direction with mock concern.

I glare as Mom turns back to me, shoving pills in my hand. "Oh my. Silly me. It's time to take your pain medication." She hands me a glass of water, while Aspen's cocky grin makes me itch to throw the contents in his face.

"I appreciate your help, Mom, but the only pain I'm having is the emotional torment of knowing how much *school* Aspen is missing by sitting here. Surely, he has tons of homework to catch up on."

My brother mouths a few choice words.

"Yes, of course. Come on, son. Sky, I'll be back to check on you in the morning."

I squeeze my mom's wrist. "I love you, Mom, but you've taken care of me long enough."

She kisses my palm. "We are only a howl away." She winks. "I promise we'll call before we barge in. I know your man friend will be living here too."

I force a yawn. "Oh, well, goodnight. Love you, guys."

Mom runs her fingertips through my hair. "My Skylar found her mate. I couldn't be happier for you. Good night, sweetie. Sleep well."

Once she walks off, Aspen gives me a bro hug and whispers *lovingly*, "Payback is a bitch."

As the door clicks shut, I deflate into the comfort of my bed. Finally, some quiet! Everything has been so chaotic. I check my phone. Carly is at the restaurant helping with the dinner rush and Azure is talking to Freddy's aunt about what she knows. I am alone—I fiddle with the sheet—but not for long. My mate will be living with me. Or will I go with him? I nibble my bottom lip as I imagine leaving my family behind. I scoot farther under the covers, shoving the negative thoughts aside as sleep overtakes me.

"Sky, it's okay. You're safe."

I scan the dark room, making sure I'm not still locked in the woods of my nightmares. Warm liquid drips on my arm. I smear it and it paints my nail in crimson. Shit! My gaze focuses on Azure's bloody nose. "Oh no! I'm so sorry." I must have elbowed him in my sleep.

He reaches towards the bedside table to grab a tissue. "It's fine, really." He pats the wound. "I should have been more careful. I jumped in to save you, not realizing you didn't need protecting."

"Trust me. I did need it." I shiver at the memory of Freddy's phantasmal hands slicing open my abdomen.

"Do you want to talk about it?"

I clear my throat, hoping it'll clear some of the nightmares with it. "No, I just want to forget about it. How was your chat with Debbie?"

"She gave us all the information she had, but it wasn't much. I read her memories, and although her actions were wrong, she mostly just used her abilities to protect herself and her family from Spike's wrath. Oh, and before I forget, what did you do with the anklet Freddy gave you?" He massages my foot.

"Uh, I think it broke somewhere. Why?"

"Let's just say: any *charms* you get in the future will need to be from individuals we trust."

That piece of shit! He's been controlling me since day fucking one. But how much of all this was part of Freddy's devious plan and how much was his aunt's? "What will be the spellcaster's punishment?"

"That is up to the authorities. But it's hard to convict a woman when she practices magic. There aren't many laws regarding its use."

"That sucks."

"Well, Luna has removed her abilities and her lineage ends with her. She has no heirs to carry on her work. So you are right. It does suck, but her reign of terror is over. And she'll have to live with the consequences of her actions."

I nuzzle into his chest hair as he holds me tight. "I'm sorry again for giving you a bloody nose."

"It was worth it, to be close to you."

I hum softly, allowing his heartbeat to lull me back to sleep.

"Sky?" he whispers softly against my ear.

"Yes?"

"After we take down the people responsible for kidnapping Sable and Maya, I'm going to retire and dedicate every waking minute to making you happy, like you deserve."

"Keep talking." I grin against his neck. "Tell me what else I deserve."

His laughter rings out and fills my heart to the brim. "You are my queen, and I'll give you the world. Anything you want. I'll move heaven and earth." His fingertips caress my arm, causing goose bumps to rise along my exposed skin.

"What your queen desires is for you to put those electric powers to good use." I snuggle into his lap and his member twitches.

"Oh, is that all?" His palms massage my thighs.

The warmth he is causing pools at my core. "It's a start, Guardian," I purr. "You can also service my lady parts with that tongue of yours. Now, lie me flat and devour me, *mate*."

His frame shivers as my words sink in, and he turns so he is towering over me. "You'll warn me if it causes you pain?"

"If you're doing it right, it'll cause some pain." I run my hand through his hair and tug as the last word drips off my lips. "But I'm not fragile."

He crushes my mouth with his and our tongues battle for control in a heated frenzy. I arch my back, begging for that same action between my legs. Azure kneads my breasts before he sucks my nipple. He teases the peak with his teeth. The pain shoots to my molten center and I yelp as my hips grind against him. "Promise me, love." His breath tickles my shoulder. "If it's too much, you'll tell me." His terms of endearment have me nearly combusting.

"I promise I'll tell you."

He grazes my hips teasingly before moving to my feet, worshiping every inch of my frame. I'm starved for his attention. But my pussy is throbbing, demanding more. While he explores, I slide my finger into my folds to help relieve some of the pressure. He stares, open-mouthed, as I glide in and out.

"Do you like watching me?" I increase the tempo and my head falls back.

He places a hand on my wrist. "I would be lying if I said I wasn't jealous of these." He suckles each of my wet nails. Then bites their tips, making me groan.

"There is more where that came from."

"Is that what you want, my queen? Or..." He guides my wrist back to my nub. "Would *you* like to continue?"

He is giving me a choice. Hmm. What *do* I want? "Does your dick have the same lines as the rest of your skin?" I blurt out the question Carly asked me earlier.

"Would you like to see for yourself?"

"And ruin the surprise?" He shimmies out of his clothes. "Come closer." I bend my pointer finger tauntingly.

"As you wish."

I inch towards the edge of the bed. "Well, *that* is pretty impressive." I run my palm over his length. He's thick. He thrusts forward, as I glide my tongue over his weeping tip. I suckle the end, lapping up the precum and enjoying the salty taste. "I wonder if you ejaculate blue too?"

He tugs his dick out of reach. His hungry gaze meets mine. "You never answered me. Are you going to continue to masturbate, or let me take over and show you how it's done?"

"Oh, trust me, nothing that you do will be any different from what Carly can do." The challenge leaves my mouth before I can stop it. I facepalm. "What I meant is…"

"You don't have to explain. I get it," he growls.

"Are you bothered by Carly and me?

"What I'm *bothered by* is you bringing her up right *now*. You're not even giving me a chance."

"I'm sorry. I don't know what came over me. Please don't make me cut her out of our lives," I ramble on, afraid he will hurt her like Freddy threatened.

Azure runs a hand over my wet cheek. "I would never ban Carly from your life. She is your best friend, business partner, and you need her just as much as she needs you." He kisses my palm.

"You aren't against what we had?"

"Had or *have*?"

I swallow, unsure of how honest I can be with him. Will he run away…? Hate Carly? "Both?"

"Sky, I trust you and will love you until the day I die. My sentiments aren't conditional. Nothing will ever change them."

"So I can continue to have relations with her?"

"If that's what makes you happy."

My jaw falls to the floor. He's too good to be true. "Why?"

"She was here before me. And, hell, she may even be here long after, considering my current line of work. I'm not going to hold that against you or her. We are mates and that was ordained by Luna. But you two chose each other of your own free will."

I run my toes between his legs. "Can she join us?"

"Now?" he chokes out.

I laugh. "Not now. But another time?"

"Can I think it over?"

"Of course." I nod.

"Would you be comfortable sleeping with Jackson?"

"What? Why would you ask me *that*? We haven't even had sex yet and you are already trying to pawn me off to another man?"

He holds my hips so I don't run. "I was only asking because I believe Jackson and Carly are together. So *I assumed* if you wanted her, they would come as a package deal."

Damn. I never thought of it that way. Jackson has been a friend and uncle figure in my life for so long. "Can I think about it?"

"Absolutely. But, for now, may I continue to please you?"

I latch on to his member and pump. "First, I need to know what color this big guy provides."

He leans into my manual attack. "Oh, Luna. You're perfect."

"Just relax and let me watch you fall apart." He allows me full access. Suddenly, his hips buck and his tip squirts wildly, the gesture accompanied by a grunt. I allow the thick cream to erupt over my belly. Marking me as his. I dip my finger into the goo. "Pity… it's the same as every other guy's."

He pins my wrists to the pillow. "Well, let me show you something that not every other guy can do."

"What's that?"

He nips at my neck. "Make you scream my name to the moon while you fall into pure ecstasy."

"Hmm. Promises, promises." He lowers his face to my hips and teasingly bites at my thigh and girly lips until I'm humping the air, trying to meet his warm tongue.

He slams his tongue inside and suckles mercilessly. The magic he weaves is nothing like what I expected. Then he teases my clit with his knuckle, my thighs quiver, and I do exactly what he predicted… scream his name, while slipping over the edge of bliss. He takes in my writhing form. "I'm going to claim that sweet pussy now." He grabs my ankles and tugs me to the end of the covers. His member caresses my opening. "Do you want this, love?"

"Yes."

He inches into me, and I'm so deliciously full. "How do you want it?"

"Fast and hard."

He pinches my nipples. "You're wish is my command." He pounds into me, gripping my hips in a bruising hold. It's amazing. I snatch his neck and claim his mouth. My juices mingle with the moisture of our tongues. "Do you like the way you taste?"

I disengage from his rod and suck our liquids from his tip. "*This* is perfection." I return to our kiss and allow him to enjoy our combined flavors. "What do you think?"

"I want to fuck you."

"Well, what if I want to fuck *you* instead?"

He lies on his back, his cock stiff and ready. "I'm all yours."

I take in my dream man and question how the hell I got so lucky…

I jump on his dick and ride him. His gaze never shifts from mine as he enjoys the show. Once I explode, my body goes limp, and he takes over. His hips serenade my center until his seed claims my core. Then we drift into a peaceful sleep, entwined in each other's arms.

## Azure

# New Position

*I* could lie here forever with this angel's form tucked into my chest and her hair fanned out against the pillow. My fingertip trails her soft breast. Even in her sleep, her body reacts to my touch. Her screams of pleasure resonate in my soul. She's my better half. My love. My life. I suck in her scent as if it's a drug. Then I nuzzle into her neck while I imagine our future endeavors.

When she mentioned her best friend, I meant what I said. If that is what she needs, I'll do whatever she wants—although she seemed unsure about sharing me. I smirk against her ear. It's all fun and games *until* she has to *share*. I adjust a lock of hair, moving it away from her eyelashes. I've never had multiple women at one time. It's a little intimidating, trying to appease two of them. And if Jackson joins… that's a whole new thing. Hopefully he can just keep to his partner and leave Sky and me alone. I clench my fist as my inner wolf bares his teeth at the thought of an unclaimed male anywhere near his fur-companion.

Sky's lids flutter open. "You're still here."

Her surprise clenches my heart. "I'll always be here for you." I caress her shoulder. "I want to fuck you, until you can't walk straight."

"Right now?"

"No, you should rest." I kiss her neck. "We have an eternity to enjoy each other's company." She shimmies under the sheets. "Sky, I mean it." The words are lost as she pops my shaft into her mouth. This woman is insatiable. I ride wave after wave of her torturous mouth-fucking, before I fill her with my seed, and she slurps down every last drop.

"You know, I'm still surprised it doesn't taste like blueberries." Her nail drags over my blue veins. She yawns and burrows into my chest. "I think this is the best day of my life."

Her groggy statement fills me with joy. I kiss the top of her head and rub her back. "And there's many more days like this to come." Then we fall into the best slumber, each in the arms of our true love.

I fumble around the covers, in search of my mate. "Sky?"

"I'm right here," she calls out and I follow the sound.

Maya and Sky are sitting at the kitchen table with coffees in hand. Maya wiggles her brow knowingly at my nude form. Sky giggles at her sister-in-law and it warms my heart to hear, so I pardon her forgetfulness in not waking me before we had an audience. I rub my face. I never sleep in. I'm always up with the sun.

"I was hoping for gender-neutral colors," Maya pushes out as she swipes through her phone. "Kind of like this."

"But don't you want to know the sex?" Sky whines. "Look how cute these gender reveals are." The excitement in her words is contagious and I find myself eagerly awaiting our own baby shower.

A knock on the entrance pulls me out of my internal thoughts. I side-glance the girls, but they don't budge. "I'll get it." I stretch and pull open the door.

Carly stumbles forward. "Uh…"

"Come on in!" Sky sings. "Just brush past Azure. He doesn't bite… *hard*."

Carly lifts her chin and does just that. "Girl, have you ever heard of coverup? Those hickeys are disgusting," she grinds out, gesturing to Sky's prominent love bites.

My mate flips the bird at her. "Just because you're not getting any attention doesn't mean you can be a bitch to everyone who is."

Maya laughs. "Ladies, can we focus please."

I step away from the estrogen-filled atmosphere and into the calm morning air. I breathe deep. The sounds of children playing and wolves panting is music to my ears. It feels good to be around a full pack again.

"Guardian." Frost lifts a palm in greeting as he approaches.

"Frost, it's good to see you." We shake hands before watching the pups wrestle in the dew-damp field.

"I bet you are eager for a litter of your own."

"I was never a family man, but Sky makes it hard to not think about settling down."

"Our mates change us, for the better. Which reminds me, when do you and Sky want to have your ceremony?"

I watch as a pup drags another by the tail. "Whenever possible."

His chuckle rings out over the playful snarls. He turns his head as laughter pours out from inside the cave. "Maya and Carly will keep Sky busy for a while."

I snort. "That's what I'm afraid of."

The alpha pats my shoulder. "While the girls play, why don't we go on a hunt? I have a batch of shifters ready for their first time."

It's been a while since I've worked with other wolves to catch prey. I normally set traps and snares when I'm hungry, because I only require small game to sustain myself. But now that I'll be a member of the Tala family, I'll be expected to contribute. "That sounds entertaining."

The alpha leads the way. "You'll make a great addition to the team. I can't wait to see what skills you have to share."

"That's high praise coming from *him*." Jackson joins us with a fur-child in his arms.

"Do I not give enough encouragement, Jackson?" Frost asks. "Should I also rub your bellies and give you bottles?"

"Yes, please." We turn to the giggling pup and he shrugs. "Hey, I'm allowed to be sarcastic too."

Jackson ruffles the child's mane and drops him to the floor. "Are you actually going to catch something this time?"

"Nope." The kid shifts and tackles the other wolves, creating a dog pile.

"A wolf who doesn't like to kill prey." Frost smacks Jackson on the back. "Good luck with him." Then he strides to the front of the group.

The beta wrinkles his nose. "He must get that from his adoptive parents!" he shouts at Frost, rubbing the back of his neck as his eyes glaze over. It must not be easy for him to have lost his mate so early in life. I recall his wife died in childbirth. I can't imagine losing Sky that way.

"Dad! I found an arrowhead!" The little boy hands it to his father.

Jackson's eyes glitter as he kneels and takes the stone. "This will fit right into your collection, Ash. Great eye." The kid skips back to his friends to show them his prize. "He has your sense of adventure,

Ashley," the beta seems to whisper to himself as he clutches the ring dangling from the chain around his neck. He stands and clears his throat. "I'm hoping the deer are grazing in the north field. Raven makes one hell of a venison chili."

"I also hear that Skylar knows how to cook an amazing venison steak."

"That's true. But if the deer won't play, we can always catch some fish." The pups moan in response. "It's better than nothing."

"But they're slimy and hard to grab," one grumbles.

"Plus, they smell funny," another gripes.

"Well then, you better stay sharp so you can attack the deer," Frost commands. "And quit yapping, or you'll alert them of our presence."

The group collectively sticks their tongues out behind the disgruntled alpha's back, then they each hold a hand over their mouths to stifle their laughter. The camaraderie of these youngsters shifts my thoughts to my nephew. Would Hunter like it here? Would Sky and Lily get along?

# New Beginnings

"Lily!" Azure hugs an approaching figure and rushes her over to me. "This is Skylar." The pride in his breathless introduction does amazing things to my girly bits.

Tonight is the big night. I have Carly as my maid of honor and Azure's sister traveled to Cold Creek to be her brother's best man… or rather woman.

"Hi, I've heard so much about you." She embraces me. "It's nice to meet you."

"Azure has been talking nonstop about you too."

"Hopefully only about the good moments." She elbows him in the stomach.

He bends and grunts. "Hey! That hurt."

"He was always a big baby." She grins. And I can't help the smile that tugs at my lips. The love they have for each other is *life goals* for sure.

I kneel and offer a palm to the little boy hiding behind Azure. "You must be Hunter." His dark eyes meet mine and he shrugs, ignoring my hand. "Do you like to whittle?" I nod to his small knife, and he clutches it tighter. I've never been great with kids, and I think he knows this. The boy screams as a group of pups bullet towards him with their tongues hanging out and tails wagging. I cringe as they tackle the newcomer and bark their enthusiasm.

"Hunter?" Lily squeals as she helps him up. "Are you okay?"

The shock plastered on his face melts into a grin. "Can I play with them?"

She blinks and nods. "Of course." He shifts and growls before chasing his new pals. Lily watches them go, catching a stray tear with her fingertip at the sight in front of her.

Azure wraps an arm around her neck. "See? I told you. There's nothing to worry about." They stand shoulder to shoulder, and I smile. Even though they are twins, Azure is taller, broader, and has those tantalizing blue veins decorating his frame. Whereas Lily is dark-skinned with a beautiful mom bod.

"Oh my! There she is!" My mother prances over, smiling at Lily. "It's a pleasure to meet you. Welcome to the family!" They hug. "Where's your little one?"

"He's getting into trouble." Lily points to the pond, then rubs her arms. "I feel like I'm missing something without him close by."

"All mothers do." Mom bumps her shoulder into mine. "Even when they grow up, they are still our babies."

"There you two are! I've been looking everywhere." Raven saunters over, adding to the growing crowd. "We're ready to begin."

"Raven, this is my sister—Lily." Azure smiles.

"Pleasure to meet you, dear. Your brother is pretty adamant that we prepare to welcome you to our pack as an official member soon. He even staked claim on a cave by Skylar's."

Lily blushes. "I wouldn't make arrangements yet. It's a long way from where we grew up and I'd have a lot to move."

"We'd have your things over here in a pinch!" Mom interjects. "Plus, free pupsitters."

"What's taking so long?" Frost grumbles. "I asked you to find them, not talk their ears off."

"Stop it." Raven smacks her husband.

"Let's get this over with." He trudges past us, muttering to himself.

Raven smirks. "Ignore him." She laughs at Lily. "This ceremony is a little different than my husband is used to."

"Oh?" Lily looks up at her brother.

"You'll see." He winks. "I'm not spoiling the surprise."

"Tonight, we gather to bring the Guardian Azure and Skylar Canis together as mates," Frost announces, and aims to move forward but Raven elbows him. "Along with Carly Smith," he mumbles. "Luna, in all her mighty wisdom, has brought them together. Thank you, Luna. We praise you." Frost sips from the ceremonial wine before he passes it to me. I watch Azure and Carly as I swallow the red liquid, mimicking the alpha's actions and handing the goblet to my mate. His eyes never leave mine as he repeats the process, then presents the wine to Carly. She hesitates as she sniffs the substance. Frost clears his throat, and she guzzles a swig before passing it to my parents. After the pack has all partaken from the goblet and it makes its way full circle to Frost, he holds it in the air. "Luna, may you bless them in holy matrimony and help us support them through their amazing journey." He meets the eyes of each of the pack members before he continues, "The grass withers and the flowers fade…"

"But the love of the pack lasts furever," everyone finishes in unison.

Then he takes the final sip and steps aside. "Azure."

My mate stands in Frost's spot, his eyes scanning the crowd until they land on me. He collects my hand and kisses it. "Skylar. I feel like I've waited an eternity for you. I'm sorry for not fighting for you in the beginning of our tale. But with Luna as my witness, I vow to never make that mistake again. I love you, and from now on, you are my world—my everything." He glances at his nephew's wolf form, and the pup prances to his side and leans in. Azure unties the ring that's around the kid's neck and slides it over my finger. "Skylar, will you make me the happiest shifter and be my wife?"

"On *one* condition."

The group chatters behind us. I pivot to grab Carly's wrist and tug her next to me. "Will you, Azure, also love, protect, and fight for the woman I love? And welcome her into our lives as an *equal* in our relationship?" Carly blubbers as she embraces me, her makeup smearing down her face until she resembles Medusa. I squeeze her. "That's also *if* she still wants me as her wife." I toss a thumb at Azure. "And if she'll deal with the Smurf too."

Giggles echo behind us. Mom sneaks over with a few tissues and she helps Carly collect herself. "I never thought this day would come." Carly pats her lashes. "Sky Bear, of course I'll be your wife. And I guess I'll *deal* with him too, if I have to." She smirks at my mate. We both stare at Azure, holding our breaths as we anxiously await his response. Will he accept both of us?

"I was going to talk to you *privately* about this, but you've given me no choice but to address the elephant in the room." Azure holds out his hand to his sister. She tiptoes closer and places an identical wedding band in his palm. He meets Carly's gaze. "You have been here for Sky when I couldn't. You even went toe to toe with a rogue shifter so you could remain by her side. Your love for her has *no* limits. Will you do us the honor and become an equal partner in our marriage? Through sickness and health *and* dirty diapers? In return, I'll love, protect, and fight for you too." He extends his hand.

Carly stares between us, her eyes watering as if she might start crying again. She swallows her sob. "You better make sure you change *your* share of diapers too, blue boy." After the laughter dies down, she adds, "I accept. And I'm honored to be a part of an incredible family." He slips on her ring. And I hug her. She pivots and smiles at our pack. "Now you all are stuck with me forever." She makes a point to wink at Frost.

"No, he didn't!" I wipe the tears from my eyes.

"He did!" My sister-in-law slurs her words. "His teeth turned this moldy green color."

"We've married a good one." Carly smirks over the rim of her wine glass.

I finish my liquid refreshment. "There he is! The *crayon* eater!"

Azure trudges over and narrows his eyes at his sister. "Really? You told them *that* story."

"It was either that one or the one when I found you jerking off…"

He slaps a hand over her mouth. "I think you've had enough to drink. Why don't I show you to your cave?" He stalks off with her giggling and drunk waving behind him. I grin at the pair. They are going to fit right in. I twirl the band on my ring finger. I'm a married woman. Who would have thought?

Carly leans her head on my shoulder. "Are you happy?"

"Yes." I lay my cheek on her hair.

"So… do I get to participate in *all* the wedding night activities?"

"I always want you by my side, Car."

She kisses my neck. Then wiggles her ring finger. I love that Azure was prepared to include Carly in our wedding too. It proves how selfless he is. And it reminds Carly that she will always be a part of my life.

"Okay, the drunk is resting." Azure chuckles as he returns. "I'm sorry. She never drinks."

"What? Why not?"

He wraps an arm around me. "When she warms up to you, she'll explain her tale. She's had to act older than her given years because she had to step up when she became a mother."

"She must be very strong."

"That she is, love. But the good thing about getting her wasted is that she finally agreed to move here."

"That's great! Hunter is adorable. I can't wait to spend more time with him." I yawn and rub my eyes. He grabs me bridal style and I squeal. We rub noses before our mouths fuse together. The bond ignites and our tongues battle for control until we are out of breath. "Can we go to bed?" I nip his bottom lip.

"Absolutely." He walks towards the cave, then tilts his head. "Are you coming wife number *two*?"

I look over his shoulder at Carly as she stirs the embers with a stick. She meets my gaze. There are tears shimmering down her face in the fire's afterglow as she stands and shrugs. "Not if you're going to call me *that*."

"How about *bitch* number two?" He grins.

She narrows her eyes. But I respond first. "She'd be bitch number one."

We all laugh, even Carly, as we enter the cave and Azure announces, "Welcome home, wives."

He lowers me to the covers, and we embrace again, in a frenzy of teeth and tongue. His hand slips over my thigh to rest on my stomach. I shiver and disengage. Carly stands, watching us, appearing unsure. I grab her wrist and pull her next to me. We lock eyes, her insecurities dissolve, and she pounces, knowing exactly where to place her lips to bring a puddle between my legs. I knead her breasts before tweaking her sensitive nipples. She arches her back, pushing farther into my hold. I gasp as Azure's tongue flicks my lower lips. Oh, this is *delicious*. A finger slips in and I clench around it. I clutch Carly's hips and guide her so she's sitting on my face. I devour her center, enjoying her moans, while Azure nips my clit and I explode, screaming into Carly's pussy.

"Lie on your back," I instruct her, and she obeys, spreading her legs wide and begging me to continue. Desire burns in my core and I must have my mate's hands on me again. He pins me next to my friend before his mouth trails along every inch of my skin. Carly's whimpers cut through my lust-filled fog and I realize this is harder than I thought. I'm trying to focus on two people at one time. "Azure," I huff. "Let me eat her out while you fuck me." We reposition ourselves so I'm nose-deep in her nectar with my ass in the air. Carly tugs my hair, then massages my scalp with her nails.

"This feels amazing," she grinds out.

Azure's palm slaps my ass and I squeal. "Raise your hips higher, mate."

My mind is melting from all this attention, and I question if this is something I can do. Carly screams my name as she vibrates her release, and Azure slams into my center, riding me fast and hard. I match his speed until we explode at the same time. Exhaustion overtakes me and I drop next to Carly. Azure tugs me to his chest, then I do the same with Carly. We all hum in perfect harmony.

Having my two favorite people by my side, in the same bed, makes my heart burst. It may take some getting used to, but we'll get there. Afterall, it's till death do us part.

# Azure

## New Life

My vision wavers, throwing off my equilibrium. Once it stabilizes, I glide my finger over a dark mahogany desk. Even if I can't feel it, I know it's cool to the touch. The door creaks and I pivot as a woman tiptoes inside.

"Carly?" She doesn't hear me. Is this a vision? It's been a long time since they've been this clear. I reach for her but my hand passes through her body, confirming that it is a premonition.

She shuffles through folders, her gaze constantly flitting towards the entrance. "Fuck. Where is it?"

I tilt my head but I'm unable to make out the documents, so I inch closer to the troublemaker. She's breathtaking. The sun glistens off the towering window, causing her wedding band to shimmer when it catches the light. It's hard to imagine I've been blessed with two amazing women. My wolf is hesitant to claim the human as his own, but if his mate accepts her, I know it's just a matter of time. Carly bends over to search the drawers. Her plump ass stretches the fabric of her skirt. Just as I reach to squeeze it, she straightens. Her *squeals of delight echo off the walls as she waves a folder around before stashing it into her jacket.*

*"I knew you had it! Now we'll find out what you're concealing."*

*I laugh at her childish antics. She's a handful for sure.*

*Suddenly she stiffens and her eyes bulge out. Her hands tremble as they wrap around a dagger protruding from her abdomen. Her eyes roll back and she crumbles into a pool of crimson.*

*Where the fuck did the knife come from? I take in the empty room. Why can't I see who wields it? I kneel and attempt to cradle her, but the vision won't allow it. "I'm here, sweetheart. It's going to be okay." Even though I'm aware it's not happening in real time, I can't stop the tears, knowing the pain she's in and the fact that she's alone in this moment.*

*That's when it hits me. This is going to happen.*

I gasp and rub the misery from my eyes. The sun is still looming below the horizon. I peek over Sky's shoulder. Carly is snuggled against her, breathing peacefully. I shiver as the phantasmal scent of blood still lingers in the air. I throw back the covers and resettle behind Carly. I tug her to my chest and kiss her hair. "I'm here, sweetheart. It's going to be okay," I whisper.

She hums and turns from Sky to curl up against my chest.

"You would think as a Guardian he'd need less sleep."

"Shh. He has to deal with us for the rest of his life. He'll need all the sleep he can get."

"True." My wives giggle. I peek through my lashes. Sky nips Carly's neck as the other woman sits in her lap with a mug cradled in her hands. Carly sets the dish down and frames Sky's face. They rub noses. "We *are* a handful."

"That we are." Their lips touch and they take their time, each exploring the depths of the other's mouth. My mate's hand grazes Carly's breast. The human swats her bestie's wrist. "You know I'm ticklish there!"

Sky returns to fondling her partner's chest. "That's *why* I do it. I love to hear you laugh." She suckles her nipples until they are peaks. "Plus, I get to hear you beg."

"Anything for you."

My erection is uncomfortable. But I can't interrupt this moment. I love observing their shared happiness. My mate slips her finger into her friend's folds. "You're always so wet."

Carly slips her nail into her wife's entrance. "And you never disappoint me with how slick you are."

"Are you hungry?" Sky asks breathlessly.

Carly leaps off her lap and swipes her arm over the kitchen table, knocking everything to the floor. She lifts her friend and lays her on the wooden surface, spreading Sky's legs wide. "I'm starving." She pulls a chair closer and sits, before tugging my she-wolf to the edge.

"I can't believe I get to wake up to this every morning."

Carly's tongue teases her partner's opening. "I couldn't ask for a better way to start my day."

My heart clenches as her words clash against remnants of my vision. If I can't stop these events, this won't last forever. Carly will die, leaving a hole in my mate's soul.

"Azure, quit being a perv and join us," Sky taunts as she flicks a look my way. "I'm sore from last night, but Carly could use some pain from your magic stick."

I throw the covers away, allowing them to take in my rod as it weeps. "I was letting you enjoy your breakfast."

"Well, how about you contribute to the meal?" Carly grins. I falter as her bleeding frame flashes in front of my eyes, causing me to stumble. "Are you okay?" She rushes to my aid.

I shake my head, unable to unsee her tragic end. "I'm just going to take a shower." I wave to my spouses. "I'm fine. Don't let me ruin the fun." I close the door and lean against the frame.

"Carly, just give him time. It's a lot to service two…"

"Whatever. I need to get ready to go soon anyway." The chair scrapes across the stone floor like nails across a chalkboard.

"We don't have to…" Sky's words melt into a moan.

I squeeze my eyes shut, enjoying their symphony of whimpers. I *will* find a way to save her.

"You don't have to go with us," Carly snips.

"Yeah, I know how much you hate shopping," my sister adds with an arched brow.

"I want to spend time with you. Is that so wrong?" Carly snorts in response. I know I hurt her feelings this morning, but I can't explain why I acted the way I did without causing unnecessary distress. "Sky is helping Maya with the baby shower again and Hunter is chilling with Ash. So I'm all yours." I wrap an arm around them. "Let's go shopping."

Carly ducks out of my embrace. "I'm driving."

"And I call shotgun!" Lily dashes to the car.

I squeeze into the back seat. Why do humans make these things so tiny? My knees crush my chest and my chin is tucked in. I could shift and beat them to the shopping center. But that would leave Carly unguarded. Plus, I don't want to offend her further by reminding her of how different she is.

"I heard you spent the night with Jackson," Carly whispers. My wolf ears prick up. *Who?*

Lily clears her throat. "It wasn't like that." *What the fuck?*

"Sure it wasn't," Carly drags out.

"I thought you and him were a thing," my sister counters with a teasing grin. "That's what the other shifters are saying anyway."

"Jackson is just a pain in my ass," Carly grinds out. "His *alpha* forced him to keep tabs on my every move, like I'm some kind of criminal."

I bristle at the pain laced in her observation. Why would Frost do that? I scratch my chin. Carly does stir up mischief.

"I'm sorry," Lily coos.

"I'm not. I'm finally living my happily ever after." My frown morphs into a grin. "With *Sky*. I know she loves me wholeheartedly." I blink as her scowl lands on me in the rearview mirror.

"You two look happy together." Lily shifts in her seat.

"We do, don't we," Carly sings. Shit. I can't be in the doghouse already. It's only the first day of my marriage.

"Not that I'm complaining, but why did you want to take me shopping?"

"Because you are the new girl in town and I want to get to know you better. Plus, you can give me all the dirt on your brother."

Yup. I'm in trouble. Lily sneaks me a pitying pout. "I'd love to get to know you better too, Carly. Especially now that we are sisters-in-law."

I wink at my twin, glad to hear she's on my side. Carly's knuckles whiten around the steering wheel. "In the spirit of getting to know each other, Ash said he found you naked in Jackson's bed this morning. What's up with that?"

Lily's neck snaps to Carly. "I was drunk!"

"I put you in *your* bed!" I growl. "How the hell did you get to the beta's house?"

"I probably had a nightmare and was searching for help."

My companion smirks at our bickering as she pulls into the parking lot. I leap out of the car and rip open Carly's door. "And why are *you* so damn concerned with Jackson? If nothing happened between you two, why is his name constantly on your lips." My fur pokes through at the thought of my spouse with another wolf.

Carly stands to meet my gaze, as best she can with the height difference. "Why do you think I have to explain myself to you?" She sizes me up. "You only want to be with your mate. I'm just scraps. A side-lay for you." She lifts her chin. "However, as long as I get to be with Sky, I don't give a fuck. But don't you dare think you have a say in what I do."

Her challenge tingles my spine. My chest crushes her against the car. "You will *not* have sex with another man or woman while you are married to us." I snatch her wrist. "This is a symbol of our promise to be loyal and devoted." I wiggle my ring in her face. "We need to hold each other accountable if we want to have a successful marriage."

The wheels are turning in her head as my words sink in. Before she can fight me, I dip my lips to hers. She stiffens as I massage her mouth with mine. My tongue moistens her seam, but she won't open. She clenches her fists and I step back to give her space. It hurts that she won't reciprocate.

But I won't force her to love me. I'll prove to her I'm worthy of her attention. No matter the cost.

# Sky

# Puppy Time

What happened? The ceremony and wedding night were perfect. Then the morning came and everything was going smoothly, until Azure shrugged off Carly. I nibble my nails. Maybe his wolf is rejecting my bestie.

"Hey, sister!" Maya skips inside with her mate on her heels. "We made sure to come over later in the day so we wouldn't interrupt any sexy time." She glances around the quiet house. "Where are your partners?"

"They went out for a bit."

"They left quicker than I thought they would." Sable drops into a chair beside me. "But it doesn't surprise me. They probably hightailed it out of here when they realized what life would look like being married to the biggest pain in the ass in the territory." He side-glances my stoic face. "Why aren't you smacking me?" he huffs.

"Ignore your big brother. He's just upset because he isn't getting any sexy time anytime soon." Maya gives him a pointed glare.

"Don't tell my little sister that!"

She waves him aside. "What's up, Sky?"

I sip my cold coffee. "Azure was acting weird this morning. Something is off and I'm afraid it has to do with Carly."

"Did he fuck her?" Sable leans in.

Maya gives him the smack he deserves than returns her attention to me. "This is new for everyone. Give it some time. I know Azure will open up and accept your friend."

"Even if he doesn't..." Sable rolls an apple in his palm. "...he'll be traveling, off being a hero, so it'll be just you and Carly anyway." He crunches into its flesh.

"But I need him to love her too," I whine.

"You can still love someone and not want to fuck them," Sable states matter-of-factly.

I rub my temples. "I just want a happy family."

"Then you have to work for it, just like everyone else." Maya squeezes my wrist. "Marriage isn't easy. And you have two partners, so it's double the trouble."

"Or double the fun," Sable grunts.

"Good afternoon!" my mom sings as she enters the room. "I have great news."

My tail wags. I asked her to look over the ultrasound I had done recently to make sure everything was working after the miscarriage. I need to know children are still an option for me, and that the risk of losing another one is slim, because I can't handle another loss.

She points to me. "You are clear and have the green light to conceive." I let out a breath. At least *that* concern is over with. She slaps down a stack of papers. "After researching the hostages' lab work, I've designed an antiserum for the General's toxin."

"Really?" Maya goes into alpha mode. "How soon can we mass produce it and vaccinate the pack members?"

"Before I can officially announce that it is in fact an antidote or preventative measure, I'll need to set up some tests. Plus, I'd feel more comfortable if I could get my hands on a vial of the poison at its full strength and not diluted by blood or tissue."

"No way. You're not going anywhere near the General," Sable announces.

Mom bristles at his tone. "I never said I was going to, son."

"I saw the gleam in your eyes. It's your signature *kick ass and ask questions later* look." He pivots to me. "Right, Sky?"

I pat my mom's hand. "He has a point."

"That's amazing work, Celeste," Maya soothes. "Thank you for your dedication."

"Thank you. And once I get closer to producing it, I'll inform the pack." She squeezes our hands. "I'm making it my priority to keep our family protected."

# Trouble in Paradise

I scan the crowded mall for any sign of danger. Some shoppers gawk and move out of my way, while others lick their lips as they take in my muscled frame.

"I need to drop into the lingerie store." Carly loops her arm with Lily's. My lip twitches at the pair. I'm glad my sister has a new buddy. Even though my wife is ignoring me, she's been gushing over my twin.

My sibling shakes her head. "You're going solo." Lily tugs on the excess skin on her abdomen. "No one wants to see this."

"Stop, you are beautiful." Carly frowns.

"No, I'm not."

"I'd have sex with you."

Lily blushes. "Thank you…?"

"Azure, you can wait at the car. We don't need you." Carly shoos me off at the store's entrance.

"I'm *not* leaving."

"Well, we don't want you following us into another clothing store. Especially one like this."

"Why? I'm going to see it anyway." I cross my arms over my chest.

She arches a brow and throws her chin at my sister. "Really?"

I stumble. "Well, not on *her*."

"And not on *me* either. I'll wear it while you're off doing whatever Guardians do." She pulls my twin into the shop, and I snarl at her departing form, causing four females to sidestep out of my path. I clench my fists.

Why is she so difficult? I slam my fingers through my hair.

My phone pings, momentarily pausing my frustrations, and I tug the device from my pocket. Sky is checking on us again. I sigh. I don't want to disappoint her, but I'm sinking here. I dial her number, eager to hear her voice.

"Hey, babe!" Her honey-laced words soothe my wolf. "How's the shopping trip going?"

I turn away from the naughty shop. "It's… *going*."

"That bad, huh?"

"Carly is mad at me, and I don't know how to fix it."

"Did you say sorry?"

"For what? She's the one with the attitude!"

"Honey, she doesn't trust men. You need to be patient."

"I'm not a man. I'm a shifter," I grind out.

"You have a penis so you're just another guy to her. Win her heart like you did mine."

"I miss you, Sky."

"I miss you too."

"Do you need me to pick anything up while I'm here?"

"Something shiny and expensive," she purrs.

I laugh, the tension leaving my body. "Fine. But Carly's not getting anything, because she's being difficult."

"You're allowed to be mad at her, but don't give up on her, okay?"

I glance back at my other wife. "Never."

"That's my man. Now go get your queens a present. Just no anklets," she reminds me.

"I love you, Skylar."

"I love you more, Azure."

I place the phone in my pocket and trudge towards the closest jewelry store. Glancing around the area, I know I'm in the right place. Everything is *shiny and expensive.* The clerk assists me in selecting a pair of gold wolf pendant necklaces. They are gorgeous, and when you connect their snouts, the fur forms a stunning heart. The associate informs me that these are known as *friendship* charms. They even provide me with a pendant of my own that fits snuggly between the two to complete the perfect marriage of the trio. I stash the goods in my cargo pants. Now my girls and I will have matching collars.

My phone blares. I answer it without looking at the caller. "Hello?"

"Just tell us where he is," a man shouts into the receiver.

"You had better release Lily right now!" I can hear Carly grind out. She must have dialed me. The hair bristles over my neck and I run towards my spouse's scent. Her fear leaves an acidic taste on my tongue. Fuck. How could I let this happen? I skid around the corner. Two men have Carly and Lily huddled in a dark hallway. My fingers tingle with electricity.

"Get your hands off them." My fangs elongate. "Now." I release a guttural growl.

They stiffen and pivot. Their hands leave the females. The taller one clears his throat. "We mean no harm. We were only asking them some questions."

Carly kicks the idiot in the nuts. When he falls to the floor, she claws at his chest like a rabid dog. "Fuck you! How dare you scare the shit out of my friend!"

The other male reaches for my spouse and my fur shreds my clothes moments before I slam him to the ground. I snap my jaw towards his ear.

"Woah! Easy!" He waves a government badge. Drool drips from my canines onto his suit. "We are investigating the murder of Brock Robinson and it's led us to his mate."

That *name*! My gaze snaps to Lily. Tears coat her cheeks. Brock's the shifter who raped my twin and left her for dead. Carly strokes my fur to hide her shaking limbs. "We don't care who you are. This is no way to conduct an investigation."

"We are just following orders."

"Who's your boss?" my partner demands. "We need to meet with them and settle this misunderstanding." She pats my shoulder. My jaw ticks before it closes around the man's neck. He squeals and fidgets. His colleague offers a business card. "We'll be by his office *tomorrow*." I release the guy. "Make sure he's available for questioning." She narrows her eyes to further emphasize her point.

They dash into the crowd, leaving us alone in the hallway. I shift, collect my sister, and stroke her hair as she cries. Carly releases a breath and joins our huddle. She burrows her face into my chest. "Why don't we head home?"

We separate and Carly cringes. "You demolished your outfit." Her gaze trails my frame as she shoves her lingerie bag into my arms. "I hope you look good in a thong."

After we return to shifter territory, I bring Lily to Frost's cave to discuss our plan of action. If government officials are after her, we need to find out *why*. But also keep the pack safe. I stroke my sister's arm. "Why are they after you?" She shakes her head. "Lily, you have to tell us. This is serious."

She tugs away. "Don't you think I know this? I was cornered and interrogated like some sort of criminal!" Her words cut deeper than her bite.

"Lil."

She stomps out of the house.

"Jackson." Frost nods to his beta. The second in command lifts his chin and follows her outside. The older man rubs his temples. "I have a bad feeling about all of this."

"They were after the kid," Carly mumbles. We meet her gaze. "They kept asking where the *offspring* was and informing us that *it* was government property," she spits out the words. "I need to meet with their boss."

"No you don't. They were just talking out of their asses." I shake my head. "There's no way a child can be property."

"Unless they believe he's one of the kids we rescued from the General's compound," Frost interjects. We are silent as the words settle between us.

"But they knew who his father was," I object. "And they thought the sperm donor was my sister's mate."

"They know nothing about shifters and their way of life. They probably assume *baby daddy* and mate are interchangeable." Carly snorts. Ever since the incident, she hasn't left my side. Even when we arrived home, she chose to stay with me instead of visiting Sky.

"We need answers." Frost stares at my partner.

"What do you have in mind, boss."

He wrinkles his nose. "Don't call me that."

"How about fur-king?" Her lip twitches.

"I'll have Jackson escort you to the location and you two can poke around."

"They're after my sister. I'll go with Carly."

"Great idea. They'll be scared shitless of you and more compelled to give us answers."

We all turn as Jackson reappears. "Lily is resting."

"What did she say?" Frost questions.

"I'm still attempting to get her to open up to me."

They exchange a look. "Guard her and her child with your life." Frost pats his back. "We are counting on you."

"Of course." Jackson pivots to me. "Hunter is asking for you." I turn on my heel, headed that way, before he adds, "They are staying in my cave and Hunter's sleeping in Ash's room."

I falter. "What?"

"Just for the time being, until we can figure out who's after them," he explains.

I bump chests with the beta. "She's my sister! She'll be staying with me."

My partner strokes my arm. "Sweets. Lily is an adult. You have to let her choose her own path."

I tug away from her. "I couldn't protect her from that monster. But I can now."

I stomp into the night air and push through Jackson's front door. "Uncle Azure!" Hunter wraps his arms around my legs. "I've missed you!"

I rub his back. "Where is your mom, buddy?"

"She's lying on the couch with a migraine, so Jackson asked us to play quietly."

I smile at the two boys. "I'm going to check on her, then I'll play a game with you."

"Yes!" he squeals.

I wait for the boys to return to their room, then kneel and take Lily's hand. She blinks at me and shakes her head. "No."

"You don't even know what I'm going to say."

"You're going to ask to see my memories." She slides her arm away. "And the answer is no. I never want to relive that moment."

"Lily, please."

"No."

"I just want to protect you." When she doesn't respond, I hear Carly's words reminding me to give my twin space. "Are you sure you want to stay here with Jackson?"

"Yes."

"Wouldn't you rather stay with Carly and Sky?"

"Their house isn't exactly *child* friendly." She gives me a pointed stare. "I love you guys, but I'm not ready to have *that* conversation with him yet."

"I understand." I caress her back. "I'm here for you, whenever you are ready to talk."

"I know." Her eyes swim with unshed tears. "Just not right now."

After a few card games with the boys, I tuck them in to bed and slip out into the night air. I lean against the stone exterior. What am I going to do? My sister is being hunted and Carly... I shiver as her painful end replays in my mind for what feels like the millionth time.

"I never meant to step on your toes." Jackson stands beside me. "It's my job to protect the pack, even the newest members."

"And it's my job to guard all the shifters, including my baby sister."

He squeezes my shoulder. "Then the pack is truly blessed to have two mighty warriors fighting for them."

"If I find out you were anything but a *gentleman* to Lily..." Electricity shimmers, lighting up my blue veins before slipping out to zap him. He tugs his arm back and shakes it. "*You'll* need protection, beta."

"There you are!" Sky embraces me. "Are you okay?"

My lips graze hers. "I'm fine. Where's Carly?"

"She said she needed to shower and wash the grime of the day away." Sky frowns at Jackson. "What happened to you?" He ignores her and stomps into his cave, slamming the door behind him. "What the hell is his problem?"

I tuck her under my arm and guide her home. "I gave him a little shock."

"What? Why?"

"To remind him of his place."

"You men and your pissing contests. Why can't you get along and be civil?" She pushes open our front door a few minutes later. "Car? We're back. Do you want me to make you some tea?"

I slump on the bed and remove the replacement clothes I had to buy before we left the mall. One thing I miss about wandering the quadrant is I never had to wear restrictive garments. But now that I'm around humans, it's different. A plastic bag on our dresser catches my attention and I snatch it up.

"What do you have there?" Carly watches me from the doorway.

I toss her a box. "Sky requested something shiny and expensive."

My mate grins before squeezing past her bestie and holding out her palm. Her eyes twinkle as she tears it open and gasps. "It's gorgeous!" She kisses me softly. "Can you put it on me?" She sweeps her hair aside. "What does yours look like, Carly?"

Our wife fiddles with her gift. "It's a wolf necklace." I frown as she sets it on the nightstand. "As if I need another reminder of how human I am." Then she stomps out.

"Carly!" Sky takes off after her bestie, and I can't help but frown. Well, that didn't go as planned...

After a few minutes, my mate returns and snuggles into my lap. "She's checking on Lily."

"I didn't mean to insult her."

"I know." She nuzzles my chest hair.

I wrap my arms around her. "Tell me what I can do to make things right between us."

"I usually just lick her pussy to make things right." She smirks at me. "Maybe you should give it a try."

"She'd probably kick me in the face."

"Nah. She'd come first. Then kick you."

"Speaking of coming…" My thumb teases her chin up and my mouth devours hers. She moans and slips her tongue inside, tasting each dip and crevice. My palm warms her thigh as it escapes under her night gown. I frisk her clit, until she's melting in a puddle of desire. She breaks our embrace to fling me onto the covers.

"You left me by myself, all day."

Once she frees her breasts, I massage them. "I missed you too, love."

She straddles me and grins. "I'm ovulating."

My dick spasms and my wolf's tail wags. I meet her smoldering gaze. "Are you sure you're ready for that?"

She pierces her pussy with my rod, moaning and throwing her head back as she sinks down. "More ready than I've ever been. Now fuck me and release your seed, mate."

I clench her hips and set our merciless pace. "You're so wet and tight," I groan as my end nears. "I love you."

The floorboards creak. We pause as our eyes shoot to the doorway to study Carly's surprised expression. "You couldn't even *wait* for me to return." Her lip trembles and she backs out. "I'm sorry I ruined the moment."

Sky leaps up and dashes after her again. "Hey! Wait up!"

My head falls back, as my dick throbs. Maybe this isn't going to work out after all.

## Azure

# The Moment of Truth

"I'm sorry about last night," Sky whispers over her rim. I only nod as I stride to the table. "Are you mad at me?"

I slam my mug on the counter. "You're damn right I'm mad. You both took off in the middle of the night and didn't even tell me where you were going. I had to call your brother to locate you!"

"We stayed at my parents' house for the night. Carly didn't want to come back here and I didn't want to leave her alone."

"We are *married*. We need to agree to talk to each other and work things out, without running away."

"I wasn't fucking running away," Carly grinds out as she enters the room.

"Then what would you call it, wife?" I roar. "You threw a fucking tantrum and *left*."

She bumps chests with me. "I was gone for two seconds to check on *your* sister and you took that opportunity to exclude me."

"I was kissing my wife! And I would have done the same thing with you if you didn't run away!"

"Fuck you," she growls before pivoting. I snatch her wrist and pin her to the wall. Her breathing hitches as she glares. "Let me go."

"I'm your husband. Not your *employee*. Show me a little more respect." She wiggles under my hold, her pulse quickens, and her arousal tempts my more primal senses. My nose grazes her neck, and she gasps while clenching her thighs. I shove my knee between hers. "Why are you fighting me?" I whisper before nibbling her ear. "Why won't you let me love you?"

"Because I'm not worthy of your affection. I'm a pathetic human. I'll never shift or bear children with fur. I'm worthless to you, Guardian. I'll never be anything more than a third wheel in this marriage."

"That's not true," Sky corrects.

"I never meant to exclude you or make you feel like you weren't worthy. You are amazing, *beautiful*, and courageous. You are worth more than you think. I'll never consider you anything less than my equal." I wipe her tears. "Damn it. Let me prove my devotion." I rip her pajama pants aside and tease my tip against her entrance. "You want furless children? Let's do it. I'll love them just as much as any pup. Whatever you want, I'll give it to you."

"I won't allow myself to be hurt again."

"How do you know I'll do that? You won't even give me a fighting chance." I release her and step back. "I never asked you to give me children or to have the ability to shift. I only requested that you love me and stay by my side," I huff. "If you want out of this relationship, let me know." When she doesn't answer, my heart splinters.

"Azure," Sky soothes.

"If she only wants to be with you, that's fine. We'll make a schedule, move her into the guest room, and attempt to share. But I won't allow her to treat me like this any longer." I stand tall. "I've done nothing wrong and demand more respect."

Carly pushes past me. "I have a meeting I need to get ready for."

Sky clutches my wrist, and we gaze into each other's eyes. "I need to head to the Wolves' Den for a few hours. Can you keep an eye on her?"

I rest my forehead on hers and we share a breath. "I'll protect her. Don't worry."

"Then, tonight, you can make me howl." She grins.

"I'm looking forward to it."

"I don't need a fucking babysitter," Carly hisses for the third time as we climb the steps leading to an office building.

"The alpha asked me to accompany you, so think of me as an escort." I readjust the suit jacket as it clings to my chest. Frost insisted that I dress in business attire so I'd fit in. But this fabric is scratchy, and the long sleeves make me sweat.

"Just stay out of my way." She straightens her skirt and takes in the expansive lobby. Then she strides towards the spiraling staircase.

"Shouldn't we check in at the reception desk?"

"Shh. Follow me," she whispers. "And act like you belong." I roll my eyes. I'd never belong in a place like this. Money-hungry politicians boil my blood. "Where is it?" she grumbles as she glances at each of the numbered doors as we pass them. "Oh!" She rests her palm on a knob, jiggles it, and grins. "Here we go." I follow her inside as she quickly presses the door closed. "Stand guard," she instructs.

The office is impressive with its picturesque window and enormous mahogany table. Papers rustle as she flips through them. I blink as I get a sudden feeling of déjà vu. Her squeals of delight echo against the walls as she waves a folder before stashing it into her jacket.

"I knew you had it! Now we'll find out what you're concealing." She prances.

*Fuck, my vision!* The entrance creaks open and a flash of silver spins in her direction. I tackle her to the ground and use my body as a shield.

"Are you okay?" When she nods, I release a snarl and charge her attacker. I keep my suit intact not wanting to draw more attention to our situation. We tumble and roll until he's under me and I crush his throat. "Who sent you?"

"The General."

"Impossible. We have him in custody."

"Obviously you've never been in the military. When one falls, *another* takes his place."

I glance at Carly. Her pale appearance lets me know I'm not hearing things. The shifters are still in danger. I slam my knuckles into his jaw, knocking him out. Footsteps approach and I zero in on the doorframe. "Get behind me so I can protect you."

"What the fuck?" Jackson skids to a halt in front of us.

"What are *you* doing here?" Carly demands.

"I told you this morning that I made an *appointment* for this afternoon to speak to the douchebag. Why are you here this early?"

"I came during their lunch break so I could snoop in their office."

"Well, great job, genius!" He waves at the body. "How are we going to explain *this*?"

I lean into Carly as my vision darkens. "Azure? Oh, no." She lifts her bloody palm to Jackson. "He's been stabbed."

I glance at my chest and laugh at the knife. "And I thought it was you who was going to get hurt."

The beta rushes to my side. "We need to get out of here. Can you walk?"

"Maybe he should shift? Don't you heal faster that way?"

"If he turns to fur with the weapon inside him, it'll cause more damage. Guardian, can you use your powers to aid in our escape?"

I clench my fists as fire burns my abdomen. "No."

Carly inspects my gash. "There's green slime coating the blade."

"Bastards," Jackson spits. "That sounds like the same serum they used on Sable. They knew we'd be here. It was a trap."

"Well, if we don't leave soon, we'll be in handcuffs." Carly rubs her neck.

"There's a back exit. I saw a janitor walk out to a dumpster—this way." Jackson tugs me forward. "I can't believe I'm saving your ass after you fucking shocked me. You better remember this moment the next time you want to use your talents on me."

"What about him?" Carly points to our attacker. "We can't just leave him in the open."

"Are *you* going to drag him out?" Jackson hisses. "It'll cause too much of a spectacle. Now let's get out of here."

Carly snatches the assailant's ankles and tugs him into the closet. "It'll buy us some time."

Jackson and Carly flank my sides, guiding me through the hallways leading to the back of the building. The passageway is clear, except for a few receptionists, but they are too busy to notice our getaway. The light blinds me as they kick open the door.

"We're almost there," Carly grinds out.

"How much do you weigh?" Jackson huffs. "You need to go on a diet."

My wife helps Jackson ease me in to the back of the vehicle. Dizziness causes my head to fall against the seat in front of me. "Hey, stay with us," her voice pleads.

"If I don't make it…" I swallow my words as images of Sky choke me. "Tell Sky I love her."

"Shut up." Carly sniffles. "You'll be fine."

I clutch my partner's wrist. "I love you too, Carly."

"I know you do, you big blue idiot."

An inferno rages through my veins and an unfamiliar darkness swallows me whole.

# Wounded

"Thank you again for coming." I walk the last guest to the door, before collapsing on the couch.

"You did an incredible job." Maya squeezes my hand. "The baby shower was absolutely perfect. Especially the pin the tail on the pup."

"I can't wait for yours." Mom elbows me. I yawn and rub my eyes. I hardly slept a wink last night. How I'm still awake is beyond me.

"Did you have fun too, Lily?" Maya coos over the newcomer.

"It was my first baby shower." Lily smooths out her dark hair. "My former pack members were a bit older."

"I'm glad you could join us. It was fun spending more time with my fur-in-laws," I add.

"Thank you for having me. It's nice to have the opportunity to meet all the ladies of the family."

Maya sips her coffee as her eyes assess Azure's sister. "Where'd Jackson go?"

"He had an appointment in the city with Carly."

My ears perk up. "I thought Azure took her?"

Lily shrugs. "I'm not sure." She fiddles with the hem of her shirt. "No one really tells me what's going on."

I bite my cheek. It's probably because everyone thinks she's hiding something, especially after the mall incident. But that's her tale to tell. And my nosey ass is eager to hear it.

We all jump as Sable bursts through the door. He scans the area before tugging Mom away from our group. The rest of us blink his way before meeting each other's worried stares.

"That jerk didn't even say hi to me!" Maya dashes out after her mate.

Our little group follows suit. Carly slams into my chest. Her frame is racked by sobs. I stroke her hair. "Sweetheart? What happened?"

"He saved my life."

"Who?"

"He threw me out of harm's way and got knifed." She meets my shocked expression. "It should have been me! I killed him." She crumbles at my feet. "I gave him such a hard time, and now I'll never have the chance to tell him how much he means to me."

My heart skips a beat as I observe Sable and Jackson carry in my unconscious mate. Azure's drenched in blood and unmoving. My knees seize, and I crumble alongside my best friend. "He'll be all right," I whisper to myself. We huddle together, blanketed by our misery while praying that our husband will see another day.

"Skylar?" Sable helps me stand, then lifts Carly to her feet as well. "Don't worry. Mom's working on patching him up." He guides us to our parents' cave and sets us on the couch. Then he rubs his face as he glances at the guest room door. "She'll update us soon."

We wait for what seems like days (though it was likely only hours) before Mom emerges with crimson-soaked clothes and sweat-drenched hair. "The good news is there wasn't any internal damage. I was able to disinfect the area and stitch him up. Now he's resting peacefully, and he'll make a full recovery." We embrace her. "The bad news is the dagger was doused in that anti-shifting serum and he can't use his Guardian powers to assist in the healing process."

"I thought you developed a cure that counteracts the effects?" Sable interjects.

"I did but I'm still in the testing phase, and until Azure's conscious and aware of the possible risks of the vaccine, I don't want to inject him without his consent."

"Can we see him?" I plead.

"Just don't wake him. He needs to sleep so his body can mend itself."

"Thank you." I give her a final squeeze before running into the room with Carly at my heels. We halt in our tracks as we take in his pale frame. I run my fingertips over his forehead. He looks older, lying in the bed like this. I miss his perfect smile and encouraging words.

"I can't believe you took a knife for me," Carly whispers as tears kiss her cheeks. "You put my life before your own." Her lips graze his. "Thank you for teaching me that not all men are the same."

I snuggle against her side. "Does this mean he's passed your test?"

She leans her head on my shoulder. "Yes, I do believe he has."

# Azure

# Waking Up

There's a horde of dizzying images. A rainbow of chaos. Then suddenly it stops, leaving me in a deafening silence.

"Sky? Carly?" I shout into the abyss.

Nothing.

A reel begins to play. The brightness makes my eyes water. It's of a little girl. She's being abused by her father. Then thrown into a den of ravenous wolves. The vision fast-forwards and her tiny body morphs into a woman. Her cackle bounces off my prison walls until she stares into my soul.

"Who are you?" I demand. "What do you want?"

"I'm going to set the world ablaze for what they've taken from me," she snarls. Before I can respond, a shadow emerges behind her. It wraps an arm around the lunatic. I rub my eyes. When I focus again, I take a step back.

"Freddy?" The grin he wears does nothing to settle my anger.

*"Stay the fuck away from us! Or I'll destroy you!"*

*His sinister laughter chills my bones. "Be ready, Guardian. The rebel's tale is slowly unfolding and we're coming for the blood that is owed to us."*

*Just as quickly as they appear, they vanish. I claw at the location they were standing. "Stop! Don't do this!"*

I jerk out of my nightmare but clutch the blaze burning in my abdomen.

"It's okay. We're here," Sky coos from my side. "You were stabbed, and Mom patched you up. But the serum is still in your system; that's why your body feels like it's on fire." I relax into the pillow as she strokes my hair. "How are you feeling?"

I clutch my aching head. "Like I was run over a few times by a semi-truck." The vision swirls behind my eyes. Was this a reaction to the poison coursing through my body? Or an actual revelation? "Where's Carly?"

Sky points to the foot of my bed. Carly is curled up with her head resting in my lap. She looks peaceful and, most importantly, *unharmed.* I let out a breath and thank Luna for allowing me to hold on to the she-devil for another day.

"You gave us quite the scare." Sky cuddles into my side.

"I'm sorry. That was never my intention."

"I know it wasn't." She tugs at the sheet. "Thank you for protecting her."

"It's my job."

"No, it was more than that. Even though she's been clawing at you, your love for her never faltered." She presses her lips to mine. "And I plan on repaying you." Her palm slithers down to my rod.

My moan causes Carly to wiggle. She yawns and stretches out like a lazy feline. When she sees that I'm awake, she crawls over me. Just when I think she's traveling to Sky, she snatches my chin and crushes me with her mouth. I'm shocked as her tongue demands entrance. I wrap my arms around her until we are chest to chest. She tastes like bubblegum. I release a growl, eliciting a shiver from her. Wetness kisses my cheek and I pull back. My thumbs caress her tears. "There's no reason to cry."

Carly smacks my chest. "You fucking idiot!"

"What?"

"Don't you ever jump in front of a weapon for me again! Do you hear me?" Her chin trembles. "Your life is worth far more than mine!"

I pull her into a hug. "Baby, you're worth so much more than what you think, and I'm going to remind you of that every single day of our lives."

Sky strokes Carly's golden locks. "I agree. You are a fucking queen. Stop being so hard on yourself."

I hold my girls close, until their even breathing tells me they are asleep. I watch their angelic expressions and chuckle. I have my paws full, and I couldn't be happier.

The sun's tendrils caress my cheeks, beckoning me to start a new day. I scan the unfamiliar room and wonder where my wives went.

"Good morning," Celeste sings as she strides in with a breakfast tray. "I made blueberry pancakes. They'll be light on your stomach and give you a natural anti-inflammatory boost." She sets the meal under my snout and I drool. "Don't fret about the girls. They are catering a fellow pack member's wedding and promise to come home as soon as they can."

"Thank you."

Celeste squeezes my hand. "No, thank you. You have done so much for my family. It's my pleasure to assist you for once."

I devour the warm cakes. It's a rare occurrence for me to eat homemade baked goods. But now that I'm bed ridden, I'm eager to try more unique treats. "Those were incredible."

"I'm glad you enjoyed them." She waves off my compliment. "But the girls can out cook me any day. You'll be fat and happy for sure."

"Has my sister stopped by?"

"Yes, she came early this morning and sat by your side for a bit. Then Hunter wanted to go hunting."

"How is she doing?"

Celeste shrugs. "Your sister has a lot of trauma that she's dealing with and that incident at the mall really spooked her. Jackson said she's not eating or sleeping." She holds up a palm as I go into big brother mode. "I prescribed her a few things that should help, and the beta promised me that he'll remind her to take them."

I clench my fists. "I don't like her staying with the unclaimed male."

"Jackson is a very tender and patient wolf. I give you my word: Lily is safe with him. Plus, Hunter and Ash have become the best of friends. You should see them together. It's heartwarming."

"I'm her brother and a Guardian; it's *my* job to watch over her, not his."

Her hand warms my knuckles. "Look at how you saved Carly, Sable, and Maya. Rest assured, mighty warrior, you're far from being pushed out of your brotherly duties. But sometimes, it's easier to divulge our sorrows to a compassionate outsider, than members of our own family."

As much as I hate to admit it, she's right. Lily will tell me what happened when she is ready. Plus, she's only living a few caves down. I could always eavesdrop or threaten Jackson to tell me what's going on.

"Has the mayor been in contact with us?"

"His office reached out to Frost, apologizing for the men at the mall but claims they were not from his administration."

"What about the assassin who was trying to attack Carly?"

"Supposedly they have him in custody. And they informed us that the individual was not working for the government."

I rub a palm over my face. This is a nightmare. No one is taking accountability for their actions because they fear the repercussions.

"The mayor did give his word that your sister will not be approached again." She strides over to a huge edible arrangement of fruit. "He even sent you a gift."

"Did Frost say if he believed him?"

"Our alpha is keeping his eyes on our borders and looking forward to speaking to the other human officials about our interactions with these supposed military leaders." She pats my leg. "But that's for another day. Let's get you mended." Her expert fingertips change and cleanse my wound. "It's too bad about the serum. You could be healing faster."

"It would be nice to be on my feet already."

She peeks through her lashes as she rebandages my cut. "Did Sky tell you I'm testing an antiserum?"

"No, she didn't. Have the trials been successful?"

"Yes, they have." She pulls the covers over my chest. "Is there anything else I can get for you?"

"I want the vaccine."

Her grin reminds me of Sky's. "Are you sure? I'm not certain of the possible side effects. It could be risky."

"It's my job to protect the shifters, right?" I hold out my arm. "Let me be one of your test subjects."

"I'll be right back." She practically dances out the door.

My wolf is clawing to run free, but with the poison in our veins, it could be months before I can shift. We don't have time for that.

"Here we are, dear." Celeste waves the needle around. "My subjects have felt better within hours." She pricks the side of my arm. "But they weren't as large as you are so it may take more time, or even a second dose." She stares at me. "How are you feeling?"

"The same."

"No rashes?" She checks me over. "How's your breathing and heart rate?" Her physician instincts have been triggered, and she scribbles notes as she asks questions.

I just hope this is the remedy I desperately need.

"Are you sure about this?"

"Yes, Sky." I scoot to the edge of the bed. "I've been glued to this room for a week and there have been no weird side effects from the shot your mom gave me."

"But we can wait a little longer."

"No. I'm ready to return to my cave." I cringe as my tender skin pulls tight against my abdomen. "Plus, your mom gave me the thumbs-up. That should be good enough for you."

Sky offers her shoulder to aid me. "We want you back home too, but…"

"No *buts*." I stand. "See?" I stride out into the blinding afternoon sun and hold my arms up, allowing my body to soak in its warmth. I've missed this. Fur pokes through my skin. My wolf is itching to be free.

Sky strokes my arm. "Carly is cooking dinner, if you are hungry."

"I'm starving." I run a palm over the side of her face. "But not for food."

"We can definitely help you with that too." She kisses my hand. "Now let's get you home, mate."

When we enter the cave, the smell of fresh meat smacks me in the face. As we turn the corner, my jaw drops. Cooking at the stove is my golden goddess wearing a royal-blue lingerie set. She waves a spatula. "Sit and I'll serve you." The fabric is see-through and her pebbled nipples are begging me to take a bite. I collect my tongue from the floor and settle in beside Sky, who is just as transfixed by the chef as I am. The timer dings and Carly bends to grab the rolls out of the oven. Her ass expands, like the perfect peach. I tilt my neck and groan at her uncovered juicy center.

"Shit." She curses and waves her seared pointer finger.

I warm her side, steal her injured digit, and pop it into my mouth. Her eyes never leave mine. Desire smolders behind her lids. I glide my palm under her breast, my thumb grazing her peak. She arches, shoving her chest into my capable grasp. I massage the other one until she is mewing. She tugs her digit away and wraps her arms around my neck.

"I'm sorry I allowed my insecurities to cloud my judgement. I do love you." She presses her lips to my ear. "And I want to have your babies, husband."

A shiver teases my spine. "Now?"

Her hips caress mine. My erection cries at her reaction. I twirl, bend her over, and place kisses up her back, before wrapping her hair around my wrist and giving her a tug. "I recall you like it rough." Her moan confirms my words. "Make sure you tell me if it's too much pain. Understand?"

She nods, but with another pull, she answers breathlessly, "Yes."

I pivot to my mate. "Do you want to join, love?"

She slinks over and lies in front of Carly, spreading her pussy like a tantalizing dessert. "Is this what you want?" Carly's breathing hitches as she takes in her wife's wet center. Sky arches her hips. "It's all I've been able to think about since our wedding night. Watching Azure fuck you, while you eat me," she purrs. "Make my dream come true."

I shove the thin material aside and tease Carly's core until my tip is covered and she's panting. "This is it, wife. There's no turning back. It's your choice. Do you wish to consummate this marriage?"

"I've never wanted anything more in my entire life." She dives between Sky's thighs. My mate's scream of pleasure fuels my thrust into Carly's tight hole. She clenches from the pressure but shakes her ass, begging for more. *Luna have mercy.* She feels amazing. I pull on her hair, removing her mouth from Sky. Then I slam into her. "Fuck," she grinds out.

Sky whimpers from the floor. But Carly's pussy is begging for attention and she's unable to concentrate on her best friend's needs. "Come on, baby. Let me see you touch yourself." She suckles her fingers before rubbing her center. "Look at us," I demand. Her eyes pop open. When she explodes, she roars my name before lying back and enjoying her high. I pick up the pace until Carly is begging for more. I slap her ass and she squeals. "When you come, you're going to cry out my name. Understand?" When she doesn't respond, I smack her other cheek. "My wolf demands you claim him as yours. He needs to know you are devoted and that he can satisfy this greedy pussy alongside his mate's."

At the mention of her title, Sky crawls to us. While I'm pumping, she licks Carly's unoccupied hole. Carly squeezes her thighs together, eliciting a delicious pressure around my cock. "Join us,

Car. You'll never have to question where you belong. We'll be your family. Always and forever." Sky tugs my dick out of her friend, gazing at me as she suckles my throbbing tip. Then she nips it, causing me to hiss as pleasure zings to my toes. She uses my dick to scrape her pussy before collecting me back into her mouth. Her eyes roll back and she moans before removing me again. "Our juices are absolutely divine."

"Let me try?" Carly begs before joining Sky.

I take a step back as my wives share my cock. "You're both incredible." It's pure torture as they take turns fucking me and licking my rod. "I'm losing it, girls. Someone please finish me off." I don't even need to open my lids to know Carly has taken the reins. I clutch her hips and exact a mind-numbing pace. "Come for me." My words are her undoing and she moans out my name, before collapsing against me. Her pussy's vibrations set off my own release. I brush her hair aside and kiss her cheek. "Thank you for putting your trust in me."

"Thank you for proving that not all men are cheating assholes."

"You're welcome."

Sky cuddles with us as we lie on the kitchen floor, drenched in each other's juices. I finger their necklaces as they rest in their cleavages, tugging on the ends until the two metal snouts touch. Then I pull mine off and place it in the center, completing the heart-shaped design.

"Welcome to our happily ever after."

# Sky

# Epilogue

"No! I said 350 degrees for fifteen minutes. *Fifteen* minutes!" I shout over the chaos. "Azure! Can you please grab James?"

Azure strides over with a baby and a pup in each arm. "Where is he?"

I point towards the couch, before returning to the call. "Yes, and I'll be there in an hour." A glass vase shatters behind me, and I cringe. "Maybe two." When I end the call, I pivot and give my family my best *mom's losing her shit* face. "Everything was calm before I answered the phone. What the hell happened?"

The door bursts open and Carly gawks in my direction. "What the fuck?"

"Oh, Mom said a bad word." Mary, our oldest, accuses in a blatant attempt at misdirection.

"I'm a grown-ass woman," Carly declares. "And I also bought everyone's favorite treat on my way home." Their noses lift into the air, and they all jump up and down. "Now sit and behave, or I'm eating everything in front of you." They all scurry to the worn kitchen table, their eyes big and drool already forming on their mouths.

"You always pick the best times to rescue me." I kiss Carly's cheek. "How was your day, darling?"

"It was good." She pulls a glob out of my hair. "I'll man the fort. You need to shower."

"James has been teething again, which makes his nose leak everywhere."

"You and I both know it is Azure's," Carly throws over her shoulder. "He explodes way too fast and misses often."

Azure narrows his eyes as he straps James into the highchair. "Look who's talking, two-second detonator!"

Carly scoffs and I raise a hand to stop their banter. "I love you both, but if I don't get a move on, I'll be *late*."

"Dear Luna, please not another baby," Carly whines in jest.

Azure tugs cheerios out of his chest hair. "I'll need a shower after you, Sky."

"Go, go. I'll take care of our beasts." Carly smirks at the little angels, still looking up at her expectantly.

Azure squeezes her ass and nips her neck. "I look forward to showing you my *immense* gratitude tonight, wife."

"Dad!" The children groan out.

"Yeah, yeah. You smell like barf. Go." She winks.

"Thanks, Car." I tug my mate towards the bathroom before she changes her mind. Once the door closes, he slams me against the wall and devours my mouth while his fingertips circle my aching clit. I melt into his tight hold as I moan against his teeth. I wish

356

our spouse could join us too, but I'll take what I can get. Once I explode, he turns the shower on and guides me beneath the scalding water.

"I want another one, love," he commands as he scrubs my frame with the soap.

"No way. We can barely handle the ones we have."

He chuckles. "I meant an orgasm."

"Oh." I grin. "That I *can* do." I shove him against the tile and ride his dick until, together, we reach our happily ever after.

# Acknowledgments

This book baby never would have been born without the many individuals who breathed life into its pages.

First and foremost, I want to thank my husband, who supports me financially and emotionally. You are my rock. Thank you for all your hard work and wonderful cover designs.

A big hug goes to all those who taught (and are still educating) me on the fact that love is *love*. Especially my uncle John and his partner Randall. Also, a tight squeeze goes to all my gal pals! You helped me create Carly and Skylar's connection and your friendship reminds me that there's nothing deeper than the love we share.

A huge shoutout to my editor, Kat Pagan. She is a word witch, and without her amazing techniques, this book wouldn't be as remarkable as it is. Thank you for sharing nachos with me.

Also, a massive thank you to all my beta and arc readers! The fact that you took time out of your already hectic schedules to read and answer feedback blows me away! Especially Courtney, for her encouraging feedback on my first ever written female-on-female sex scene. Alicia, for the nickname change from 'Sky Boo' to 'Sky Bear' and removing a ton of *digits* from the manuscript. Rae, for the idea to a add a beautiful wedding ceremony scene in. Jennifer, for suggesting more Azure scenes and less abrupt chapter beginnings. Also, Heather, for her advice on the reservation hospital and insisting who Carly should be with.

Finally, thank **YOU**! Without readers, I couldn't continue my writing dreams.

Welcome to the pack!

# Additional Titles by the Author

**Feathered Dreams Series (a rags-to-riches, clean romance):**

Join Ann and be swept into a world of swoon-worthy characters, glittering gowns, and unrelenting intrigue.

Ann is beginning to see how naïve she has been, though by no fault of her own. Farming side by side with her father, away from the drama of the outside world, is what she has always loved most. But now that she is at the Palace, she is forced to focus on other people and their daily struggles. In the midst of her personal growth, she starts to realize how cruel the world can be. Will she shy away and run back to the familiarity of her old life? Or can she share her unique sense of compassion and fierce loyalty to help those in need?

Feathered Dreams (Book 1)

Plucked (Book 2)

Molting (Book 3)

Split Feather (Book 4)

To Be Titled (Book 5) TBA 2023

**Wolves of Cold Creek (18+, paranormal romance):**

The Cold Creek packs are loyal—while bursting with mouthwatering, unclaimed shifters—all just waiting for their mates. Why not drop in and enjoy the picturesque views by day and scorching fires at night? Don't be shy. They don't bite… hard.

Scarlett's Tail

Sky's Tail

Lily's Tail TBA

The General's Report TBA

Rebel's Revenge TBA

The Spellcaster TBA

**Cooking Up Disaster (slow-burn romance):**

Step into the Decadent Cup and grab something hot!

Blake has a tough exterior but a heart of gold. In the small town of Jasper, he owns the Decadent Cup café where he's selling handcrafted coffee, baking killer banana nut muffins, and staying the hell away from long-term relationships.

Amy's a struggling single mom with no time for love, because she had it with her deceased husband. When her best friend asks her for a favor, she jumps at the chance. But this change in events brews a challenging new blend of trouble, and she'll be cooking up a disaster with the town alpha.

Available now only on Kindle Vella.

# About the Author

Brittany Putzer is a stay-at-home multitasker, living in Florida with her husband, two sons, and mini zoo. She turns to books to escape the world because it's easier to pretend to be a shifter, princess, wizard, vampire, or damsel in need of an alpha. Although she enjoys reading, her passion is writing. And in 2020, she published her first book: *Feathered Dreams*. Her writing style is a creative blend of dark and light themes, sprinkled with sarcasm, humor, romance, and intrigue.

Scan the QR code to chat with Brittany on social media, **review** her books, get signed paperbacks, check out merchandise, and join her newsletter for freebies and sneak peeks.